Jasmine

Jasmine

Passion

Darshan

PARTRIDGE

To order additional copies of this book, contact
Partridge India
000 800 10062 62
orders.india@partridgepublishing.com

www.partridgepublishing.com/india

Best Complements

The author has been a very nice colleague of mine. I have been observing him since his first creative endeavor "A Smile Takes Life". What makes me appreciate him is his absolute dedication to his writing and his sincere and pure will to give his readers a wonderful and delightful experience of reading. "A Smile Takes Life" is a delightful book with novel and innovative themes. His new book "Jasmine" is also capable enough to touch to the right chords of the readers. The book is written in such way that it would compel the readers with its reading mirth to welcome it. As a nice colleague of the author, I extend my good wishes to his long lasting literary journey. As a reader, I appeal the readers all over the world to pay their eyes to the books. I am sure they would be delighted.

Ms. Darshana Salvi
(Author's Colleague)

Review:

Madhushala: Out of frustration in love, a youth starts a Madhushala where many frustrated lovers and beloveds come and live together and finally meet their life partners. Eventually he also gets his lost beloved and lead their lives for the sake of Madhushala.

A Mistake: It is a story of a doctor who is obsessed to take revenge on his beloved who denies marrying him. Luckily he gets the opportunity when his beloved comes to him as a patient. He wants to be loyal to the principles of his profession and save her life but in conflict he makes a mistake and becomes responsible for the death of his beloved.

Kite: It is a story of an extra-marital relationship and shows how extramarital- relationship compel the people to behave inhumanly with their blood relations.

Nandini: A young doctor girl gets affected by handling a leprosy patient. The family which loved her so much turns out to be her bitterest enemy and makes her suffer for her sacrifice done to the family.

Well Done My Son: A married writer gets fascinated towards his fan and develops extramarital relationship with her which results in the birth of a son. The same son becomes responsible for the death of the Writer.

Falling Star: It shows how the blind faiths and superstitions deeply rooted in Indian culture have strong hold on the minds of the Indian people. It is a story of a film actor who attains stardom and eventually dies due too much faith in superstitions which is related to his life.

Butcher: Butcher narrates the story of a progressive Muslim youth who wishes to bring about social reforms for the interest of the people. But as usual he has to confront with those anti-reforms forces and eventually meets his end.

Jasmine: A school going girl has great fascination and love for flowers. Once she happens to see a flower of Jasmine. She falls in love with it. She is so much emotionally involved in it that she cannot live without it. The end of Jasmine brings about the end of the girl.

Chillum: a youth from a Harijan Community who is victimized by the deeply rooted racism in the society gets provoked to take revenge on the society with the help of a chillum. He succeeds in his motive but meets a tragic end.

Scientist: it is a story of a black scientist who becomes a victim of an unexpected blast in the laboratory and has to keep his research in an incomplete state. But fortune smiles upon him and his schoolmate comes to his help. He continues his research with the helping hands of his friend which ultimately brings him Nobel Prize

Widow: It is an emotional story of the lovers who could not meet in their youths. They don't come together but remain face to face till they attain their old age. Eventually they meet and leave the place which remains hostile to their union.

Passion: It is a story of an excellent stage actor who is known for his too much love for art and wine. His passion for art is so powerful that while performing a death scene he dies.

Lajvanti: It is story of a married shepherd who with his melodious flute art attains a beloved. His repute as a poet spreads everywhere and the king honours him as a poet laureate. But the moment he loses beloved, he loses his genius as a poet and the honour. When his wife comes to know about his weakness, he searches his beloved and calls her home and performs their marriage.

Nargis: It is an emotional love story of a flower selling girl who is told that her fortune will smile upon her and she will have rich husband when she will see a complete rainbow in the sky. When she is on the verge of the death, the prediction comes true and she meets her life partner.

Acknowledgement

In my newly flowered career as an author, I observe the presence of many well wishers and inspiring forces. I would like take the serious note of their presence in my note of gratitude. Their presence is ever recorded with inspiring voice at every turn of my life. I would like to take the note of such striking and ever present who support me in my writing journey and pray for its literary success. There are some significant people who contributed a lot to my professional career. The first and the foremost among them is Hon. Shri. Ravindraji Mane, former Minister of the State of Maharashtra and the Chairman of Probodhan Shikshan Prasarak Sanstha (PSPS), Ambav, Devrukh, Ratnagiri Maharashtra and Mrs.Neha Mane his better half who are responsible for my bread and butter. I always feel in their debt as they gave me their helping hand in my adverse and discouraging circumstances. They offered me a hope to stand and continue my life in criticalities.

There are some people who have given their outstanding contribution to my academic achievements. The first and the foremost is Dr.Chauhan A. S., Ph.D. guide of Rashtrasant Tukdoji Maharaj University, Nagpur whose valuable contribution made my Ph.D. submission possible. I am also thankful to Ramesh Belsare, an official in Ph.D.

Cell, Rashtrasant Tukdoji Maharaj University, Nagpur who gave me his helping hand during my entire Ph.D. process.

My family has been a vital force in my literary journey. Ceaseless inspiration of my loving departed father Lt. Ishwar Naroba Wakde who taught me the lessons of innocence, honesty, dedication and devotion and always wanted me to be different from him. My mother Mrs. Parvati Ishwar Wakde who always wishes to see her son standing quite high in the esteem of the world always supports me in my adventure and never let me get disheartened in my courage stealing and frustration inculcating blows of the destiny. Her love and care energies and revitalizes my every step towards adventures. I always feel rather lucky guy to have very supporting, encouraging and understandable wife Mrs. Asha Wakde whose presence at every literary discussion gives me creative acceleration and new vision of diverse and unknown literary ideas. She is always ready with her helping hand whenever and wherever she finds me to be tumbling in gyre of complexities of life. Without her, the work would have been just a seen but never fulfilled dream. I am very thankful to my loving kids Aryan and Rajveer Balasaheb Wakde who deprived themselves from fatherly love, affection and care as I could not spare time for them being engaged in my work. There are some other family members who are always ready with their thumbs up gestures to my mission in life to whom I am grateful are my elder brother Mr. Laxman Ishwar Wakde his entire family and my loving and caring sister Mrs. Aruna Balaji Bhoite.

Eventually there are some friendly faces to whom I cannot afford to ignore in my feel of gratitude. The first and foremost is my friend Ms. Darshana Salvi who is the most respectable, estimable and adorable professional colleague of mine. I always have literary discourse with her. She is a great well-wisher of mine and emotional support in my professional career and personal life. She supports me in my every creative work and acts like a ceaseless fountain of inspiration and courage which enables me   to enjoy life with all its colours.

Prof. Ashok Jadhav and Prof. Shivnarayan Waghmare, close friends of mine, gave a very significant contribution during manuscript revision process. Mr. Rajesh Jadhav, Dr. Sudarshan Awasthi, Mr. Kishore Khatane, Mr. Sandip Kotwal are some of the friendly faces in the never ending queue of well-wishers to my literary and creative journey. I pay my sincerest thanks to them for their love, affection and care.

Contents

Madhushala

It was winter and was giving its severe whips to the lives in Belapur. It whipped very severely to the families which had been feeding on the textile industry in Belapur for years. The textile industry had been a boon to many families in Belapur and it had been responsible for enhancing the existence of Belapur which once upon time was like a village. Now the industry had become an old and counting its last breaths. Considering the loss and response of the market, its management decided to close the industry without bothering for the lives relied upon it. One day morning when the workers came at the gate of the factory to report on duty, they got shocked to see that the gate was locked and feared to see the placard having message 'Industry Is Closed'. The workers got frustrated and some of the annoyed came forward started shouting against the management and demanding their rehabilitation. Some of the mature and understandable workers were there who knew that there was no meaning in blaming the management as it was faultless. They knew the fact that when the industry was in good swing, the management facilitated all that they could do but now they were helpless. The workers who were conscious of it, they came out of the striking mob of the workers and started searching for new way of survival. Most of them were on the verge of retirement and some were of middle aged scared about the impossibility of getting any source of employment at this late turn of life.

Suddenly emerged circumstances exposed number of families relied upon it to unbearable adversities. One of such families was of Ramchandra Dwivedi a supervisor in that textile industry who had to take imposed retirement. Adversities and financial crisis whipped the poor family. Ramchandra was leaving no stone unturned to survive the family in such critical circumstances. Anyhow he managed to get a job as a security guard which relieved the tension for some time. What gave him relief in these blood sucking and courage stealing circumstances was his educating son Bharat not very talented but great hard worker, keeping alive the hopes of the family. He had a great wish to join higher education but being fully aware of the financial conditions and limiting his high flying aspirations started searching for job. Luckily once he received an interview call from the local post-office. He gave the interview with all that possible potential and was waiting for the response.

The financial condition of the family was growing worse day by day as the earning of the father was not able to meet the requirements of the family. The family was just surviving and not flourishing with meager earning of Ramchandra. It was at that critical moment, the luck smiled upon them and Bharat was called in the post office. Bharat was optimistic that something good was stored in his lot and it was that was calling him there. He reached to the post-office where he was given an appointment letter and was told to join the office from the very next day. He was absolutely astonished. Bharat returned home with great excitement and shared the news of his accomplishment with his family.

Ramchandra was at home as he had night shift. He became very happy over that achievement of his son and happily gave a pat on his back.

The first day was very pleasant for Bharat as he got acquainted with new faces and new working conditions and shouldered the new responsibility. He thoroughly understood what he had to do. He took with him some letters and other post documents to be distributed on the very next day. Ringing the bell of the bicycle and dancing his lips on the tune of a song, the young, bachelor and newly recruited postman at the post office marched towards his various destinations.

Within a month's time he became well acquainted with each and every nook and corner of Belapur as he had to visit each and everyone's house in the town. Every person in the town knew him. Slowly his popularity as a postman began to grow.

He was fondly called 'Bharat Postman' by the people actually his name was Bharatbhushan Ramchandra Dwivedi. Bharat was very happy with this job as it offered him a unique happiness to meet people and deliver their long and eagerly awaited messages. When Bharat rang the bell of his bicycle, the entire Belapur used to get up as if it was in the sound slumber dreaming of their near and dear ones and waiting for their messages. When he entered the town ringing the bell of his bicycle, people engaged in the house hurriedly came out and looked at him with great expectation that he would have brought some letters for them. When they found nothing for them they happily bid him farewell with the hope that he would definitely bring something for them tomorrow. Old ladies sitting in the front yard of their house or in *veranad* happily asked him, "Bharat any letter for us." If it was there, he got down from his bicycle and delivered whatever he had for them. If they were not able to read as they were illiterate, they used to ask him to read them out. Bharat kept his bicycle aside, drinking the glass of water offered, read out the messages sometimes becoming grave in reading and sometimes bringing a smile and laughing at the writing in the letters. When he commented on the writing and errors in the letters, both laughed a lot. Reading faulty letters was a great fun for both. If he found any ominous thing in the letter, he very calmly put his supporting hand on the shoulder of the person and conveyed the news in such way that nothing serious had happened. His approach towards the people made him very popular. When he came in the town ceaselessly ringing his bell, children playing around started chasing him shouting "postman came, Postman came' and bid farewell to him as his bicycle ran ahead.

One day he was distributing letters. He reached at a small size house with a door closed and window half open. He shouted, "Is anybody there? I have a letter for you." He waited there for some moments but none opened the door. He shouted again but no response came out and finally he decided to leave the letters. He was about to push the door but he thought that it would be wrong thing to open someone's door without his permission. He took a look at the half opened window and got shocked to see that hand of someone came out of the window to take the letter. He went to the window which was curtained. He tried to peep in to see the face of the person but being curtained, he could not see it. What charmed him a lot was the half fair hand.

He was wise enough to understand that it was of a girl not of a lady or man. It looked strange to him but enhanced his curiosity to know who was behind the curtain and why it was curtained. At least twice or thrice in a month he used to visit that and all the times he found that no one opened the door and the fair hand came out collected the letters got disappeared behind the curtain.

During all his visits to that house, he never felt the manly presence and never heard any human voice. Strong will to see the world inside overpowered him number of times but at last moment he withdrew himself from the thought. Once it happened that he reached to the window to hand over the letter while receiving the letter, the letter slipped out of that half fair hand and Bharat bent down to pick it up meanwhile the girl behind the curtain removed the curtain with the thought that the Postman might have gone. Bharat got up with the letter and got shocked and astonished to see that curtain was half removed and a beautiful girl was there staring at him. The girl collected the letter and hurriedly closed the curtain. It was the first time Bharat got the chance to solve the riddle behind the half fair hand. He went back to keep all the undelivered documents in the office and returned home. He took his dinner and retired for bed. When he was lying on the bed, the unveiled face of the girl came on the canvas of his mind and he got engaged in watching it. The beautiful face of the girl made him think of her. The next day he went to the office and started searching whether any letter was to be delivered at her address. Luckily he got it and he became so eager to deliver the letter and he took the letters and directly reached to her house. Accidently or by chance the window was opened and the girl was sitting at the window. For the first time he got the chance to see the girl. He hurriedly reached to the window. When Bharat stood at the window and engrossed in watching her beauty the girl asked, "Have you brought any letter for me?" Bharat did not answer the question as he was deeply engrossed in watching her beauty. Realizing that he was not alert she asked him, "Hello! What did I ask you? Do you have any letter for me?" When the words fell on his ears, he came out of her charm and handed over the letter. Both exchanged smile. Girl gave him a normal smile but Bharat took it to be something else and fell in her love. Longing to meet her became his passion.

When there was no letter for her, he became uneasy and could not understand what to do? He knew that without any reason, he could not visit her house. When he had no letter for her, he deliberately passed through the lane riding bicycle slowly and taking pauses as her house approached. When he reached in front of her house, he deliberately looked at her window to get a glimpse of her. But most of the time it happened that he found the door locked and window curtained. Sometimes when it was opened, the girl was not there. He got bored. He wanted to go near the window but he could not dare to do so as he had no reason for visit. One day he found the letter and hurriedly reached to her house. Frequent visits of Bharat developed a good relation with the girl. The girl was now exposed to him and became well acquainted with him. Bharat mustered his courage and opened his mouth. "Hello! I am Bharat. I work in the local post office. May I know your name please?" The girl answered, "I am Rani." Suddenly someone shouted from inside, "Rani, who is there and with whom you are talking?"

Rani closed the window. Bharat took his bicycle and went to the next lane where he delivered some letters and went back to home. Now he had become completely obsessed with the girl. He began to question himself how to meet her and where when there was no letter for her. Suddenly an idea clicked in his mind, "Let's make fake letters if no letter came." He was very happy with the idea.

Gradually their meeting increased and the girl fell in love with him. She too became habitual to wait for him. Both became eager to meet each other. They started searching for ways to spend a lot of time together. Bharat also did an idea that he delivered the letters of the others first and then he came to the house of Rani where he spent lot of hours together talking about this and that. As her house was at the end of the lane and no one passed by, it provided enough room for them to speak. Once it happened that there was no letter for Rani. He made a false letter and reached to the house. Rani was also waiting for him. She became very happy when she saw him coming. Bharat hurriedly came at the window and delivered the fake letter. They looked at each other and exchanged a smile. Bharat asked her, "Why don't you come out? Why do you remain confined in this room?" Rani became emotional and said, "It is my father who does it. He has confined me in this room because he suspects that I may do something disgraceful to him." He questioned further, "What does he do and when does he come back?" He is a supervisor in an ice factory and he comes quite late in the evening." Bharat felt strange and questioned, "Who accompanies you whole day?" "It is my grandmother," replied Rani." Bharat asked with greater eagerness, "How is she?" Rani answered reluctantly as she was a great burden for her. "She is very suspicious and short tempered woman. She has been sick for months and never let me speak with anyone. Whenever I sit at the window and when a human voice falls on her ear, she questions me with a doubt, "Was any stranger there?" I was really fed up with these questions and confinement and I wanted to come out." Bharat realized the intensity of her boredom. "Don't worry. I would free you from this confinement. Trust me." All of sudden there appeared her father. Seeing the postman very close to the window, he doubted something was going on. He shouted at him, "What are you doing?" Controlling the situation Bharat said, "I am delivering the letter and nothing else." Luckily a true letter had come on that day which saved the situation otherwise he would have been in trouble. Hearing this father calm down and asked Rani to shut the window. Already scared Rani shut the window. Bharat left the place went to the office thinking over what could happen to Rani. That night he could not sleep as he was deeply engaged in thinking over Rani's situation and determined to elope with Rani. Bharat's love for Rani was at its zenith. He wanted to attain her. For a few days he did not visit the house as he thought that father might be at home and since there was no letter for her it would be doubtful to visit her.

One day he took a fake letter and directly reached to Rani's house got shocked to see the door was locked. He felt strange but he doubted something undesirable. He grew restless. Consoling himself he went back with a hope that she might return shortly. On the very next day, he took out his bicycle and went to Rani's house again he got shocked to see that door was still locked. His uneasiness grew. He questioned himself, "Where she could be? Why didn't she inform me about her going? Would she come?" Once again he consoled himself that she might be out of station for a few days and might return very soon. Every day he took a round around the house of Rani but all the times he got disappointed to see the permanent state of the door. He sunk in despair he parked his bicycle on the side of the road and sat watching at the closed window of Rani's house. He sat there till late in the evening with a hope that Rani would return. But hope turned into disappointment. A passerby asked him, "Bharat what are you doing here at this hour of darkness? What made you sit like this? Don't you want to go back home?" Bharat replied somewhat terrifyingly, "Nothing, I have been waiting here for my acquaintance. I would meet him and depart soon." The passerby doubted and without poking his nose, he left saying, "Go back home it was late." Bharat nodded positively, watching him disappearing in the cell of darkness. Bharat waited there hopefully that she would be back. He looked at his wrist watch and got shocked to see that it was 11 O' clock and thought that his family might be waiting for him. He went back home. It was for the first time, Bharat arrived home late. Father shockingly asked, "Where have you been? Why are you late? It never happened previously." He tried to avoid unnecessary questions saying, "There was a lot of work today. So……" Thus shutting his mouth, he entered his bedroom saying that he had his dinner and not to wait. He shut the door. He opened the window of his room and stared outside as if he was searching for Rani in the deep and dark room of darkness. He stood there endlessly thinking over Rani till dawn.

Late night awakening, reporting late to the duty and taking unnecessary rounds in the lane of Rani waiting hopelessly became his daily troubled routine. Locked door of Rani's house became his bitter memory. One day while returning home from his office he saw wine shop having placard of "Thandi beer Angreji Sharab." He thought to enter the shop but avoided as the thought of his family corroded him. He spent whole night sleeplessly. The next day he took a round in the lane of Rani and as usual he found the door to be as it was other day. He confirmed that it would be in vain to expect Rani's return. He grew indifferent and negligent to everything around him. Family, job and everything which pleased him previously, now started displeasing. It was already late in the office. When he left the office, he decided to visit Rani's house. He forcefully made his mind to think positively, but when he reached Rani's house, he got drowned in frustration. He felt very sad to see a big lock was hung to the door. While going back home, once again the board of the wine allured him and that time he could not avoid the attraction. He kept his bicycle aside and entered the shop. He over drank and left the shop with staggering legs. Suddenly it started to rain; with an uncontrolled steps and mind he reached his bicycle. He came under the spell of wine so much that he was not able hold the bicycle properly. Twice or thrice he fell down and his dress got spotted with mud. Anyhow he reached home. Parents got shocked to see the condition of their son. Father tried to know the reason of this change in his behavior but Bharat did not responded.

Slowly he came under the spell of wine. One day he over-drank and went to the office and started quarrelling and abusing the officials. Finally he was suspended for two years.

When the father came to know about the suspension of Bharat, he could not bear the shock he caught bed permanently. One day it was around 10 o'clock. Bharat's father grew serious and started counting his last breaths. He missed his son very much but unfortunately he could not see him and died. When Bharat returned home in fully drunken state, he was totally uncontrolled and without noticing the noisy scene and people crying loudly. He went in his bedroom and lay on the cot. The next morning, when he got up, he got shocked to see the rush of people and some people crying at the dead body of his father. He felt sorry. He did all funeral rituals and kept himself away from wine for next fifteen days.

Gradually the memory of Rani overpowered the memory of his dead father. The more he tried to forget her, the more he got involved in it. His body demanding wine and willingly or unwillingly he got fascinated towards the wine shop. He drank to forget the grief of separation from Rani. He realized how much relief wine gave the people. Suddenly an idea clicked in his mind liked him very much, how many people would be there drowned in grief. Let's do something which would lessen their pain. He thought that it was wine which could be the best medicine to give relief to broken hearts. So he decided to start Madhushala where people would come and enjoy relief from their personal grief. He did not have money. A question to collect money started troubling him. Suddenly an idea clicked his mind. he published some pamphlets distributed among the people and pasted on walls and space available. The matter on the pamphlet was quite interesting one "Free Madhushala for the frustrated lovers." Funds Required. Donate liberally. The content on the pamphlet attracted the people especially the failed lovers and luckily appeal of Bharat received tremendous response from the people and thus he received a ceaseless fountain of funds from the frustrated lovers.

He used the funds to start a capacious Madhushala. He bought an acre of land and started construction. Within the period of a year, a splendid Madhushala came into existence and soon became the talk of the town. Frustrated lovers in an around Belapur started gathering in Madhushala. It became great enjoyment for them. They got all sort of wines and recreations. It was a great enjoyment for them as people living in the same boat were there.

The first troubled heart to get registered in Madhushala was Ramesh. Immediately after him there came a girl Nayana and one more middle aged man Ramnaresh. Bharat was very happy with arrival of those people and was happy that his Madhushala was getting popular. Madhushala didn't mean only drinking; Bharat had managed many indoor amusements which kept those frustrated people happy. As it was opening days of the Madhushala, there was no crowd but the popularity was increasing as people were making calls to Bharat to know a lot about the endeavor he started. It was morning time, Ramesh, Nayana, Ramnaresh were sitting on the table and waiting for the wine to be served. Meanwhile they started their conversation. Ramesh expressed his wish to know what made them come here. Then one by one started revealing their past. The question was who would begin. They made lots and Bharat was asked to declare the lot. He did his job and a lot fell on Nayana.

All became anxious and gave their ears to Nayana to see and listen what happened in the life of her which brought her in Madhushala.

"I was in the final year of graduation in an arts college. One day I was attending a lecture when my eyes fell on a boy sitting at the window and looking at me drawing something on his note. Next day when I was going through the corridor, I was surprised to see crowd of the students at the notice board. I went there to know what important thing was there which students were watching. When I went there, suddenly I heard one of them saying, "What a sketch? Wonderful!" They were shocked to see that the name was not written there. One of them shouted, "Nayana come here! Someone has sketched you." Finding the way through the crowd, I reached to the notice board and really got surprised to see my sketch. It was drawn so nicely that I got impressed. On the next day same thing happened when I was taking down note, I took a look at the window found the same thing. I got suspected that it was the boy who could be sketching me. The next day morning again I found the crowd at the notice board and saw students appreciating the sketch. That day I decided to talk to the boy and to know why did he sketch me and display it on the notice board without writing his name. During recess he was sitting in the garden. When I was approaching him, I observed his movements and understood that he was little scared. When I looked at him he bowed down his head as if he had done something wrong. I introduced myself, "Hi! I am Nayana. May I know your name, please?" Controlling his pressure and scared breath he replied, "I am Rohit and started looking down." I asked him about his stares at me and demanded his note book. Initially he refused but when I became obstinate he handed over his note book. I was really surprised to see that he had drawn number of sketches of mine in his note book. The sketches were very beautifully drawn that I got fascinated towards him."

From the very next day we became good friends and then slowly well and then close friends. Our friendship turned into love and we became mad for each other. Bunking lectures, spending hours at the canteen and sometimes going at isolated places where we could make love became our regular ritual. One day my father unexpectedly visited the institute and got shocked to see me absent. When I went home, he investigated about my absence. That time I managed by telling him a sheer lie that I had been to the birthday party of my friend. But I read the facial expressions of the father and found lines of doubts on his forehead. I was really scared.

I tell you, my father was very influential person in the town and he never liked anyone damaging his reputation. He was searching a boy for me in a very high class. It had come to my ears that they had got a very nice boy who was to come shortly to see me.

My liking and love for Rohit was at its zenith. Spending a single moment without his presence was really impossible. The attraction for each other was so grew that most of the times we remained absent at the college and passed times in some remote place. One day the institute sent a letter of attendance at home. Seeing attendance report, father got shocked and he confirmed his doubt. Knowing that my father would not approve our marriage, we decided to elope. One day it was afternoon I received a call from Rohit that he was waiting for me at the railway station. I took my college bag remove all the books and put some dress and money and ornaments which I had and telling that there was some function in the college I left the home. I hired an auto rickshaw and went to the railway station. As there was a time for the arrival of the train, we sat in the waiting room so that none could see us. I did not understand and how my father got the wind of it he came there took me forcefully in his motorcar.

I was really scared and thought he would give me severe beating but nothing happened like that. He talked to me sweetly as if I had done nothing disgracing. He asked me with sweet tongue, "Who was that boy? Where were you going? Did you love him? Did you want to marry him?" When he uttered the last question suddenly the word yes slipped out of my mouth. I told him everything and he assured me that he would do as I wished. I never doubted his sweet tongue and started imaging the possibility of my dream. One day he asked me to call the boy for diner and conditioned me that he should be alone.

Next day I went to college and met him in the canteen and conveyed the message of the father. He doubted my father's intention but I convinced him that nothing worth suspecting was there. He came on the planned day. My father received him very warmly and cordially asked a lot about his family and his future plan. My father created such conditions that I thought he was absolutely happy with my choice. They had enough talk and after that they sat for dinner. After dinner again they had friendly talk then Rohit departed. Before going to bed my father called me in his bedroom and asked me to get ready to go out of station for some days. He took entire family to a hill station where we spent almost a weeks' time. During our stay outside, one day my father told me that he would have my marriage with Rohit after completion of my graduation. It made me very happy. I fully trusted what he said there was no room to doubt his statement in my mind. I started dreaming of marriage and became eager to convey the message to Rohit. I wanted to call him but I thought it would be happier if I tell him on his face.

We returned home after a week's time. One day I went to college and got shocked to see that he was not in the class. One of my friends told me about the sudden demise of Rohit. I got shocked to hear. When I was going through the corridor, I saw a notice on the board about unexpected demise of Rohit. I was thinking to go to Rohit's house to know how it happened but I could not dare to go alone. I took some of my friends with me and went to Rohit's house. His house was full of guests and neighbor who were there to console the family. His father had been out for some purpose. His mother was there. When she looked at us, she became emotional and started crying loudly. We tried to support her. She told us how it happened. There I came to know that Rohit's death was caused due to food poisoning and it happened immediately on the next day when he had come to us for dinner. Suddenly my mind doubted father's sweet tongue. Since that I stopped going to college. I lost my interest in everything. Father realized the reason but he preferred to keep quiet on the issue. One day at the hour of evening, I saw police van at the gate. Police sub-inspector along with his constable came in to see my father. They directly entered the bedroom of my father. But unknowingly they kept the door slightly open. It was all strange to me as it happened never previously. I dared to go to the door to overhear the conversation. I heard the police inspector demanding five lakh rupees for suppressing the matter. My father agreed. The matter was settled. It was really a shock to me that my father talked so sweetly could go to such an extent. One day I was told that a boy was coming to see me. I refused to marry. My father got angry over me and confined me in a room and was forcing me to get married. One day my mother forgot to lock the door of the room where I was confined. Taking the advantage of it I ran away and came directly here." Listening to the story of Nayana everyone got shocked and consoled Nayana for whatever happened to her. When all were silent Bharat questioned her how she came to know about the address of Madhushala? Nayana replied to him that when she was on outing with his family, she happened to see the advertisement of Madhusala and a pamphlet. When Nayana ended the story, tears started rolling down her cheeks. Everyone supported her and consoled her.

Bharat took the chit and declared that now it was the turn of Ramesh to unfold his life story. Everyone was looking curiously what Ramesh would tell.

"I belonged to a very poor family. My father was a shoe maker. He did all that he could to impart me education which I aspired for. I was very sincere and sharp in studies since my school days that were pride for me and for father as well. He stood top in the school in matriculation and again in the twelfth. Luckily I scored well in twelfth and got admitted in M.B.B.S. Actually my father was not in position to finance but the family relatives came to my help and my dream to get admitted for M.B.B.S. came true. It was the first lecture which was almost half finished, suddenly a girl having fairy like beauty came at the door of the class and said, "May I come in Sir?". The Professor stopped his teaching and entire class stared at her. For some moments he forgot that he is in the class. Entire class stared at her as her beauty was so enchanting. She came in and greeted everyone "Good Morning" and sat at on her table. Her beauty became the subject of talk everywhere at the canteen in study room and wherever the students gather they talk about her. The first semester finished and result came out. Luckily I stood first in the college. Since then my name came into discussion especially in the girl section. Slowly girls in the class started approaching to me for the sake of notes or other purpose. We formed a good friend circle. Soon she joined our group. Through meetings and other things talk enhanced and fascination for each other grew. We fell in love with each other. She wanted to propose me but I was so eager before she did it I proposed her and within no time she gave her confirmation. We decided to marry after completion of education.

Passion to meet each other grew and then we started eliminating other friends to have privacy. Our clandestine meetings enhanced. It was Sunday most of the students were at their natives. I made a phone call to her at her ladies hostel and proposed for outing. She gave her confirmation. I took out my bike reached to our secret point. She came there and then we went to near tourist point. It was hilly area and road was crooked so I was driving the bike rather consciously. Sitting at my back, she was doing mischief and singing songs loudly. She started tickling me and I lost my concentration and control on my bike. All of a sudden container came from the front side and within a moment what happened I did not understand. I remembered that my bike dashed against it." Suddenly Ramesh started crying loudly. His voiced got blocked. It was silence everywhere. All became serious. Bharat came forward and put his hand on his shoulder consoled him. All tried to make him silent. After sometime, he began the remaining story. All became serious and attentive to listen what he would say the next.

Wiping out his watery eyes with a handkerchief Ramesh continued, "The dash was so powerful that I fell on the other side of the road and Hema got crushed under the tire of the container." The accident became the headline of the newspaper. It was a great shock to everyone and defamed everyone who was associated with us. The police came on the spot made the enquiry and I was taken to the police station. All were there including Hema's parents, my family and the Principal of the institute. I felt ashamed of myself and I could not see into eyes of anyone. My father was very angry and better not to think about Hema's parents. I was really scared and dying for the end of the investigation. It continued for a week or two. It was the most traumatic period in my life. One day I received a letter from the college which confirmed my detention. It was one more jolt which I and of course my family could not bear. Seeing the letter my father angrily asked me, "What is that? Read it out loudly." I read out the letter and explained to him the content." He lost his temper and slapped me and shouted, "Get out you difficult child! You *Nalayak*! You disgraced us and defamed us. You made our lives difficult to lead. Get out of my sight! I don't want to see your face." It hurt me a lot. I was really confused what to do and how to face the world with my deed. There was nothing but love is always a crime in the eyes of the world. One day wandering through the town, I happened to see the pamphlet stuck on the wall. It was about Madhushala. Noting down the address of Madhushala I returned home. My deed was so defaming to my family that no one preferred to talk to me. I was really fed up with that silent life. That night I packed my bag and decided to join Madhushala to come out of this traumatic experience. It was a great shock to all. When the story came to an end, Ramesh began to cry. Everyone tried to make him silent. Bharat offered him drink. He drank it a little as he had to peep into the life book of Ramnaresh."

"Really friends you have suffered a lot in your life and I really sympathize with you. I graduated in commerce and I remember that day when I luckily joined the local company as a supervisor. When the family relatives came to know about my job accomplishment, they started approaching my family for their daughters. Finally a family was fixed and I got married with a girl named Bharati. We had married for ten years and we had no children. Perhaps this concern was corroding Bharati. She was growing pale and weak day by day I never blamed her for this childless situation. Life was going on as per its fixed pattern. One day I was preparing for going to office. Suddenly I heard vomiting sound of Bharati and I was shocked to see that there was blood. We consulted with the local doctor. Report came and I sunk in despair as it was blood cancer. My mind took a deep dive into sea of frustration and for a moment imagined my life without Bharati. It troubled me a lot. I did all that I could do but everything went in vain. Doctor declared that she would live only for next six month. It was great shock to me. I was just counting days. It was a very delicate and sensitive period of my life. Much of the time I spent with Bharati. Period of six month slipped out of hand so rapidly that I did not understand when the last day of Bharati's life came. She had become very thin, pale and immovable consistently staring at me as if she was begging me for leaving me in the middle of the life and leaving no mark of their union behind. Day began to count its last breath with that Bharati too. A moment came when darkness spread all over and in the darkness Bharati's soul got disappeared. That was the darkest night in my life. The next morning cremation ritual was performed. The next days were boring and frustrating. The memory of Bharati was corroding me and making me restless. I told my parents that I was going out for climate change it might take month or two to return. They had great understanding of my state of mind and they let me did what I wished. I packed my back and came here."

Listening to the story of Ramnaresh, Ramesh exclaims, "Life is really strange!" Everyone agreed with him. It was late they eat drank and went to bed. Madhushala was nothing but school of recreation where you could do anything and everything. Drinking, eating playing all sorts of games playing antakshari, organizing *maiphils* were some of the things which made the people forget whatever happened in their lives. It taught them a new of way life. Anyone who joined Madhushala left it with new approach to life that was, "Whatever happens, happens for good in life." Slowly new people were joining Madhushala. Slowly it took the form of fair. People from all over world took the note of it and came to enjoy life in Madhushala. Everyone appreciated the endeavor of Bharat. The interesting thing about it was that in Madhushala spoiled lives were reconstructed. New pairs were formed. Frustrated lover fell in love with another beloved and they got married and left Madhushala to play the new inning of life with the principle of acceptance.

Meanwhile Ramesh and Nayana came closer and got married. Ramnaresh met a widow and married her and settled in their lives. Madhushala turned into a marriage bureau. Popularity of Mahdushala was rapidly growing with the crowd of people also. Considering the need and demand of the people, he expanded Madhushala in acres. There was no dearth of funds as the numbers of frustrated lovers were not less in a huge country like India. It was being funded from all over. Bharat was really happy that he could do something to bring relief in people's life. But the thought to find a partner himself never touched his mind. Perhaps he might not have found a woman of his life. It was morning when he was engaged in arranging wine bottles in shelf. All of a sudden woman greeted him, "Hello!" He turned back and got shocked to see a widow with a bag was standing at the counter. He stared at her for sometime because it was Rani. Both recognized each other became very happy. Bharat felt very unhappy over how much she suffered in her personal life due to drunkard husband who ultimately died due to over consumption of alcohol. Rani asked him, "Postman, didn't you marry?" Bharat happily replied 'No'. "Why?" Rani asked. Bharat humorously answered, "I was waiting for you." Rani blushed. They sat at the table talked a lot wiped out each other's tears and eventually Bharat put his hand on Rani. They joined hands and lived for the sake of Madhushala.

Kite

Playing sound of humans as if they were playing a hide and seek game was coming from a huge Bungalow. It was a bungalow of a Professor Dr. Janardan teaching in some university in the city, Mumbai. He had just come out from a setback in his life. His wife Shanti died in a car accident leaving a twelve year old daughter Seeta behind. It was a huge bungalow deprived of a motherly affection. Dr. Janardan was absolutely collapsed but what made him survive the question that who will look after his loving daughter Seeta after him.

The memories of his dear departed wife Shanti troubled him a lot. In day time, its impact was less as he was engaged in his responsibilities but as the darkness fell, the interiors of the bungalow turned silent, the silence terrified him. What terrified him the most was the questioning daughter, Seeta. All the time she questioned him, "Where is my mother and when will she be back?" When Shanti died, Seeta was kept deliberately away from the cremation ritual as Dr. Janardan feared that she won't bear the abrupt death of her mother. When she had asked about her mother, she was told that her mother had been to U.S.A. for her research work and would take a few years to return. Thus she was silenced that time. Hoping that her mother would come soon, she learnt to live without her but missed her a lot. Whenever she missed her, she troubled her father a lot. This was the trouble which was somewhat unbearable to him.

Much of his time he spent with her playing this or that game. When bored at home, he took her for outing sometimes to the garden, or a moll to buy something or a nearby hill station. Thus he took all possible pains to amuse her and make her forget her mother. It continued for a year or two. But he realized that he could not fill the hollow caused due to sudden departure of his wife. It was noon, the doctor was lying on the bed and Seeta was reading her textbook. Suddenly somebody knocked at the door which disturbed them. Seeta ran towards the door saying, "Papa, I think it is mummy." The words hurt him and made his wife's memory alive. He knew that it was not her Mummy. Not to make her feel discouraged, he said, "Please open the door quickly, perhaps it might be your Mummy." Seeta opened the door and astonished to see that a beautiful girl well dressed having an identity card hanging around her neck and with some product standing at the door. Seeta questioned, "Who are you and what do you want?" "I am Shaila, an executive from a Johnson and Johnson Private Limited and wish to inform you about the product I have." "Is anybody there either your Papa or Mummy?" Seeta replied, "My father is there." "Call him please." She shouted, "Papa, someone has come to see you." Dr. Janardan came and saw an executive was standing with a heavy bag with an engaged hand with some cosmetics. He called her in. They sat on the sofa. He asked Seeta to get some water for the guest. Seeta went in the kitchen and brought a glass of water. Meanwhile they began their chat. She introduced herself, "I am Shaila Kumar an executive of Johnson and Johnson

Private Limited." "I am Dr. Janardan, working as a Professor in a university." "I have some products which I wish to show to you." said Shaila. She kept the box on the tea table and started opening it. Doctor asked her, "What product?" "I sell cosmetics. Perhaps your wife may need it." The moment she uttered the name wife, his face turned pale his talking tongue became silent. Changed facial expression hurt her and made her to question him. "Doctor, is anything wrong? Have my words hurt you?" "It is not like that. Actually I lost my wife in a car accident recently. I stay here along with my daughter Seeta." "How tragedy occurred?" "My wife was also a Professor in Science. She had got enrolled herself for research work in some university in America. When she was on her way to airport to go abroad for her work, her car met an accident on the way and she lost her life." "I am really sorry Professor. I hurt your feelings." "Don't think like that. You questioned out of ignorance. That is not the fault of yours." "Does Seeta know it?" "She has been kept ignorant about it." "You did it greatly otherwise it would have an adverse impact on her." "You are right."

Seeta became very friendly with her. In the first meeting, they got emotionally attached with each other. Shaila was sweet talker and with her skill she won the hearts of both in the first meeting. Seeta became such a great fan of her that she called her to stay with her. Seeta asked her, "Aunty why don't you come and stay with us. Pappa goes to his college and half of the day I am alone. If you join, I will get a companion." "It is my pleasure to be with you but it is not possible as I have to do a job. But If I get the time, I will be there with you." Dr. Janardan also requested her to come off and on as per convenience. He also did not forget to add that it was a cordial invitation and not the force." Reacting to this she said, "I can understand it. It is your goodness that you have invited me here. I tell you very frankly I would like to be with you, if I get the time." Seeta made interference in the conversation and said, "Shaila aunty, please come. We will have a great fun together." Shaila got overwhelmed by this cordial invitation. She lovingly said to Seeta, "I can understand it. But I am helpless. But don't worry I will come to play with you at least once in a week, probably on every Sunday." "Really!" "Yes!" Seeta became happy with this assurance and said, "How loving and cordial you are!" Shaila looked at her wristwatch and said, "It is too late. I have to report the office." She looked at the Professor and said, "Sorry sir I hurt your sentiments." "It does not matter." Seeta took her cell number and said, "Won't you mind if I call you?" "No you can call whenever you wish. I won't mind contrary I would be happy if I get the chance to have a talk with a sweet girl like you." Seeta thanked her.

Seeta became a great fan of Shaila. Whenever she was bored at home, she called her and call continued for hours. When it became routine, Shaila had to stop her saying, "I am in the office not at home. Let me go home, I will talk for hours. Before going to bed, Seeta called her and talked for late in the evening. Shaila too liked the girl perhaps it might be out of her motherless situation. Seeta troubled her lot at home and in the office by ceaseless calls, but she never shouted at her or had never been harsh to her. She also had a great attraction for Seeta. The calls brought them close. On every Sunday, Shaila came to play with Seeta. Visits of Shaila became frequent with that grew intimacy. Shaila became almost a family member. Initially Dr. Janardan and

Shaila were formal with each other. They maintained good distance from each other. But as the distance lessened, they grew informal. Whenever she came, she directly entered the kitchen and took the complete charge of it. She made good dishes for them and had it together. Sometimes they went out for picnic or visited some moll or garden.

Dr. Janardan gave her some gifts. Initially she refused it but she could no longer say no to him as she was also greatly impressed by the goodness of the professor. Dr. Janaradan made such an impression on her that Shaila knowingly or unknowingly fell in love with him. She was young, charming and dynamic. Professor too loved her at heart but never disclosed it as he feared that she might take it otherwise. When the intimacy grew, they started making such gestures that they understood its meaning. Whenever Seeta was engaged in something else or playing with something or engaged in her studies, they began to find some private moments.

It was Sunday, the Professor was at home. Seeta told him, "Pappa there is a function in the school I have to go." Dr. Janardan told his driver to drop Seeta at school. Immediately after half an hour, Shiala came there. It offered them a chance to be together. They started liking each other's company. Whenever Shaila was free, she called him. They met at secret place. Attraction grew and the time came when they found they could not live without each other. They were so fascinated towards each other that started ignoring Seeta or kept her engaged so that they can have their moments. Gradually Seeta's eyes caught the change in their conduct. She realized that they are excluding her or trying to isolate her. The change hurt her a lot. She thought a few days back both had great interest in her, now that interest was disappeared. They talked to her, enquired of her studies took her out but now they are going together leaving her. A fear that her father was being stolen by Shaila started making her restless. She thought Shalia was selfish and money minded woman. Slowly she turned negative of her and started observing silently whenever she came. They had become so lusty that they unnoticed the silence of Seeta. Once her father was reading a news paper.

She said to her father, "I don't like Shaila aunty. If possible ask her not to come. Her intention is not good." Dr. Janardan raised his eyebrows and said, "Why have you become negative of her. She is good, loving and caring. Don't think like that." Dr. Janardan had become blind in her love. He was unknowingly becoming irresponsible towards his duties as a father. Shaila had captured him in such a way that she forgot that he is the father and needed to be with her. But Shaila's love was making him indifferent towards the sentiments of his daughter. Slowly he started ignoring her. Whenever Seeta wanted him to play with her he gave an excuse or shouted at her. Once it happened that she was requesting him to play suddenly Shaila came there directly entered into the bedroom. Janardan totally ignored her and was about to leave. She tightly held his hand and said, "Don't go. Play with me. I feel alone here." He angrily left her hand and said, "I don't have time to play with you. I have an urgent work. If you can't play yourself better you burry yourself in the books. But don't disturb me. I am going in." He went in and forgot to lock the door. Accidently, he kept the door half open. Seeta bored with books missed his company a lot. She could not control herself and saw something undesirable and shouted, "Papa I am missing you." Shaila got irritated at this. She left the room hurriedly without talking a single word with him. Dr. Janardan felt hurt. He got angry at her and said, "You stupid girl why did you come here? I had warned you not to disturb." All of a sudden his anger reached at its extreme, he slapped her vehemently. She fell down. Dr. Janardan went in his bedroom dressed himself and left out hurriedly. Seeta was absolutely bewildered with this drastic change in his father. She realized that Shaila had stolen her place in her father's life. She felt miserable at her own plight.

Dr. Janardan went out and called her on phone. But he became restless as she did not pick up the phone. Her rejection made him restless. He came quite late in the afternoon. Seeta was watching some program on television. She looked at him with a hope that he would come and say sorry but nothing happened like that. He was so obsessed with Shaila that he paid no heed at waiting Seeta and directly went to his bedroom. Again this strange behavior of her father made her miserable. She began to feel insecure. House became hot. She could not understand what to do and how to convince her father that whatever was happening had an adverse impact on her relation. She knew it if she told him he would get angry as he was not in mood to listen a single word about her.

She was crying. She thought that she must meet her father and tell him that things at home had become unbearable to her and suffocating. She got up and moved towards the bedroom but she felt sorry that he had shut the door. She returned disappointedly and sat for her studies. Dr. Janardan consistently tried to call Shaila but she did not respond. He grew impatient and restless. At about 7 PM he opened the door and came out and found that Seeta was lying. He woke her up. He took her out for meal. But during the meal, he spoke not a single word. Seeta was afraid of his angry face. She scared that if she spoke anything, he might slap her again as he did it previously. Bitter memory of it was still alive in her mind. They returned home silently. He asked her to sleep in her bedroom. He sat in the drawing hall watching some program. At late hours of the evening he received a phone from Shaila which made him at ease. They spoke for a long time and ended the meeting with a word to meet soon.

Shaila left her office and came directly to Dr. Janardan's house. Dr. Janardan was engaged in doing some work while Seeta was doing her studies. Shaila greeted her, "Good evening Seeta." Seeta looked at her with a disgusting face and unnoticed her. It hurt Shaila. Janardan asked her to make something for meal. Shaila entered the kitchen and made some dish. They gathered at the dining hall and sat together. She served Seeta which she refused saying, "I don't want to have it." Dr. Janardan asked, "What is the reason?" "I don't like her." It created a grave silence there. Shaila felt insulted and left the dining hall. Dr. Janardan got angry at Seeta but instead of wasting his time on her, he went after to convince Shaila. She was weeping in the corner of the kitchen. She said, "I won't come here hereafter. She insulted me. I think she doesn't like my presence in the house. You decide what to do? Whether you want her or me? If you want me here, you have to keep her away from you. If you agree, I will come otherwise never." "He was fumbled with this demand of Shaila. He tried to convince her. "She is little girl. Ignore her." "I can't bear insult." "If you can't do it better you forget me." She pretended to leave. He stopped her saying, "Darling, don't leave. Give me some time. I will do something." "Promise?" Doctor helplessly promised her, "Yes. Give me some time." Shaila told him, "She will not meet him till he manages the things." Doctor got disturbed what to do?" That night he thought over the issue but he was not able to get the solution over it. One day he called Shaila and told her that he was not getting any idea what to do with her. She gave him a hint, "she does not want to see her whenever she comes there. If possible shift her from here" Doctor got the path. He began to think over it. Seeta observed that her father was completely changed and had turned flint hearted towards her feelings. He started feeling insecure from him. When she looked at his face, she thought something evil is going on in his mind perhaps about her. Doctor stopped talking to her. They dined together and spoke rarely as he looked at her as a disturbance in his path. The evil mind in him wanted to remove this hurdle at any cost.

He took his car driver, Babu, in confidence and paid him hugely. He said, "You know I can't live without Shaila. She too loves me and wants to marry me but she strongly disapproves to the presence of Seeta. What can you do? Can we shift her to somewhere else?" Babu joined hands with hands and voice with voice and said, "Give me a day's time; I will see what can be done in this connection." Babu took a round in his colony and found an old and dilapidated building which was marooned by the people as many suicide cases were reported there. It was the faith of the people of the families who went to live in that ominous building, suffered a lot. Out of this rumor, no one preferred to stay there. A kind of fear was deeply rooted in the minds of the people. Babu had the information of it, but never had the opportunity to see the building. He deliberately went there. He entered the building and found entire building had taken dirty look. It was turned into a dust bin as it was not swept for years. Pigeons and bats had made it their residence and spiders had free walks everywhere. He went up the last floor where he found single room perhaps built for the purpose of storage. He found it to be suitable place. He took a glance at it and found some raw material was scattered there and open space behind. He went up the terrace and found it to be tallest building in the colony. From its terrace, entire town could be seen. He also noticed that there was no rush of the people.

He was happy that he could find a place as he desired. He happily returned to his Master and reported him. One day both Dr. Janardan and Babu visited the building confirmed its safety and secrecy. Dr. Janardan loved his daughter Seeta; but he had become mad for Shaila. Out of that madness, he got ready to do such inhuman act with his daughter. If Shaila had stretched the matter further, perhaps he would have killed her but luckily the matter was not stretched as her demand was to shift her somewhere else. Dr. Janardan was so mad for Shaila that he did not bear single minutes presence of Seeta. He told his driver to take the motor car out as he had to go urgently. He said, "Babu, I wish to see the place. How far it is from here?" "It is not far from here. It will take hardly ten to fifteen minutes" "Let's go then" "As you wish." Babu turned the car towards the colony. By parking car at some distance, they came towards the building. Seeing that no one is watching, secretly they entered the building. After confirming it to be the best and secure place for confinement, they returned. On the way they stopped at the hotel. Doctor Janardan ordered coffee and some snacks. Doctor opened his mind, "Babu, I want you to shoulder the responsibility. I am a father and I am not that much flint hearted to do such act with my daughter. So I want you do it. You take whatever the amount you want. But do it." Babu replied, "Don't worry. For your sake I will do it." "Remember you have to take care that she should remain alive. Feed her properly, for this you will get the money." "I won't let it happen. I will feed her and would take all possible care." "It is ok then."

Shaila had told him that as long as Seeta was there in the house, she would not come. She remained firm on it. It troubled Dr. Janardan who could not tolerate it. He wanted to bring her home at any cost. It made him hurry in shifting Seeta. He called Babu to do it tomorrow itself. "Don't worry. Leave it to me. I will please you." The next day at around 9 PM Babu came up. "Sir, I am ready. Where is Seeta? She is in." He entered her room. He asked Seeta, "Would you like to come with me to have ice-cream." The moment she heard the name of ice-cream, her mouth started watering. "Babu, I would like to come." "Let's go then." Babu took her. While going, he smiled villainously at his little mistress." Babu took out the car. First they went to the ice-cream parlor and then they had a round around the city. Babu was deliberately passing the time as it was too early to shift her there.

At around 9 PM, he turned the motor car towards the building. Seeta felt scared and asked him, "Where are you taking me? This road does not go to our house. Stop the car. Your intentions are not good. Stop the car otherwise I will shout. Babu hurriedly stopped the car. First forcefully bandaged her mouth and with a rope he tied her hands. Seeta was absolutely frightened with this abrupt happening. She struggled hard but poor creature could do nothing but to keep quiet like a corpse. He speedily took the car towards building. He lifted her and hastily stepped in the building. He took her in and took care that she should not shout or come out. Before leaving the room, he confirmed that the knot of the hands and legs are tightened. He locked her in and left the building silently.

The moment Seeta was shifted; passionate and eager Dr. Janardan called Shaila. She happily came. They secretly got married and continued their life leaving Seeta suffer in the confinement of the room. The couple was so engaged in the life that they never thought of Seeta and they never tried to know in what condition she was living.

Everything was going on smoothly. The couple was happy without any disturbance; and Seeta was suffering silently like a corpse with no protest. How could she protest as her voice was silenced?

One day at the early hours of the morning, Babu entered building where Seeta was confined. He uncovered her mouth, and freed her hands and legs and let her eat. Seeta finished her meal. He bandaged her mouth and he was about to tie her hands and legs, suddenly his mobile rang. Seeing it an urgent call, he left the room thinking that she had been tied properly. He locked the door and went out. It was the first time Seeta felt free. She stood up and had a walk in the room. There was window which was kept open. She peeped through window and saw a jungle of houses and saw at some distance some children along with the parents were taking pleasure of flying the kites.

It was the occasion of kite festival. The town was engaged in flying kites. Wherever they got open space, they started flying kites. Rahul a little boy was also flying a kite. They were standing exactly opposite the building where Seeta was confined. Their kite was going up and high in the direction of the building. Accidently it got stuck to the window of the building. Rahul tried to free it but he could not. Seeta saw it. She picked a charcoal which was lying there and wrote 'Save Me' and freed the kite. Rahul took it back and checked whether it was torn. He turned the kite; he found some letters written with charcoal. He hurriedly called his father and said, "See, Pappa, someone has written 'save me' on this kite." His father saw it and said, "Have you written this" "No. I haven't written it." A doubt was raised in the mind of the father. Father asked him where it got stuck. He answered it pointing the remote building. Father said, "Rahul, there is something doubtful. Let's follow me." They hurriedly stepped in the direction of the building. Father asked him, "Rahul, at which window the kite got entangled. Rahul anxiously pointed his index finger, "There, there, the first window from the top." Father hurriedly reached up. While going up almost all the doors and windows were open. But when he reached the room at the top, he got shocked to see that only that room was locked. It made him think why was it so? His curiosity to see what was there inside grew. He peeped through crack of the door and shocked to see that a girl was taking walk. He found something doubtful in that. He did not break the door nor did he shout. He called the police. The police came there in sometime. Together they broke the door and freed Seeta.

All reached to the police station. Seeta told everything. Sometimes later, a police van reached to the bungalow of the Professor and arrested the couple on the charges of harassment. The couple realized their mistake but it was too late. Police brought them to the police station. At police station, they met each other. Dr. Janardan could not dare to look into the eyes of Seeta; nor Seeta showed any interest in them. She happily joined hands with Rahul and his father and stayed with them. Rahul's father took the responsibility of looking after her. The couple was given five years imprisonment.

Five years later, the couple realized their mistake. They reached Rahul's house and told them that they wanted their Seeta back. Rahul's father took no objection. He called Seeta who was in. "Seeta, See who has come to see you?" Seeta came out and was not surprised but shocked to see her parents there. Doctor said, "Seeta, we have come to take you with us." She looked at them with great disgust and said, "When I was with you, you treated me as a hindrance in your relation. Why do you want to carry this disturbance home? It will disturb you again. I am happy here. Let me be here only." The couple felt dead and went out with guilty hearts.

A Mistake

It was the month of March. The sun was enjoying its golden childhood. The last breaths of the winter were being burnt in the warmth and heat of the burning Sun. The trees were undressing themselves to put on the new garments. The roads were almost eclipsed and turned yellow with dead and yellow leaves. The city was rising from its sound slumber of the last night. The city had taken a calm look as the people were still to come out of their homes. There was a huge campus at the outside of the city having huge buildings scattered in acres. It was the campus of a medical college in Raipur. It was very calm and secluded place completely cut off from the hustle and bustle of the city. A motorcycle or motorcar was seen disturbing silent life of the city. Some vehicles were seen going towards the college. The entrance was just opened and a security guard was there on his duty giving passage to the visitors, students and the officials going in. There was huge and capacious canteen in one corner of the college. It was the early hours of the morning and the canteen was just opened. The owner of the canteen was worshiping the photo frame of the Goddess Lakshmi, goddess of money. He garlanded the photo frame and lighted the incense stick which rejuvenated dead look of the canteen. Cooks were seen busy in making breakfast meal.

Suddenly the man at the canteen got engaged in conversation with a student. "Hello! Rahul, you have come so early today and you are alone and where is your partner and friend." Rahul replied lovingly and respectfully, "Yes! Uncle I am feeling hungry. I am expecting my friend shortly." The canteen owner said little bit calmly, "Rahul there is time for breakfast and tea also as the canteen is just opened. Will you wait till then?" Rahul replied with an unhurried tone, "Uncle I am not in hurry. You take your own time. I will sit in the corner and wait for my friend." He took out his cell phone and made his fingers dance on the keypad of the mobile. Off and on he was taking cell phone to his ears and taking it back and sometimes muttering, "Oh shut where you are, yarr! I am not getting you." Then again his finger began to dance on the key pad of the mobile. Suddenly his disappointed face wore a smile as he got connected with his friend. "Where are you. Jann? I am waiting for you in the canteen. I have ordered for you please come early. Don't make me wait." He took down the phone with a satisfactory smile and got himself engaged playing some games in his mobile. Suddenly someone greeted him with a great enthusiasm, "Hello! Rahul. Sorry for making you wait." Rahul with dancing heart lovingly greeted. "It does not matter. Have a seat please, Suchitra." "What would you prefer?" "Anything you would offer." "What is your plan for coming Sunday?" "I have not fixed anything yet. Probably I would finish the studies and remaining will be decided then. Why did you ask? Do you have any plan?" Rahul joyfully said, "I am planning to take you out? Would you like to accompany me?" "Sure! Why not? But where you planned to go?" "There is a hill station some kilometers away from here. There is a very popular temple of Lord Shankara. I have heard that whatever you demand there, it gets fulfilled. Many love birds prefer this place." "How nice to see it!" After finishing their coffee, they went to the library as Suchitra had to return some books and take some new reference books. Meanwhile Rahul took a look at the newspaper. Suchitra did her job and asked Rahul to go. They came out of the library and took a walk in the campus. They finished their job in the library and took a long walk in the campus talking this and that. Before departing, Rahul reminded her of the plan of Sunday. "Suchitra, don't forget the plan of Sunday. Remember you have to be there at the bus-stop at 9 AM." "Don't worry I will be there. Ok then."

It was Sunday. Rahul got up early in the morning. He visited his friend staying in another building and requested for the key of his bike. He took the bike, filled petrol and came at the bus stop. He did not find Suchitra there. He parked his motorcycle made a phone call to her. "Hello! Suchitra, where are you? You are coming na!" Suchitra replied rather hurriedly, "I am preparing. I will be there in ten to fifteen minutes. Please wait." After some time, Suchtira reached the bustop. Rahul became very happy. They moved towards their destination. They had a great fun while driving. Singing this and that song tickling each other and making amorous gestures and postures they reached at the top of the hill. Seeing the landscape and scenery there, Suchitra reacted, "Why didn't you plan it previously?! How pleasant to be here! There were a few couples here and there. Seeing them both felt comfortable. They moved towards the temple.

While going towards the temple, Suchitra said, "Rahul what are you going to demand God?" "I will tell you later on. What have you decided?" "How do you expect me tell you? It is secret?" Rahul said somewhat indifferently, "It is ok. Don't tell." Suchitra laughed at him somewhat funnily. They went in and stood together paying homage postures in front of the God. They took a round around the temple and came out sat in one corner. They looked at each other and gave a blushing smile. Forgetting what talked previously, Rahul said, "Suchitra what did you demand to God?" "I won't tell you. You tell first." "I asked God to give me Suchitra as a wife." Suchtira smiled and asked, "Are you sure you would get what you demanded?" "I am positive and of course I would be blessed with you." "Let's forget about me. I am eager to know what have you asked for" "Nothing special, a good husband?" "What do you mean by a good husband?" "I mean a person who would love, care and respect me as an individual." "Does it mean that I don't do it?" "Don't take it otherwise. It is just expectation and nothing else. It does not mean that I think of other person as my life partner. That fellow might be you. Why are you so disheartened as if I am dreaming of anybody else?" Holding his cheeks with her soft hands and funnily says, "You, *Buddhu,* I demanded you only." The moment these words fell on his ears Rahul, got excited and with great joy he thanked Suchitra, "For a moment I was really shocked and disheartened. Thank you for making me happy. You are simply great!"

Assuming that none is there to keep check on their clandestine gestures and postures, Rahul dragged her and enjoyed some romantic moments. They came back in realism. Rahul's passion for her grew stronger and in an excitement he proposed Suchitra, "Dear, you know how much I love you. I wish to immortalize our love and make my all dreams come true by marrying with you. Will you marry me?" Suchitra being a mature and little practical knew that Rahul was growing emotional. She took care that his sentiments shouldn't be hurt and encouraged him, "My dear I am equally in love with you. I am as eager and passionate to have you as you are. I think this is not time to be carried away ourselves in such feelings which put a question mark to our futurity. To be frank, my mind says we need to rein our emotions otherwise we will be nowhere. I don't want that we should be fooled by our emotions. I think it is practical approach of the time that we need to focus on our career. Once we do it, it would be more convenient for us to come together. Am I right or wrong *tell na?*" Rahul nodded positively, "But…." Suchitra stopped him by shutting his mouth with her palms and said, "No more buts. I will marry you, Promise!" This assurance brought a smile on his face. They took a round around the temple and talked this and that and after exchanging love feelings they left the temple. As their examinations came closer, their meetings got shortened. When they were not able to meet due to their hectic study schedule, they preferred to please each other by having long talk on phone till late in the night. Rahul had greatly involved in her but aspiration to have her made him study.

At the end of every paper, they had a brief meetings and talks about their performance. It was the last paper. Among the crowd of the college students, Rahul was looking for Suchitra. She was a little bit late. Rahul met her at the gate and conveyed the message that he wanted to have an important talk with her. As there was a little time to have a talk and the paper was about to start, Suchitra said, "Let's go we will get late. I will surely meet you after the examination." It was around 5:30 PM their paper finished and they came out and went to the canteen. They sat in a corner giving up a high sigh of relief. The waiter came and disturbed them. "What would you prefer?" "Coffee and some snacks," replied Rahul. Directing his attention to Suchitra, Rahul opened his heart. "I received a call from home regarding my marriage. Suchitra curiously said, "Why your family is in such hurry? It is the last year of your M.B.B.S. a crucial year. Don't they understand it? Is it a time to marry?" "It is not my family forcing me for marriage. You know my family was not in position to support me financially for higher studies. It was my maternal uncle who financed my education and now he wants me to marry his daughter." "Suchitra, tell me what should I do? I want to marry you. I want you to discuss our marriage with your parents." "Don't worry. I will leave for my native tomorrow. I will let you know. Till then you silence your maternal uncle. Tell him candidly I love someone else and I will marry her only. Rest I will see." The next day he left Raipur for his native.

When maternal uncle came to know that Rahul was returned, he visited his house and put his proposal for marriage. Rahul with great courage and igniting force from Suchitra responded to his maternal uncle, "This is not possible. I can't marry your daughter." Uncle got irritated and questioned, "What is the problem? Let me know?" Rahul with a heavy heart replied, "I love someone else? She is my friend and classmate. We love each other." This reaction moved the ground under the feet of his uncle. Uncle got irritated and threatened either you marry my daughter or repay me with interest" He left the house with eyes turned red. The family felt little bit discouraged with this threat. But the parents did not impose their will on him. Once, the family was taking dinner. Father questioned him. "Who is the girl?" "It is Suchitra, my friend and classmate. "What is her family background?" "She belongs to a well to do family. I think her father has business." "Are you sure she will marry you?" "I am confident and fully sure that affirmation will come?" "Let's see then."

It was late in the evening. Rahul tried to call Suchitra. Initially he found her phone to be out of coverage area. After waiting some time, phone began to ring. It was Suchitra. "Hello, Rahul! How are you?" "I am fine and how are you? And where are you?" "I am just fine and enjoying picnic with family away from home." Rahul curiously questioned, "Have you discussed the issue with your parents?" "Not yet. Give me some time. I will hit the iron when it is hot. Don't worry. I will inform you at the earliest." Rahul got little bit disheartened but hiding his nervousness he said, "I am not in hurry. Take your own time. But please inform me immediately if any affirmation comes from your side." "Yes! Of course! I won't stretch your curiosity." Rahul kept the handset in his pocket and got engrossed in thinking about the certainty and uncertainty of Suchitra's decision.

Whole vacations went in waiting for her reply. Rahul waited till the last day of the vacation but no response came. He tried to reach to her number of times but her phone was switched off. It strengthened his doubt of marriage possibility and also sowed seeds of inner conflict which troubled him throughout his life. Rahul reached to Raipur one day before. The last semester was to start from the next day. Rahul got prepared earlier and directly went to the canteen. As it was too early, the canteen was yet to open. Rahul was growing eager and nervous to see Suchitra. What made him anxious was that her phone was switched off. There was cement chair outside the canteen. Rahul sat on it and was waiting for the canteen to open. After sometime; the owner of the canteen came and disturbed him, "Good Morning! Rahul. You came early. How was your vacation?" "Yes! It was a great enjoyment." He sat in his favorite corner chair and waited hopelessly that Suchitra would come and join him. He took his breakfast and went to attend the class. While entering the class he took a look at the class to check out the presence of Suchitra but became nervous when his eyes could not find her. A week passed but there was no news of Suchitra. Tension began to corrode Rahul. What troubled him was not her absence but her switched off phone. One day he mustered his courage and asked his Professor about the absence of Suchitra. Professor told him that due to some unavoidable circumstances she won't be able to report to college for a week or two.

One day he was coming to attend the lectures, he saw the crowd of the students reading something on the notice board. Finding way through the crowd of the viewers, he reached at the notice board and found that the students were reading the marriage invitation card. He got shocked and almost collapsed to find that it was the marriage invitation card of Suchitra. "Oh! My God! I am deceived." It was an unbearable shock to him. It was so severe that he could not bear it. He did not attend the lecture and directly went to the hostel. He lied on the cot and began to move his fingers on his mobile and dialing the number of Suchitra throughout the day. He was so depressed by the feeling of being deceived that he forgot to have his food. He lost his interest in his studies. Whole day he spent on thinking over unexpected stand of Suchitra. He was so engrossed in his thinking that off and on he muttered, "Suchitra you have deceived me. You are a murderer. You spoiled my dream. I hate you! Hate you for being so callous and inhuman to me. I will never pardon for what you have done to me." He stopped attending lectures and paid no attention to his diet. Late night awakening and no diet made him physically weak. When he found that he may fall sick at any moment. He packed his bag left for his native giving excuse of illness to the institute.

Sudden coming of Rahul created tension at home. Parents were worried not about his absence at the college but of the health. He had grown so weak and thin that parents could not bear it. For many days, he observed silence. Father tried to ask him but he gave no response to him. It enhanced their worries. Much of the time he spent out of home visiting this friend and that friend. One day Rahul came late. Anxious and annoyed father asked Rahul, "What is going on? Considering your health, I kept mum so far but now water is going over head. Be serious otherwise your reckless and selfish behavior makes us serious. Tell me what have you decided? What about your studies? Are you going to continue it or not?" Rahul preferred to keep silence over all these questions. Finally father got angry and said, "Forget about all these questions and tell me what about Suchitra? Do you want to marry her? If it is the reason, I will talk to her father." The moment he uttered her name, Rahul began to cry. Father spotted the frustration hidden in his loud cry. Putting his hand on his shoulder and making him feel to be with him said, "What made you cry? Is anything wrong with you?" Intensifying his loud cry he said, "Pappa, Suchitra got married and since then she neither met me nor contacted me. I am absolutely frustrated. I feel everything disinterested? The more I try to forget, the more I remember her. Her memory hurts and wounds me a lot. Papa, tell na what should I do" I can understand it my son. It is not your fault. Love makes one mad." I can do nothing but advice you as a father. If possible forget her. The more you remember her, the more it will trouble you. Engage yourself in some other activities. It will make you forget her and regain your mood. If possible accept the reality that she is married and she will never come to you. If you accept it will pain you for sometime but if you don't it will pain throughout your life."

The advice of the father had short time impact on Rahul. Very soon the memory of Suchitra overpowered him. He visited this and that friend, this and that relative and watched this and that movie and nowhere could he find his mind. The betrayal of Suchitra made him uneasy. One day father asked him, "Rahul, what about your academics? Are you not willing to rejoin the college?" Rahul purposefully avoided this question. When he was feeling uncomfortable, he took round around the city. He watched this movie and that movie. When he was fed up with it, he visited this relative and that relative. He visited his old friends to kill the time. But these sources of amusement made no charm on him. One day he was taking round on the farm of his friend. There was a hut where he found some pesticide. His evil mind began to work. He sent his friend to bring something meanwhile he managed to get some pesticide in a small bottle. He came home and hid the bottle at a secret place. He was completely sunk in despair and found no way out of it. No way and by no means could he forget Suchitra. He determined to end his life. Most of the nights passed sleepless. The inscribed image of Suchitra and the moments he spent with her troubled him a lot. He lost interest in everything as everything stopped appealing and pleasing him. Frustration took a strong hold of his mind and provoking him to lead his life to commit suicide.

It was at the stroke of midnight, Rahul suddenly got up as some nightmare of Suchitra frightened him. His body was sweating. He found his parents resting on floor. He entered the room with silent step as a thief did. He took out the bottle and came back on his cot. He found the bottle of pesticide dearer than his parents who were resting after a hard work of the day. He opened the cap and was about to pour pesticide. Suddenly his eyes caught holes on the banyan of his father and patched sari of his mother. It laid him into the life of poverty and frugality of his father and made him understand how much parents sacrifice for the sake of their children. Holes and patches and on the clothes of his parents made him realize the suffering and troubles they were taking to change the destitute destiny of the family. It made him realize the hopes for which they were taking all the pain and doing hard work. Finally he felt pitied with the miserable and poor condition of his parents. He thought if they could sacrifice every pleasure for the sake of their son's happiness, couldn't I forget Suchitra, that selfish Suchitra, who got married without having a thought what would happen to me. He muttered, "How much they have suffered and pained for me. They offered new clothes to me and wore torn. How selfless they are and how selfish I am! For the sake of a selfish girl, I was going to miss and trouble my loving parents. If I end my life, for whom will they lead their lives? What will be their hope and what will they dream of? For the sake of a selfish girl I was murdering not myself but my parents also. It is ridiculous and absolutely disgusting." He climbed down from his cot, came outside and threw the bottle away. He returned to his room and touched his parent's feet and slept with determination, "Suchitra is dead for me now. If she meets me alive at any turn of life, I won't leave her. With this midnight revengeful determination, he entered the nest of sleep. After many days, Rahul had night full of sleep. He got up early in the morning. He told his parents he was going back to college to continue his studies. It was the most delightful day for the parents. Father embraced him and cried a lot. Both cried a lot. Father exclaimed, "My son. No more mistake now! Be happy and make others happy! There is never late to amend!" He clung to his mother both wept for a long time. Eventually Rahul took his bag and left the house. He came to Raipur completed all the process of filling up examination form and fully dedicated himself to his studies. He turned nights into days and appeared for the examination. Hard work and dedication brought success to him and laurels to his parents. He finished his M.B.B.S. successfully and became a doctor.

He had his hospital in Raipur and with his outstanding surgery skills and service to the patients emerged as the most successful surgeon of Raipur. In this race of making name and making money, he had not forgotten that revengeful thought of Suchitra. Even today in some deep corner of his mind he thought of Suchitra and the way she betrayed him. Whenever he was alone and used to brood, "God bless me an opportunity to have revenge on Suchitra who pained me a lot and for her own self left me in the world of suffering." When he became a successful doctor many families coming with the proposal for marriage, but Rahul denied and convinced his parents to let him lead life of a bachelor as long as he wanted. It was at morning tea, father asked him, "My dear loving son you have given me a lot and just one thing I expect from you if you do it, it would give us a sigh of relief." "What is that you have not been given so far?" Father put forward his demand, "I want you to marry?" "Papa, let me get settled in my life and let me earn enough. There is time for it. Let it come I will do it." Father realized that Rahul was avoiding the issue of marriage. Father got irritated at him, "Marry whenever you want. I won't go after you."

One day parents asked him for going on pilgrimage. Rahul had no objection to it. Rahul managed everything from booking ticket and lodging. On the day of departure he came at the spot where travels office was located. He happily bid them farewell. Off and on he used to receive phone calls from his parents. Sometimes he phoned them to know about progress. One day it was around 9 PM Rahul received a phone call from his father. Father told him that it was raining cat and dog here. They were having meal in a hotel near Kedarnath temple in Uttrarakhand. All of a sudden the phone got disconnected due to some cacophonous sound. Rahul's mind began to think ominously as the sound in the mobile was somewhat terrific. He tried ceaselessly to be in touch with them but he could not contact his parents. Whole night he was restless. It was a sleepless night for him. When he got up and turned on the television he was absolutely terrified and shocked to watch the news of calamity and loss of human lives and public property due to cloud bursting. He hurriedly dressed himself and went to the travel agency. There was already crowd of near and dear ones of the passengers who got trapped in the calamity. Some relatives were making a loud cry over the death of their relatives. Everywhere there was a scene of *Matam*. Rahul making his way through the angry, frustrated, sad and lamenting relatives he reached to the person at the counter. Controlling his scared breath said, "Hello! Gentleman, could you please tell me about my parents?" The person at the counter questioned, "Have you brought their photographs and other details?" Rahul hurriedly took out his wallet and took out his parents' photographs and details and handed over it to the person. The person took it and began to search for it on his personal counter. Rahul was in hurry to know about his parents as the thought of safety of parents was troubling him. Rahul was ceaselessly staring at his face and observed the changes taking place in his facial expressions. Rahul began to realize that something ominous happened to his parents.

The face of person at the counter turned pale and serious as he was unable to hide it. When Rahul found that the man is delaying to answer, Rahul annoyingly questioned, "Hello! Why don't you answer? I am speaking to you. Are my parents safe?" The man at the counter opened his mouth, "I am sorry to say that the bus which carried you parents has been reported to be missing and the passengers in it are also missing. No idea about their whereabouts. Search operation is on. If I get any news, I will let you know. Don't worry." Rahul felt almost dead. He returned home in a completely frustrated state of mind. He turned on the television and kept watching the news of mishap. He wished to go there but cancelled the plan as all the roads to Kedarnath temple were damaged and blocked for safety purpose. Rahul was absolutely frustrated with this loss and as a consequence he was unable to focus on his profession. He asked his subordinates to take care of it for time being.

More than two months passed, no news of parents came. One day he went to travels agency to collect the news about the parents. The man at the counter said to him, "If you don't mind, you accept the fact that your parents are no more. Almost two months are over and we are not getting any news of the passengers. I think they are either trapped in the mud or carried away to nearby sea where they might have been eaten by the fish. Report says the dead bodies found were in very worst condition. Such dead bodies were cremated on the spot considering hygienic issues of the people living around. Better you give up the hope of their being survived. If they were alive, they would have come back or at least contacted me or you." Rahul did not get angry with him and said, "You are right gentleman. Better I should give up the hope of their survival." He returned home and began his normal routine. After many days he attended his hospital. Patients were eagerly waiting for him as they had less faith in the medicinal capabilities of other doctors. He focused on his profession and patiently waited to accept the lot as it came to him. But he was consistently watching the news on the television and contacted the travel agency.

Almost year passed. Rahul had become habitual to his routine life. Loneliness of life was corroding him but he never let it overpower him. One day he got up quite late. He informed the hospital about his late coming. He went to the kitchen to make coffee. Suddenly his cell phone began to ring. It was the call of his subordinate doctor. He said, "Please come urgently. There is a serious patient. If you delay it can cause harm to her life. I can't see her condition. She is extremely uncomfortable with physical pain. Please see how you can come early. Her relatives are troubling me a lot." Rahul said, "Don't worry, I will come shortly till then you give her some pain killers." Rahul reached the hospital in some minutes. He put on his uniform and sat in his chair and called his subordinate. He came there and reported, "It might be a case of appendix or some intestine problem." Rahul hastily got up from his chair and walked towards the room where the patient was admitted. Rahul came closer to the patient and got shocked and surprised to see that it was Suchitra. Suchitra looked at him and bowed down and never dared to look into his eyes."

The dormant desire to take revenge and teach lesson to the killer of his emotions and dream got accelerated. He began to grow revengeful and made determination not to leave her at any cost. He thought "Criminal is in my dock. I am the judge. I will decide either to punish her or to leave her. But whatever may happen, she had to pay for what she had done to me. I won't let her go so easily. She brought grief and suffering in my life how can I see her to be so happy. Let her bear the pangs of agony then she would understand how much I suffered at her hands. Let her get burnt in my anger. Previously my life was in her hand. She punished me for my no fault. God had offered me an opportunity to punish for her fault. Whatever may happen, her fault won't be pardoned. I won't let it happen. I will do with her what she did with her. Hurry up! Prey is trapped. Do take chance otherwise; she may get slipped out of your trap." Suddenly he stopped and called his subordinate and said, "Your guess is right. It is case of an appendix and it is in its last stage. She needs an immediate operation. If delayed, it can cause risk to her life. Get ready for operation. It will be performed at 5 PM." After giving the necessary instructions he returned to the cabin and got engrossed in the world of revenge. He began to think "What to do with her? How to behave with her? The girl whom I loved the most in return she behaved so cunningly and craftily with me how she can expect me to give her life. But I am a doctor and I should not forget that saving life is my duty and principle of the profession says that I should not let my personal will enter in my profession." Suddenly his evil mind empowered him and said, "Keep your professional principles aside and don't give life to the girl who made your life unhappy."

He prepared two syringes. In one syringe he loaded life saving medicine and in the second he loaded poison. His conflict began which should be selected? As the time of operation came near, his conflict got intensified. He did not want that other should not get wind of his intentions. So he asked his subordinate that he was going to perform operation individually and if he needed he would call him. He instructed him that only nurse should remain present. Subordinate nodded positively. Sharp at 5 PM operation began. Only two nurses were there. He finished the operation within half an hour. Eventually his hands moved towards two syringes one was a pain killer and other contained poison. He took the first syringe which contained poison and was about to inject it, suddenly he stopped. His conscience stopped and said, "It is not fair. You are doing an injustice with the patient who trusted you." He withdrew his hand back and picked up the second one and was about to inject. Suddenly his revengeful mind overpowered him and said, "It is not injustice. You are doing justice with yourself. Justice says she should die. Let her die. She has lost her right to live." Again he picked up the poisoned syringe was to inject suddenly his conscience overpowered him stopped him saying, No! Stop it! You are a doctor and as a doctor, it is your commitment to save her. Forget your personal emotions. Save her. If you do it, it will be loyalty to your profession and will make you happy." Thus he did it number of times. He got so confused in this conflict of fair and foul. Eventually his conscience overpowered his evil mind and prepared him to save life. But he was so confused in the conflict that he wanted to save her but unconsciously he picked up the syringe having poison taking it to be the life saving and injected. He came out of the operation theatre. His body was sweating and he picked up his handkerchief began to wipe it out." He came and sat in his cabin with the satisfaction that he saved her life."

He called the nurses in. While coming towards the doctor's cabin, a nurse said to the other, "Did you observe any change in the doctor?" The second nurse said, "Yes! He seemed to be confused and his hands were trembling while injecting as if he was doing something wrong with the life of the patient." "I thought the same." said the second nurse. They entered the cabin and said, "Did you call us?" "Yes!

I called to inform you that I have given her the pain killer. She would take a few hours to regain her consciousness. Be there with her and if needed please call me." The nurses said in one voice, "Yes Sir! Don't worry. We will take absolute care of her." Half an hour later, the doctor got up from his chair and hurriedly stepped towards Operation Theater." He went closer and got shocked to see the life saving injection was still there and fully loaded and the syringe which had poison was empty. He exclaimed, "Oh! My God! What I did. I made a mistake. I killed her! I am a murderer." The mistake hurt him a lot and he was totally bewildered. He told his subordinate doctor that he was going on important mission and he might not come back to the hospital. He shouldered him the responsibility of looking after Suchitra and he left the office hastily and frighteningly. Time passed very quickly. Nandini became shut the main door and entered in his bedroom. He was absolutely scared and had turned diffident. He knew the consequence of his deed. He was unrest at heart. After some hours, he received a phone call from his subordinate doctor stating that patient did not wake up. "It made all of us serious. Patents' relatives are making commotions and troubling with lot of questions. We can't do anything but to silence our tongues and face their anger. If possible come and convince the relatives. We have failed." The doctor asked his subordinate to check pulse rate and inform him. The subordinate doctor did it; he got shocked to find the patient dead. All of them got shocked as it was not expected. With sweaty hands and sweaty body he made one more phone call to the doctor and reported, "Sir, Patient is no more." Doctor asked him to inform the patients' relatives about the death and he switched off his phone. When the subordinate doctor informed the relatives about the death of the patients, they grew aggressive and violent. Some of them started breaking the cabin of the doctor and broke some artifacts provided lot of damage to the hospital. One of them came forward and slapped the subordinate doctor and demanded an immediate presence of the doctor. They threatened the subordinate doctor if the doctor did not come, they will call the police here and register a case of murder against him. The subordinate doctor was totally scared. He was absolutely helpless to take any action. He took out the phone and made a call. His scare reached to its zenith as he found the doctor's phone to be switched off. One of them angrily asked, "What happened? Is he coming or not? Why are you silent?" The relatives understood and one of them called the police.

A police van came at the hospital and made necessary investigation. They tried to calm down the angry mob convincing them that if the doctor found guilty in this matter, they won't leave him. Those words of the police silenced the angry mob. The police tried to call the doctor number of times but they failed. Finally the police van moved towards the doctor's residence. The van stopped at bungalow of the doctor. There was a security guard. The police asked him about the doctor's presence. He said, "Sahab is there in the bungalow." The police got down from the van, walked towards the main entrance." They gave a big thumbing at the inner door. They did it ceaselessly with the expectation that if the doctor was slept, he would open it after hearing this big thumbing, but they received no response. They smelt something ominous in it. They tried to reach him on phone again they found his phone to be off. Finally they called the security and ordered him to open the door. He brought some instrument and broke the door. The police reached to the bedroom of the doctor. It was slightly opened. When they pushed the bedroom door in they got shocked to see, the doctor's body was hanging to the ceiling fan. They took him down and found him to be dead. On the cot they found a piece of paper which spoke like this." "Suchitra was my love. But she betrayed me. I wanted to take revenge on her but my principles and ideals of my profession came in my way. I was so troubled in dilemma whether to kill her or give her a life. Eventually when I decided to be loyal to my profession, my confused mind made a mistake and I injected wrongly. Really I made a mistake, A Great Mistake."

Nandini

It was the time of sunset. The tired sun was stepping slowly and powerlessly towards its destination. The vigorous darkness was growing eager to furnish him shelter. The departure of the Sun left its despairing marks in the darkness. Perhaps it might be reason why the darkness of the eve did not seem to be that much hopeful. It seemed to be somewhat sad at its heart. Perhaps it anticipated something painful happening in its presence. The gloomy darkness was covering a town Sitamadi in its black blanket. The town was getting silenced with the arrival of darkness. The street lights and home lights reported on their work. The entire town was almost silent as majority of people were engaged in their households. A small sized house was there in one of the lanes of Sitamadi. People were seen coming and going out of the house muttering slowly. It was the house of a clerk Mohandas in Muncipalty of Sitamadi. Entry into the house showed that a woman was lying on the bed and people were sitting around her. Mohandas was sitting at her pillow and at her foot there was a girl. The woman lying on the bed was Suchitra, the wife of Mohandas. Silent interiors of the house were being disturbed due to her speedily breathing which resulted in her aching sound. Suchitra had been suffering from asthma from last some years. She was under treatment but her body had become so weak that she could not respond to the medicines. That eve her illness had gripped her with its full might strangulating her and robbing her of her breaths. The trouble was so painful that Suchitra was dying to die and the disease was dying to have her. Crowd of the people was breaking the frontiers of the small sized house. Everyone was staring at her with gloomy face and a question mark indicating what would happen. Suchitra's breathes were getting tired almost all were reached home except one which was taking time. Before it reached its home, she called her daughter Nandini and handed over her hand to her father who was at her pillow. The last breath of Suchitra reached to its destination and silent interiors got disturbed with lamenting sounds of mourners.

Nandini was just twelve years old when she lost her mother. Mohandas had to attend office leaving Nandini alone. Her schooling was going on. But when she returned from the school, she was all alone and felt bored. Mohandas too was well known with situation but he was helpless as he had no option but to keep her alone at home. After coming from school, she sat for her studies. As she was not mature, she could not do cooking and all those things which woman could do. As she was little and no one was to accompany her, out of fear she confined herself in the house. When a stranger knocked the door, she got scared and avoided to speak to him. It was Sunday. Mohandas was at home. Nandini came to him and began to weep. "My dear Nandini, what is the problem and why these tears for?" "Papa, when you are away, I miss you. I feel lonely and above all scared. When someone knocks at the door, I get scared and don't dare to open the door. Please do something otherwise the grave silence will kill me." Mohandas realized and understood the feeling of his lonely daughter." He assured her, "Don't worry. Have patience. Everything will be alright." Suddenly someone knocked the door. Both looked at the door. It was a distant relative of Mohandas. He recognized him and cordially invited him in. "Hello Badri! How are you?" "I am alright. Thank you. What about you? Sorry I could not come to attend the funeral of your wife. I feel very sorry for that." "It is ok. Thanks for being curious to know about my life." "I think it is humanity." "If you don't mind if I suggest." "No! Go ahead." "You are still young and alone. Why don't you marry? It will end your concerns and it will bring happiness to you and your little daughter will get a mother?" The very reference of Nandini made him serious about the proposal of Badri." "But who will marry a person who is a widower?" "Leave it to me I will take care of it. Just I want to know whether you are ready if anyone accepts you." Looking at little miserable Nandini he said, "Yes".

Within a week, he returned back with proposal which was eventually accepted. Sitamadi also sympathized with him and stood with him. The people of Sitamadi came forward and arranged his marriage. Each and every member of the family in the town gave his presence at the marriage ceremony. Saroja entered as the second wife of Mohandas. Once again the silent interiors of the house began to speak. Happiness was there everywhere and Nandini felt happy that she got someone to accompany her and make her feel fearless at home. Soon Saroja and Nandini became one with each other. Saroja was soft hearted loving woman. She loved and cared Nandini. She took her studies and played with her whenever was possible. Nandini was good at studies. It was at the hour of noon, Nandini was busy in reading her text. Saroja finished her work and came to accompany her. "Nandini what are you reading?" "A poem." "What poem?" "Mother" and began to weep. Saroja put her hand on her head and asked, "Do you remember your mother?" "Yes. A lot" "How was she?" "She was a never ending fountain of love and affection. She never scolded and punished me. Always smiled and caressed me with care. What a woman never seen before! When I used to sit for studies, she came near and read with me loudly. We recited a poem together. Her voice was very sweet. Whenever I remember her, I read that poem which we read together. It makes me cry." "You loved her a lot." "Yes. But one thing I wish to tell you since you have come in the house, I have become little oblivion to her and find you to be very close to her." When Saroja heard this, she took her close and told her, "I know I am not your mother. But whatever the love and care I could shower on you, I will do." Nandini kissed on her cheek. Tears began to enhance the shining of their faces.

Life was going on very smoothly. Saroja became pregnant and the happiness of the family knew no bound. All are waiting for the arrival of the new member in the family. Nandini was also very happy as she was going to get a companion. The period of pregnancy was very delightful for both. It brought them very close to each other. Previously Saroja cared Nandini lot now Nandini became her caretaker. Though she was not mature girl, she helped her a lot. Keeping her studies aside, she helped her mother in doing all the household activities. Soon Saroja delivered a male child. All were happy. Much of her time Nandini spent with him caring and playing. Saroja always took care that Nandini should never feel to be isolated. She doubled her love for Nandini. When the baby rested, Saroja did her house work and sat with Nandini for studies. One day Nandini was busy in reading something, Saroja questioned her, "Nandini what do you wish to be in your coming life?" "I wish to be a doctor." "Why do you wish to be a doctor" "To love and care the people. When you were not there, I suffered a lot on account of mother's unexpected departure. Pappa had to be away and at home I was totally deprived of love and care of a mother. There are many people in this huge world who really need love and care of their near and dear ones but on account of some reasons they are deprived. I have well realized the value of love and care. That is why I always wish to give it wholeheartedly." "It is really idealistic."

Time passed very quickly. Nandini became mature and one of the responsible member of the family. She was appearing for her H.S.C. examination. Saroja faced one more pregnancy in the course of the time and gave a daughter to the family. Her first son Rohit was going to school and the second was on the verge of it. As it was the most important year, Nandini turned nights into days for her study and fortunately came up with flying colors in the examination. Her percentage was so high that she easily got admitted in for M.B.B.S. It was a great honor for the family. Mohandas spent all that he had earned in his life on the education of his loving daughter and fulfilled her dream. Mohandas, a poor clerk, took a huge loan which he could not repay. It took years but the burden was not lessened. Financial tensions started mounting over the family. Mohandas took it very seriously and one day when he was on duty received a severe heart attack. He died on the spot. His dead body was brought home. Unfortunately Nandini was not there to receive it. Saroja was almost collapsed with this event. It was a great shock and caused an irrevocable damage to the family.

Nandini had been to her college to do some official work. When she received a call from home that such thing happened, she began to cry there only. Without spending a single moment, she returned home. Seeing the serious and lamenting face of the crowd at home, she could not control her cry and she entered the house shouting, "Pappa, I can't believe that you are no more. You left us alone in this world, now at who we should look at as our support. Wake up. We need you a lot." She embraced Saroja and carried away in emotions. Funeral was done in tearful condition. It was the most memorable and painful day in the life of the family. They were not ready to believe that the father was not there in the family. For some days Relatives were there who consoled them. Soon the crowd of the relatives and enquirers lessened and the absence of Mohandas began to trouble them. The question of survival became a great trouble to them.

Fortune smiled upon the bereaved family. Nandini's result came and she passed M.B.B.S. exam with good marks. Within a few days, she joined as a doctor at local hospital which gave great financial relief to the bereaved family. That change in the family relived them from the sorrow of the departed father. It was a job of good salary. Nandini emerged as a strong support of the family. All were happy as the family got a strong financial source. Saroja's children were growing. Saroja was happy with the way Nandini was taking care of the family. She became the father of the family. Whole day a just one name dominated the family and that was Nandini. Nandini too was happy with her status in the family and felt proud that she could do something for the sake of her family.

Saroja was cautious that Nandini was attaining marriageable age. Everyday someone come with the proposal for marriage. She wanted to get her married off but she was troubled with question that who will look after her family in case Nandini got married? Saroja knew that family still depended on her. If that support lost, the family would get disturbed. So she was postponing the marriage of Nandini. She thought let her son complete his education got settled, and then marriage of Nandini would be seriously considered. Saroja was sleeping and became uneasy with the memory of Mohandas. She realized the worth of a husband in woman's life. It made her realize the emotional and physical needs of Nandini. The next day when they came together she happily asked, "Nandini, you have done a good job for the sake of the family. Now the family wants to do something for you." "What is that you want do?" "I wish to see your marriage. Good proposals are coming and accept one of them." "Mother, why are you hurrying for marriage? Are you fed up with me?" "It is not like that one day or other, it is to be done. Why not now then?" "No. I am not ready for it now. I think there is lot for me to do for the sake of the family. Very soon Rohit will finish his studies. I have to do something for his settlement. When he gets job and start earning money, I will ask to perform my marriage."

At heart Nandini also wished to free herself from the responsibilities of the family and lead life for herself. But time was the barrier and homely responsibilities were there she had to perform. Time was passing with giving little ease to Nandini. Saroja's son completed his studies and luckily he got a job as an engineer in a local industry. Nandini was very happy with the happening. She offered a dinner to all in a hotel to celebrate the accomplishment of Rohit. When they were enjoying dinner, Saroja touched to the right chord of Nandini's heart. "Nandini, get ready for marriage. I have seen a boy who is also a doctor. He is coming to see you next week. I have a photograph which I will show to you. I have seen him. The boy is handsome. I hope you will prefer him. It is great responsibility which I wish to perform at the earliest. As a woman I can understand how much you would be suffering at heart." Nandini was quite happy at heart. She accepted the proposal without any negation. "Mummy, I also think that the time has come for me to get married. If you have seen a boy from my field, it is well and good. I am ready."

One day Nandini took a leave stayed home as the boy was coming to see her. She was very happy at heart and willing to see him. At 1:00pm a motor making sound came in front of their house and became silent. A cultured family with handsome young man got down and marched towards their house. Nandini who was very eager to see how the boy looked stood at the window keeping it slightly open so that none could see her. Through the slightly open window she looked at him became very happy as the boy was very handsome. Girl seeing ceremony took place in delightful atmosphere. Boy was so impressed by Nandini that he conveyed his affirmation to his parents there only. Parents of the boy informed Saroja that their son Rajendra liked Nandini and they wished to have the marriage at the earliest possible. Saroja happily agreed and got ready for marriage.

On a Sunday, the engagement ceremony was arranged. For the first time Rajendra and Nandini got the chance to talk to each other. They talked with each other in a room became one with each other. Since then everyday calling was there. Rajendra came home to talk to her. If she was in hospital, he went there and had a talk. It was going on very nicely. At home Saroja was very busy in marriage preparation. As she was not able to handle the responsibility, she appointed a maid servant Kashibai who was middle aged, widow a good natured woman. With her good temperament and her skilled work she became one of the members of family. Nandini had special attachment for her as she had never had the chance to enjoy the love and affection of her grandmother. Every one respected her and fondly called her grandma. Saroja asked Kashibai, "Grandma, who is there at your home?" "I am alone. I lost my husband a few years back he was a great drunkard." "Sorry! What about your children?" "I had a son?" "What do you mean by that?" "It is not like that. My husband was very short tempered. He used to come home fully drunk and beat us. We were tired of his everyday beating. My son Sanjay was very scared of him. One day he came home and began to beat me. Sanjay came to save me. He threw me down and began to beat him. Sanjay was so scared that he ran away from the house and never returned then. No news of him. I don't know whether he was dead or alive." Kashibai's narration made all silent. All sympathized with her. "Nandini had tears in her eyes and requested her, "Grandma why don't you stay with us then? We too want a grandma for this house who will love and care us?" All supported Nandini. Kashibai accepted the proposal and came to stay with them.

One day Nandini was busy in checking the patients. Almost all the patients were examined and last was there who was sitting there on the chair outside. He had covered himself with a blanket so that none could see his appearance. Nandini asked the nurse "Is anybody there outside?" The nurse said, "Mam, just one is left. Call him quickly. I am in hurry to go home." The man came in. Both felt strange about the man. He was absolutely covered. He took the chair and sat silently and was unwilling to uncover him. Nandini understood it. She questioned, "Why don't you uncover yourself, gentleman?" He replied, "I am afraid you don't like it." "It won't." The gentleman slowly uncovered himself. The nurse who saw him got scared and went outside. For a moment, Nandini too got frightened. His face was very ugly and his body had received cracks through which blood was coming. For a moment she too was not willing to examine him. But she could not do so. The patient begged, "I can't bear the trouble and I am scared of my own appearance. There are doctors. I visited them but none of them liked to treat me. When I went to them they avoided me made me wait for a long time and when my number came they left hospital or got themselves engaged in some work. I felt insulted. I determined not to go to the doctor bear what pangs of agony are there in lot. But since morning, I am experiencing lot of pain and a lot of blood is coming out of the wounds. Your hospital was new and not visited previously so I became hopeful and came here. At least you should not say no to me. Give me some medicine or tablets which would offer me some relief." Nandini was extremely moved by his suffering. She called the nurse in but she was not there. Nandini realized. She took some cotton and began to dry the wounds on his hands and face. She applied some creams and bandaged his fingers which were releasing blood. After giving him treatment, she sat on her chair and prescribed him some medicines. "You take the medicines and tablets which I suggest. It will give you some relief from the pain." Patient looked at her and said, "You are Goddess for me. I am really moved by the way you treated me. You are really a doctor who believes in her professional religion. Thank you and god bless you with a long and happy life" She treated so many patients but she never had satisfaction like this. The words of the patients really pleased her and made her felt that she was a doctor in a real sense.

The meeting was over but it left such marks behind that Nandini had to bear it. It might be her misfortune that she got infected by the patient of leprosy. Slowly she began to observe the symptoms of that horrible disease in her. She was frightened. She took medicines but they could do no magic. Slowly the disease was spreading its roots on her body and giving a lot of cracks to her body. One day Rajendra came to see her and he observed the change in her appearance. Being a doctor, he realized it in a second. Without making mention of it and avoided talking to her, he left her there. Nandini understood. She felt sorry but spoke not a word. Since then she never saw his face. One day the family members of Rajendra informed Sujata that due to some reason, they had to break the marriage. It was a great shock to Saroja as whole preparation was done. She sat on the chair with absolute frustration. All were shocked. Kashibai asked, "What happened? Why are you silent?" "Marriage is broken." It silenced Kashibai.

Saroja was in problem and tension how to break the news to Nandini. What an impact it will have on her. Soon Nandini returned home. All were silent. Nandini understood but spoke not a single word. Seeing the grave faces of the family members, she asked as if she knew nothing. "What happened? Why your faces are looking so horrible?" Saroja broke the news. "There was a call a from Rajendra's house that they have broken the marriage." Nandini showed no response just she laughed reluctantly. It does not matter for me. I am really happy to accept the decision. You should too. Don't feel sorry over that. It was destined." All were in mourning mood as if someone was dead at home. It was a sleepless night for all. Saroja thought, "Why this sudden denial for? Everything was alright till last few days. What happened suddenly that they came to the decision of denial? There might be something that Rajendra's family objected. She thought she must ask Rajenrdra's mother. Suddenly she changed her thought as she was aware that it won't change their minds. There might be something serious which made them took such a drastic decision." Whole night passed in confusion but nothing could come out except to accept the decision of negation. It was a disgrace to the family. Saroja thought a lot over it and when she looked at the wall, the wall clock stroke 6 O'clock. She got up and began to work. She was feeling restless.

The family could not digest the rejection. It had a worse impact on the family and above all Nandini. It contributed a lot to the exposure of the disease. Gradually the disease began to show its real colors and the colors were so dark that the eyes hated them all. Saroja ignorant so far took a serious note of her disease. One day Saroja was cooking.

She asked Nandini to wash utensils. When Nandini was washing utensils, Saroja's eyes fell on her hand and she got shocked. "Stop, Nandini! What happened to your fingers? They are bleeding. Show me." Nandini felt shame of it and tried to hide it but she could not. Finally she had to show it to Saroja. Saroja was wise enough to understand what disease it is. She shouted, "Nandini, it is leprosy. You have hidden it from us. You have done great wrong to us. Has Rajendra an idea of it?" Nandini nodded positively. Saroja understood it was the reason of the refusal.

The word leprosy was horrible to hear and more horrible to see it. It changed Saroja's mind. Saroja took the disease to the heart and felt insecure. The word changed the minds of all in the family except Kashibai. Saroja who loved Nandini so much till yesterday, turned hostile to and started avoiding her, maintaining safe distance from her and avoided to use things of hers. She lessened her contacts with her and warned her children to be away from her. She also warned Kashibai to be away from her. Nandini was observing that change in her family. She felt very sorry over this change. She realized that people were changed. Love was replaced by hatred. Eyes were throwing out the fire of hatred. She knew that very soon she would be thrown out of the house or completely ignored. She thought to leave the house but where to go was the problem. So she continued bearing every ill treatment at the hands of those who loved her so much till yesterday and for whom she liked to live. Single word leprosy changed the lives of the family. Relation broken and people separated and a grave silence came to stay in the life of Nandini. None spoke with her. Nandini became almost a walking shadow.

Saroja was growing hostile day by day as if she did not like Nandini's presence. Nandini too took this change to her heart. Her disease was taking a grave form stealing her beauty and spoiling her life. Disease was painting her with horrible colors. Her face was completely changed. It was looking so horrible that no one preferred to see her face. Realizing the danger of it and its contagious nature, Saroja confined her in a room and warned her not to open the door and told her that whole day she had to be within the room. She would get everything there only. So far Kashibai kept quiet but when she observed the cruelty of Saroja was growing, she interfered, "Stop Saroja! It is too much. I can't imagine one can be so inhuman to someone who sacrificed her life. I know it is horrible disease and can affect the people if they come in contact. But she is not a stranger. She is one of the members of family. We should treat her like ours?" Saroja shouted at her, "Kashibai, I respect you but better you keep quiet in this matter. It is serious matter and can harm us. I can't afford to put my family in unnecessary trouble." Kashibai was well aware of her position in the family after all she was stranger and too much interference would bring crack in their relationship.

One day Saroja had been to market with her children. Kashibai got the chance to talk to Nandini. "Nandini you are really an unfortunate child of the destiny. Sometimes I feel that you are paying for your goodness." Hearing this, Nandini could not control herself and began to cry. Kashi affectionately took her close and moved her hand very loving over head. Nandini embraced her and said, "Kashibai, what should I do now? Leprosy has made my life horrible and lifeless. No one loves, cares me and worst thing is that no one talks to me. You tell me how one can spend his whole life in silence." "I can understand it my dear child. But you're helpless. You have to bear it as long as god wishes but believe that God is not cruel that much to leave you in this state permanently. Be hopeful that something positive would come out it." Saroja came shouting in, "Kashibai, I told you not to talk to Nandini. I did not like this." "Kashibai kept quiet and went into the bedroom. Nandini could not tolerate this and ran towards her bedroom and locked herself. Kashibai felt very sorry over the miserable plight of Nandini. She wished to do something but she could not.

Saroja was growing very harsh and merciless towards Nandini. She locked the door of Nandini's room so that she should not come out. One day she called the carpenter and asked him to cut bottom of the door sufficiently so that she could push the food through it. She wanted no contact with Nandini and warned everyone in the house especially Kashibai whatever may happen nobody will dare to open the door. Everyone followed the instruction strictly. Kashibai disliked the way Saroja was treating Nandini. But like a helpless creature she was watching the things done to Nandini. Saroja managed separate utensils for Nandini in which food was served. She never touched them. She asked Kashibai to serve the food and asked her to wash them off. A merciless villain in Saroja took the hold of her mind and began to display its villainy through her every act. Sarojawas really fed up with Nandini. She wanted to get rid of her. So she lessened food served to Nandini. Previously food was offered twice to Nandini along with breakfast. Slowly she stopped giving breakfast, then giving lunch off and on. Sometimes Nandini had to live with one time food. Hunger and pain of disease made her a miserable creature. The moment she was not able bear the pain of hunger and disease, she shouted, "Giving me food. I am dying. Either have mercy on me or kill me." Saroja heard the cries of Nandini but she deliberately unnoticed it. Kashibai disgusted Saroja's villainy. She knew that Saroja did not have good intentions. She realized that Saroja was doing it deliberately so that Nandini should die soon.

One day Nandini was crying very loudly and demanding food. Kashibai could not tolerate it. She went to the kitchen and brought some food for Nandini and was about to push through the gap of the door. Saroja saw and came there snatched away the dish. Said, "Let her die. I don't want her." "I won't." "You have to if you wish to continue here. It is my home and I know better how to run it. You are a servant and live within your position. If you can't better you leave the house and if possible take her with you. I want none of you." Kashibai got annoyed at the way Saroja treated her. She angrily said, "I know that it is not my house and never expected it to be. It was your selfishness that kept me here. I am leaving and not alone. Nandini will go with me." Saroja gave a smirk to her. Kashibai opened the door of Nandini who was lying on the bed almost dead. She covered her body with a blanket and supporting her she took her out. She looked at Saroja and said, "Thank You for this day" Saroja again smirked at her. Seeing them going, Saroja exclaimed, "Finally trouble left the house!" and laughed loudly.

Kashibai took her to her house. It was not big and comfortable. But it was enough for two persons. She saw Nandini was turned very horrible. Her face received a lot of cracks which changed her face. Kashibai felt very sorry for her. She gave her bath with hot water and mixed some leaves in it. It gave her some relief and made her feel fresh. Nandini felt very happy and indebted. Kashibai cooked and served to Nandini. She enjoyed it and said to her, "Kashibai, how kind you are! Really I saw the image of my mother in you. If she had been alive, she would have taken care of me like you." "Let it be. I am with you everything will be alright." Nandini smiled after a long time. She embraced her and said, "Don't you think you will be affected by me." Kashibai laughed at her and said, "I don't care. I am an old woman and I don't know how long this body will be alive. If not leprosy some other disease will live on it. Why not leprosy, then? I wished to be so. It will make me your true companion." Both laughed at each other. "Nandini, you take rest for some time. I am going out to see my old friend."

Kashibai knew a woman who was her old friend who kept good knowledge of Homeopathy. She went in search of her and luckily someone gave her the address of her friend. She reached to her house which was closed. Kashibai knocked at the door and a young woman opened the door. "Who are you? What do you want?" "I am Kashibai. Does Savitri live here?" I am her old friend." The woman gave her a smile and said, "She lives here. Come in please. Sit there comfortably. I will send her." She went in and gave the message to her mother in law. Savitri came out and surprised to see Kashibai sitting on the sofa. Both smiled at each other. Savitri enquired, "Where had you been so long? I visited your house number of times but all the time I found it locked." "I had been staying with my relatives in the town." "Is everything ok?" "Everything is fine and I hope the same with you." "Yes. It seems to me that you want something."

"Yes." Kashibai shared the problem with her. Savitri went in and brought a paste of some leaves and told her how to apply. She instructed her if you apply it for six months or more, I am sure it will cure the disease." Kashibai thanked her.

Kashibai returned home in cheerful mood. Nandini asked her where she had been so long." "I had been to my old friend. Do you know what she has given me? "What?" she opened a carry bag and showed paste to her and said, "This is medicine for you. My friend has advised me that if I apply this paste to your body for six months or more, it may cure your disease." "Are you sure it will create that magic." "Not only I but also the entire town believed in her medicinal powers. It has shown results. A lot of stories told that how people are benefited. Let's try it. What magic is there in attempting it? I am sure that it won't cause any loss too." "Kashibai, I have full trust in you and know that you always love my interest. Do as you wish."

Like a mother Kashibai began to apply the paste. Luckily that paste began to show its magic. Both were happy with it. Kashibai continued it for more than six months and fortune smile upon Nandini. Paste did its magic and Nandini got cured. She regained her lost beauty. She looked at the mirror and exclaimed, "Kashibai you are genius. You are not less than a God. You have given me new life and new hope. You made me alive. Tell what you want in return." Kashibai smiled and said, "Mother never expects anything from her daughter but gives. You are not like my daughter but daughter in real sense. If at all you wish to give anything to me then do one thing be with me if I need you in old my age." "You have done such a wonderful job for me I am really indebted. You have done a lot for me and now it's my turn to do something for you."

Nandini rejoined her service as a civil surgeon. She was earning good salary. In a year or two she accumulated a good amount which she used for reconstructing the old house of Kashibai. In a few months, an old cottage of Kashibai turned it into a well furnished and capacious house with a title 'Kashibai'. A house warming ceremony was arranged and half of the town attended the ceremony. Kashibai was on the seven heavens. It was a hectic day. Whole day there was hustle and bustle everywhere. Both were tired due to day's activities. She took dinner and before going to bed had chat. Kashibai took her close, kissed her and said, "You are daughter as well as my son. I don't understand why people are mad for sons when daughters are there like you." Nandini gave smile with a great pride. She looked at her wrist watch and shouted, "Kashibai, it is quarter to one. It's really late. I have to go to office tomorrow." Nandini switched off the lights and slept. Usually, Kashibai woke earlier than Nandini and did all the household activities. That day she did not leave her bed. Nandini got up and saw that Kashibai was still in bed. She shocked that it never happened. She went close to her and found that Kashibai body was sweating and she had chest pain. She understood that it was mild heart attack. She instantly shifted her to the hospital. As there was risk to bring her back home so she continued her stay in the hospital for some days.

One day a young, handsome, and well dressed young man came in the lane of Kashibai asking an address to the people who met in the way. Finally he reached to the house of Kashibai and felt disheartened to see the house was locked. He enquired to the neighbor. The neighbor informed him that she had a mild heart attack and admitted in the local civil hospital. He hurriedly stepped towards the civil hospital. He reached to the ward where Kashibai was shifted. Nandini was checking the patients. A nurse was passing through the corridor. He asked her about Kashibai. She asked him to accompany her. Finally they entered in room of Kashibai. Nurse said, "Kashibai, get up. See someone has come to see you." Kashibai who was resting slowly opened the eyes saw a young man was standing in front of her with bouquet. Mother is mother. Within a minute, she identified him to make confirmation of it she questioned, "Are you Sanjay?" Sanjay smiled and cried loudly, "Aai!" Both embraced each other. He offered her a bouquet. She enquired, "Where had you been so long? Years passed never missed me." "I did but I was afraid of Pappa. Where is he?" Kashibai looked down and said, "He died a few days after your departure. Let's forget those painful memories. It is delightful moment. Tell me about you and your survival." "I have been staying in Mumbai running business with good earning." "What made you come here?" "I missed you a lot. It is love and strong desire to see you brought me here." "Will you stay here or go back." "I am fed up the city and its life. I have sold out my property and come here to be with you and start my own business here."

Suddenly Nandini came there which disturbed their conversation. Giving a big smile to Nandini she exclaimed, "Nandini see who has come to see me" "Who?" "He is my long lost son Sanjay." Nandini exclaimed with a joy, "What a surprise! Is it a dream or a reality? I can't believe. How can it be possible?" Kashibai happily touched his hand and said

I have touched him. It has become possible. It is reality." All smiled at one another. Looking at Sanjay she asked, "What about your marriage? Are you married or a bachelor?" "I am still bachelor." Kashibai looked at Nandini and passed the message. Nandini smiled. They got married and the whole family lived happily thereafter.

Well Done My Son

It was 11 AM. The air was releasing smell of some pleasant happening. There was hustle and bustle everywhere in a college at Raybareli, as there was Golden Jubilee Year celebration of the oldest educational institute. To add to the color in the celebration, the trust of the institute had invited an internationally acclaimed young Indian Writer popularly known with his pen name Siddhartha. The writer had rocked and shaken English Literary Sphere with his innovative and novel writing. In short span of time and at an early age, he had attained ample celebrity at an international level with his creative writing. In his short career, he had created wonderful and commendable literary creations which made him emerging and twinkling star in the galaxy of Indian English Writing. He delivered his acceptance to attend the celebration as he was the former student of the institute and to revive the memories of the childhood and to see the transformation brought about in the appearance of the city. The city was garnished with banners, flex and pamphlets with writer's photographs. The institute left no stone unturned to advertise the occasion and give publicity to the writer to catch the maximum crowd for the function. The news of impending arrival of the world famous writer caught the ear of the people, the sea of the people, poets, writers and lovers of literature began to make the crowd there. The writer became the talk of the town. The coming of the Writer had become the talk of the town as the crowd at the tea stall, pan stall and all other sorts of shops were seen discussing and talking about arrival of the writer. Everyone present over there had had his eyes on the arrival of the writer. There was an enthusiastic leader of the girl's group was heard addressing, "The moment the writer will get down from his car we catch him and take his autograph. Let's be the bees to get his autograph. All said in one voice, 'Yes, Sarojini'

The passage which went towards the main building of the institute where the function was to be held was fully crowded. The students were standing on both the sides of the road to welcome the guest and at the main building there was huge crowd of the youngsters standing with waiting stance. Suddenly a luxurious car entered through the main gate accompanied by a police van. The crowd which was on the both sides of the road started chasing the car. When the writer got down from the car, the crowd of lovers attacked on him as honeybees attack their object. The writer got overwhelmed by this welcome. He was trying to please everyone with his autograph as it was getting late; he had to disappoint most of them. As it was getting late to the function and his fans were not ready to leave him; the police took him out of the gyre of the crowd. But the lovers chased him till he reached on the dais. After completing initial formality, the anchor announced, "Ladies and Gentlemen and all the lovers of Hon. Siddhartha, your long awaited moment to listen to your darling writer has come. Before I invite, I would like appeal you to give him a big applause. All stood and gave him a standing ovation and clapped in such way that the entire hall got vibrated. The writer felt extremely overwhelmed with this grand welcome. The anchor said, "I would like to invite Sir to address his fans, lovers, admirers and the readers. There was a pin drop silence in the hall. All had dedicated their ears, minds and hearts to the Writer. There was a proud smile on the face when he was moving towards the mike. The way he moved towards mike was really very impressive. The gestures and postures of his personality caught the attention of all. The way he held his mike in his hand and stood in a confident stature fascinated and impressed all. He began. "Hon. Founder Mr. Brijlal, all the trustees on the dais and respected teachers who taught me, all the respected teachers whom I don't know, Ladies and gentlemen and all my fans. I exist just because of you. You read me and immortalize me. I am a parasite who depends on your love, appreciation and motivation. I write it and you read. If you are not there to value it, it is just paper colored with black shapes. It is you who read it and while reading you add your heart and soul in it and make it alive. It is you who give me life........." He spoke for more than half an hour. Every word in his elocution touched to the right chord of the heart of the audience. There was a pin drop silence till the end of his speech. It died when the clapping of the audience attacked and finished it. In the first row, there was a girl who had become almost one with him. She was staring ceaselessly at him. She was so engrossed in his speech that she could not understand when his speech came to an end. She got up from her world of fascination when the clapping sound of the audience knocked at its door. The function came to an end on happy note and the anchor announced that the honorable Sir has committed to give an hour's time to his fans and it will be after lunch. The announcement pleased all the fans of the Sir are requested to have this chance to communicate with their darling writer. Again there was huge a clapping sound and all faces looked beautiful as it brought a smile on their faces. There was a huge seminar hall where all the fans and lovers of the writer were waiting for him. After an hour the writer came there in new costumes which really befitted to a writer. He dressed in white shirt and white trouser with pink sleeveless jacket. He sat on the chair quite comfortably and looked at the audience. He was pleased to see that the hall was replete with interested audience who wish to communicate to him.

The dialogues began. The writer was answering questions quite silently. What made him think was the ever smiling and indicative face of a girl sitting in the front row of the audience. While answering the questions, the Writer found himself somewhere imprisoned in the captivating gestures of the girl. He understood its meaning. He thought that she would question him but she preferred to be silent. She was ceaselessly staring at him till the end of the gathering. The writer felt little bit awkward but realized what she had in her mind. When gathering dispersed, the girl came close to him and said, "Hello! Sir, I am Sarojini, a student studying in the final year of graduation. I wish to tell you that I have read your books and have become your ardent fan." "It is my pleasure to see you, Sarojini. Have you read all my books? How have you found them to be?" Sarojini replied very enthusiastically, "I read most of them and I tell you very honestly that they are really heart touching." Someone disturbed them in middle, "Sir, you have been invited in the founder's Cabin." Siddhartha left the conversation in the middle and was about to leave. Suddenly Sarojini stopped and requested him for his cell number. The writer gave her the cell number and hurriedly went towards the founder's cabin. Being reluctant with the disturbed conversation, She followed him and asked him, "If you don't mind, May I call you this evening?" The writer said, "of course why not?" It pleased her very much and in a great excitement she said, "Thank you Sir! Please receive the call." Siddhartha smiled at her which raised her hopes.

Gathering was dispersed. Sarojini was very happy that she had got the autograph of her favorite writer. What made her the happiest was the cell phone and permission to talk to him. When Sarojini saw the Writer leaving in a motor car along with the Police, she left for her house with her friends. When she reached home it was around 4 o'clock. She was very tired with the hectic schedule of the day. She wished to have a nap but the memories of the program did not let her do it. She became restless. She got up and went towards the study table where she had kept the note book which contained the writer's cell number and his autograph. The autograph caught her eyes and she kissed it number of times and ceaselessly stared at the cell number. She was getting eager to call him but controlled her will. She closed her eyes and got engaged in the writer's fantasy. She remained in the same state for more than hour. Her mother called, "Sarojini, get up. I have made tea for you. Get fresh and come in the kitchen. We shall have it together." Sarojini came out of the fantasy of the Writer and answered, "Yes Mummy, I will be there shortly." When she entered the kitchen, she took the notebook along with her to show her mother what she had got. Mother enquired, "What is there in the notebook?" Sarojini replied, "Wait I will show to you. It has something special." She hastily started turning the pages of the notebook finally reached on the page. She reversed the notebook and told with great excitement, "Mummy, see what is this?" Mother questioned, "Signature, whose is it?" "It is an autograph of Siddhartha, my writer, my favorite writer." Mother tickled her saying, "That is why you are in so jubilant mood today." Sarojini blushed as if mother had understood the hidden feeling of her for the Writer." There was the cell number of the writer which she deliberately hid it as she was afraid that mother would catch her.

Sarojini's mother was mature enough to read and understand the mind of her daughter. In order to divert her from that world of fantasy and impossibility, she said, "Sarojini, there is a lot of work and I think I won't be able to do it alone. Will you join me please?" Sarojini replied rather willingly, "Why not mother? Tell me what to do?" Both got engrossed in cooking. They had dinner together. After dinner Sarojini went to her bed room and shut the door so that none should get wind of her clandestine world inside her bed room. It was around 9 PM, Sarojini made a phone call to Siddharth. "Hello! Siddharth sir, this is Sarojini. I met you at the seminar hall and took your number and you promised me you would receive the call." "Sarojini, I got it now. How are you?" "I am quite fine and have been missing you since your departure." "I understand it. Really you are ardent fan of mine. Sorry I could not talk to you at the end of the session as there was an urgent call form the founder of the institute." "Don't say sorry. It is not needed. You are great person and should not say sorry to an ordinary fan like me. I should say sorry to you as I have disturbed you at this odd hour of the evening." "It is not an odd hour. You are great fan of mine and for people like you there is no prohibiting time that you should call me during this or that period of the day. For fans like you, I am available for all hours of the day." Sarojini heard someone calling the Writer. She got disturbed with woman's voice. She questioned, "Whose voice is that?" "It is my wife, Geetanjali." Sarojini felt discouraged and her enthusiasm began to come down. "Ok then." Siddharth understood the frustration hidden behind her silence. He said, "Sarojini, why don't you speak?" Suddenly the phone got disconnected. Siddhartha tried many times but he found her cell to be switched off. Sarojini kept her phone on the study table and began to weep. She felt very sad and thought that she should not have called him with that expectation. What hurt her most was that the writer was married and was happy in his life. She determined that she would not call him hereafter and disturb his peaceful marital life. It was a night of a great pain and frustration. She passed her night with wide open eyes. The next day she got up quite late in the morning. Mother went to her bed room to wake her up, "Sarojini, haven't you seen the clock. It is around 11 PM, you have missed your college. Don't you want to attend the college?" Srojini replied with a yawning. "Mummy, I am feeling little bit tired. I won't go to the college today. I would prefer to take rest at home. She got fresh lunch and took out her note book to write something. Coincidentally she picked up the same note book which contained the autograph and cell number of the writer. It pained her lot. The more she tried to ignore it, the more it came in front of her. She closed the note book and slept on the bed and began to weep. Whole day she spent like that.

In the evening, she had some shopping with her Mummy. But her mind was engaged in the thought of Siddhartha. She thought that she had wrongly expected from the writer and trying to come out of the yesterday's memory. They returned home but Sarojini found no interest in anything. It was also observed by her Mummy. "Sarojini, if you don't mind, it seems to me that you have been engaged in some serious thought. Its frustrating shadow has eclipsed your face. Is anything wrong? Please share with me. It will relax you." Smiling artificially, Sarojini said, "Nothing Mummy. There is nothing like that. I did not have sound slumber last night. It might be the reason of it." Mother felt careless and said, "If it is the reason, then ok." They cooked and ate together. It might be around 9:30 of the evening; Sarojini was sitting at the study table and was turning the pages of the book suddenly the phone began to rig. She hurriedly took the phone and got surprised and happy inwardly to see it was Siddhartha. Suddenly she thought not to receive the phone but she could not save herself from the attraction of the Writer and received it. She put the phone to the ears and got pleased to hear him. "What is the problem? Other day you disconnected the phone? I wished to talk. I tried many times but it was switched off. Was anything wrong there at the other end or had I said anything which hurt you?" Sarojini replied with a great respect and being trapped in the debt of his words, "There was nothing like that. My mummy had called. So I disconnected the phone." They talked for a very long time. "So it was the thing, I thought something else disturbed you. So, Sarojini I feel very proud of myself that I have such ardent fans like you. Sarojini, what have you decided for future?" "Nothing aspiring to take the examination of graduation and after the consultation with the parents, I will decide the future course of action." "It's good thing but I would like to suggest you to come to Bombay to do higher studies. I will be there to support you. I have good acquaintances which can help you a lot." "If you are going to support me then I would definitely come to Bombay. But before that I have to seek the permission of the parents. But I am sure that my parents won't object to my going. After all they too want that their daughter should grow and stand quite high in the esteem of the world. If possible, I would discuss the matter with my parents tomorrow itself and let you know at the earliest possible." "It will be the most pleasant thing for me if I could do anything for you." They bid farewell to each other with a promise that they make a call tomorrow. It became their ritual to call each other every evening.

Regular talk brought them into intimate zone. Gradually, Sarojini became indifferent to the fact that the writer is married and has a wife and children. She was dreaming of him. The way he talked to her trapped her in his words and she became so eager to listen to him as if he was not a stranger but someone who was very close and dearest to her. Once Siddhartha asked, "Sarojini, have you asked your parents?' "Yes" "What is their stand? Have they agreed to your coming to Bombay?" "Yes I have a serious discussion with my parents and they want me to complete exam. If the result is good they would consider my plan otherwise they will seriously consider the issue of my marriage." "So, what is your stand?" "I have told them very candidly that after the completion of my graduation, I will go for my higher studies and I won't marry unless I complete my higher studies." Suddenly, the Writer's wife came in the bedroom of the Writer. He got disturbed and he disconnected the phone and sent a message that he would call her soon." Sarojini tried number of times but all the times she found his cell phone to be switched off." No call came. Sarojini was absolutely disappointed. She got angry and decided not to call him. But next morning she received a call from the Writer which softened her anger. Slowly their daily calls brought them physically and emotionally close with each other. Now they were kissing and touching and doing all that husband and wife do in their bedroom. Both became eager to see each other. The time came when they were calling rather frequently making calls fifteen times in a day and late night calls were extended to till dawn.

It was the month of April; Sarojini was taking her examination of the final year. She had informed him that she won't take his phones till the end of the examination as his calls divert her. The author too understood the significance of it and controlled his passion for calling her. Sarojini had told him that she would call him immediately after the end of the examination. It was the final paper and since morning, her eagerness to call him was troubling her. Anyhow she controlled it and took the examination. She came out of the examination hall and seeing a corner in the premise of the institute she stood there and gave a ring to him. The author received the call. A smile bloomed on her face as a new flower gets bloomed on the tree. They talked for a long. Before she ended the talk, she promised him that she would call him after the dinner. It was a free evening for her as her examination period was over. Sarojini took the dinner and went to bed. She shut the door as usual.

She picked the phone up and gave ring. The author too responded the phone instantly and their love episode began ceaselessly. "So how was your examination?" "It was fine. All papers were easy. I am sure of success." "It's well and good. Congratulations in advance." "Thank you. Siddhartha, I am dying to see you. I had not seen your face since the function." "Why don't you come to Bombay?" "When?" "In vacation." "But how is it possible? What an excuse should I give to my parents?" Tell them that you wish to make an enquiry of the course that you have to do as later on you won't get enough time." "Will they believe?" "I am sure they will." "She became a silent over the question where to stay and what to do?" "Hello! Where have you lost? What question troubles you?" "Where should I stay? As there is no work, what should I do there?" "Don't worry about all these silly questions." You come to stay with me on my bungalow? I will manage some job here which you can join later on when your result will be declared." "Job! What job are you going to manage for me?" "I have managed a job for you which will give you good salary." "How nice of you! Your offer has enhanced my curiosity to come to Bombay." "Come then who stopped you?" "I will discuss the matter with my parents and I will you let you know about the conformation?"

It was at dinner, Sarojini raised the issue. "Mummy I am planning to go to Bombay." "For what?" "To make enquiry about the course which I am likely to choose and there is also an interview for a job. If I get it, I think it will give me good salary." "It is good thing. I won't come in the way of your ambition. But see what your father says in this matter." Her father worked as a supervisor in a steel company which was distant from the house. He used to come once or twice in a month. Mother informed her that he was coming tomorrow. They meet at the dinner. Sarojini said, "Papa my result will come soon. If I do well in the examination, I am planning to go to Bombay for further studies and there is an interview for a job also. If I get the job, I will get salary which I would utilize for my studies. I want you to permit me to go." Father said in somewhat anxious tone, "How are you going to manage alone? We don't have any acquaintance there? Where will you stay? Who will take care of you? You are a girl? I am worried." "Don't worry Papa. I will manage rest of the things. Just I want to know whether you will let me go or not?" "If you are so obstinate, I don't want you to change your mind." "I have some friends there who will help me in staying there." "If you are so sure and confident, I will stop you no way." Sarojini got excited and kissed her father, "How nice of you! Thank you." "But Beta, do take care of you. I won't be there to bid farewell to you." "I will manage."

Sarojini finished her dinner and entered her bedroom. She picked up the phone and dialed the number of the Writer. "Hello! What are you doing?" "I am writing something. Have you finalized the issue?" "For this I have called. Parents have permeated me to go." "What a pleasant surprise! Tell me when are you coming to Bombay?" "If possible, I'll come on coming Saturday." "OK! It is nice. How long will stay here?" "I will be there for a few days." Then they came on the routine track and train stopped quite late in the night."

It was Friday the day before her departure. She informed the writer about her coming. "Hello Sir I am leaving for Bombay tomorrow evening. Will you be there to receive me?" "It is fine. Surely I will be there. There is no question of it. After all you are my guest." The talk continued for a long time. It was late night. Both were not willing to discontinue their routine talk. Sarojini had to wake up early in the morning as she had to make preparation. So Sarojini took initiative to end the conversation putting the excuse of preparation. Since they were intimate to each other, they were very informal to each other. In a formal tone Sarojini said, "Hello! Dear it is too late. I had to prepare for tomorrow. I will call you tomorrow if possible." "You are right. It is late. I will wait for your call." She woke up quite late. Whole day she was engaged in her preparation. Finding time from busy schedule she called her father and informed him about her departure. "Papa I am leaving for Bombay this evening." "It is ok my dear. What about accommodation and other things?" "Papa, I have a friend there. She will manage everything for me. There is nothing to worry. Everything will be absolutely fine." "Ok then. Take care" "Yes, Papa. I will call you after reaching there."

It was 7:30 of the evening. Sarojini along with her mother came to the bus stop. As there was time for its coming, both engaged in conversation. Sarojini's mother had become emotional as it was for the first time that Sarojini was going away from her. She was so emotional that she was getting difficult to speak. Looking at her and wiping her tears Sarojini said, "Don't weep. I am not going permanently. I will be back shortly." "What matters for me is that you are alone. None is there who know you. In a big city like Bombay you will be alone. How you will find the things you want. We don't know how the people there are. I have heard that they are very smart and dangerous.

It makes me feel concerned about you." Oh! Mamma you are unnecessarily feeling concerned. I am not a child to be lost to be worried. I am educated and I know everything. I have every details of the journey. So there is nothing to worry." Suddenly the bus came. Sarojini got on the bus. Her seat was at the window. Mother stood at the window." "Sarojini, be careful and don't talk with the stranger. Call me immediately after reaching there. "Yes, mamma. Don't worry. I will manage there. Take care of yourself." "You should also. I am at home. But you are going away." Mother standing outside was shading tears. Sarojini too became emotional. With tearful eyes they bid farewell to each other. The bus got disappeared and disappointed mother returned to her lonely house. Sarojini took out a phone and called the Writer. "I am coming tomorrow morning to Dadar. I will reach there around 6 AM. Be there otherwise I will get disturbed." "Don't worry. I will reach there earlier than you." The writer had some important work so he could not have a long ritual like every day."

The next day morning, Sarojini got down at Dadar. The writer had parked his motor car there and smoking a cigar standing at the pan-shop continuously keeping watch at passengers. Suddenly the writer's phone began to ring. "Hello! Sarojini, where are you?" "I have reached at the auto rickshaw stand of Dadar." "Wait. I will be there in few minutes. The writer walked some distance before that he extinguished his burning cigar. Sarojini was staring at the opposite end of the road. The writer identified her and reached to her and said, "Hello! Sarojini" Sarojini got surprised. "Sir, I am pleased to see you." "Let's go." "How?" "In my car." "In your car?" "Yes I have a car. It has been parked at the other side of the road. We have to walk up to there." "You have a car." "Yes. What surprising there in a car. In Bombay every ordinary fellow had a car." Sarojini took pride in it. They both crossed the road. The writer opened the door." "Sarojini felt proud of it. She got engaged in imagination that it was her husband who was opening door for her." Sarojini occupied her seat. The writer came in from other side and took the steering in his hands. Both exchanged smile at each other." Sarojini asked, "Where were you waiting for me?" "I came earlier than you. I was standing at the Pan shop and keeping watch on everyone coming and going there." "I was really scared in the crowd of the strangers." "What scared you?" "The thought." 'What thought?" "If you do not come there, then?" "How such a foolish thought can touch your mind? "I don't know how such uncertain thought disturbed and scared my mind." "It came out of mistrust." "Let's forget it." The motorcar was parked at one sky touching building in a posh colony. She was absolutely wondered as she had never seen such shining and awakened city with sky touching buildings." Both got down. The writer took her in a lift." When they got confined in the lift, both looked at each other and they read the feelings in each other's eyes. When the writer looked at her, Sarojini blushed and looked down with a smile. The lift stopped at the flat on 11th floors. They marched towards a locked flat. The writer took out the key to open it. Sarojini surprisingly asked him, "Why is it locked? Where is your family?" "She has been to her father's house. She would return after a few days." It made her feel awkward. But she did not let it show to him." "Sarojini, you might be tired and experienced loss of sleep. Do one thing there is my wife's bedroom. You can use it. You rest there as long as you wish. I am also feeling sleepy. I would also like to take rest. You go in and shut the door. If you need anything just call me. I will be there in your service." "If required I will call you." It was around 9:00 am; Sarojini came out of her bedroom. She was surprised to see the writer at the coffee table. Seeing her said, "Good Morning Sarojini. Come and join me for coffee. I have made coffee for you. May I serve it?" "Will you let me do it?" 'No. it is my duty. Let me enjoy it." All these actions of the writer whether it was opening door of the motor car or making coffee enhanced her attractions for him." That day she preferred to take rest on the flat of the Writer. As there were important engagements, the Writer left the house after having the breakfast. While departing he asked her she had to cook for herself as he won't be there for lunch. He would be back at evening. "Get ready I will take you for outing." Sarojini nodded positively.

Seeing the posh flat and colony of the author, Sarojini got impressed. What impressed her was the life style of the Writer. Cooking in such posh kitchen was really a delightful experience for her. She was little confused as everything was new to her and she was not getting things for cooking as she did not know where the things were she required for cooking. Anyhow she managed things and cooked. She took her lunch and again retired to bed. Sound of the bell disturbed her and she understood it was the writer. She got up and went towards the door. Seeing him standing at the door, she felt pleased. "Are you not ready? Have you forgotten that we have to go out?" "Let's have coffee first. You might be tired. Meanwhile I prepare myself." "Hurry up!" "Give me ten to fifteen minutes only."

The writer took the car to a moll where he purchased some articles and costumes for her. She forced him not to have it for but he did not listen to her and went on buying one thing after the other. Finally she held his hand tightly and said, "Stop! How much you buy for me. It is enough. I don't need all these things." When they were shopping, the people around them took notice of them. Among them were some fans of the Writer. A crowd of his fans approached and demanded his autograph. He wanted to avoid them but he could not as they were growing obstinate. It consumed his time till then Sarojini had to wait. "Sorry, Sarojini. I isolated you. Wherever I go, this problem occurs. That is why I avoid visiting public places." Sarojini smiled at him. He too did it in return. Then he took her to a huge garden. There they had sweets and eatables. There was hut where they sat for some time and exchanged some words. Again some fans caught him and they demanded his autograph. It made Sarojini feel proud of him. His name, fame and recognition allured her towards him. The writer thought that she might be bored with this trouble. So he left the garden and took her to a five star hotel for dinner. Seeing the Hotel, She got astonished. The splendid look of the hotel made her close her eyes. Everything was a new experience to her. She had never had merry making and delightful experiences. Seeing the interiors of the hotel and people there, she grew shy and silenced. She thought of herself and muttered, "Do I deserve this?" When she was engaged in her brooding, the Writer disturbed her in the middle and said, "Sarojini, where have you lost? Putting the menu card in front of her asked, "What would you prefer?" She was absolutely confused. She took a look at the menu and got confused as she had had never

such items in her life. Seeing confusing gestures on her face, he questioned, "You are giving order Na?" Helplessly looking at him she said, "I am confused. Better you order. I have never had such items." Understanding that she was not comfortable, he said, "It does not matter. He ordered some items." The attendant came there. Seeing the Writer he requested, "Don't give me tip but give me your autograph before leaving the table." The writer got pleased with this. He asked him give me your diary, I will do it now." The attendant became so happy that he hurriedly went in and brought a diary and put on the table. The writer signed on it. The attendant happily exclaimed, "How lucky I am to see you and have your autograph." The writer said it is my pleasure too." Sarojini was silently and admirably watching all these things. With every event, the writer was growing bigger and bigger in her esteem. The attendant took the order the writer looked at her and asked, "Where are you?" "No I was thinking how celebrated you are and I am ordinary girl. You have given this honor to be with you. Really I deserve this? It makes me feel awkward." "Stop your baffling. Don't belittle yourself. Be happy and smile please." They enjoyed the dinner and returned home at about 11:00am. She carried the articles in the bedroom. The writer changed his dress and sat in front of the home theater to watch a movie. Soon she too joined him. She sat little close to the writer and began to watch. Knowingly or unknowingly her hand fell on the Writer's and the Writer took it to be the invitation dragged her and rest is ....
It continued for next two three days.

One day he took her to a company office and managed a job of a clerk for her. She was very happy with this. Once when they were in the bed, the Writer asked her, "Sarojini, do one thing. You go back home and tell your parents that you have got a job and you have to join on the very next day. In the next week I would be leaving for Himachal Pardesh for my writing purpose. I will take you with me. You come soon." Sarojini nodded but raised a doubt, "What about the job?" "Don't worry. The boss is my fan and I will tell him you will join two months late." She mingled her voice in the Writer's. The next day he dropped Sarojini at the bus stop. He accompanied her till the bus left the station." The next morning, she reached to her home. When her mother saw her, she became very happy. Both embraced each other. Sarojini said, "Mummy, the visit was pleasant and I have also got the job. I am very tired and I need rest. Let me rest now. I will speak a lot to you later." She kept her bag in the corner and directly went to her bedroom.

They met at the lunch. Sarojini spoke, "Mummy, the visit was very pleasant and my friend helped a lot. Luckily I have a good salaried job as a clerk in a company. I am expected to join within a week's time." Mother became happy with this but sad at heart as her daughter would go away and she would miss her company. She advised her, "Better you talk to your father regarding your job. He is coming tomorrow. If he permits you, you can join but if he refuses, I won't convince him." Sarojini said, "Don't worry Mummy, I will convince him. I am sure he won't say no to me." "Is it necessary to go to Bombay and do a job? Really speaking, I don't like it. We are thinking of your marriage, and you are insisting on doing job and continuing education. It will be late and then we won't get good boy for you. "Mamma, you are in hurry. Is it an age to get married?

Let me be free and enjoy the job and complete my education, then I will give my confirmation." Listening to the strong negation, Sarojini's mother kept quiet. She understood that none can change her obstinate mind.

Father came on the desired day. They sat for dinner. While having dinner, Sarojini raised the issue. Father asked, "How long will you do the job? What about the marriage? Will you be there permanently?" She was little confused with the series of the questions." "Not fixed anything yet. But for a few years I wish to do the job and along with it I would continue my education." "I have no objection if you are so determined." "Thank you, Papa." "Take care. You are going away." "Yes. Nothing to worry." That night she spent for preparing her departure. The next day her parents came to see her off at the bust stop. The bus was already there. Sarojini took her seat in the bus. They had talk till the bus left the station. It was an emotional moment for all. Bus had just left the city. Sarojini took out the mobile from the purse and called the Writer. "I have just left my native and will reach to Bombay tomorrow morning." "Don't worry. I will be there. Have you convinced the parents?" "Yes I have done it." "It is well and good. They continued their talk till late in the evening."

The bus reached to Dadar at its usual timing. Siddhartha was already there. He took her but by different way. He took her to different complex where he had managed a flat for her." Sarojini felt it to be somewhat strange. Why this change? "My wife is there at home." "It's ok then." "You take rest. I will be back in the afternoon." "You will get everything there in the flat." "It is so I will manage the things." The writer left there." Meanwhile she took rest for some hours. She got up quite late and had coffee and then lunch and waited for Siddhartha to come. He came at 2:00pm. He told her that she had to go to the company to receive the order which will be post dated. They took the lunch together. Gradually their eyes began to talk. The writer touched her and the ritual performed. In the evening they went out in his car at an isolated place so that the fans of the writer should not disturb them. "Remember tomorrow evening we have to leave to Himachal Pradesh." "For how many days?" "It may be for a few months. That depends on the situation." "What about your family? What an excuse have you given to her?" "I told her that I am going to Himachal Pradesh to write a book on the lives of people there" It will take at six months time." "What was her reaction?" "Nothing. She told me that she would go to her father's home." "You have done a good job "While returning home they had dinner in a hotel."

At about 9 PM they returned to their flat. He made a phone call to his wife telling her that he would come rather late in the evening as he had to attend party of his close friend. Not to wait. The Writer was with Sarojini till late in the evening. It was around 1 PM he left her room telling her to get ready. He would come here to take her with him. Sarojini nodded positively. Next day Sarojini visited her office and collected the order of the job which was post dated for next three months. It was around 6: pm, the writer reached at the flat. Sarojini was prepared. He took her luggage and kept in the taxi. He asked the taxi driver to take taxi to the airport.

They reached at Manali airport quite late in the night. The Writer's friend was there with a bouquet to welcome them. Seeing the friend, the Writer became happy. The Writer introduced Sarojini to his friend. "Hi! Mahesh, meet my wife Sarojini." Sarojini exchanged a smile with him with Namaste posture. "Sarojini, he is friend cum fan of mine. He had managed everything for us here." Mahesh took them to parking and then they left towards their destination. The late night scenario of Manali pleased Sarojini. For the first time in her life that she could see the city at sleep in darkness of the midnight hours and in warmth of street lights. She was very pleased with this late night beauty of the city. She wondered, "How beautiful it looks! Really, it is a pleasant experience. It will be life long memory for me. Thank You, Siddhartha." He smiled at her and said, "For me also. It is just beginning. Reserve your memory for many more things to come." Sarojini smiled at him.

The motorcar moved towards an isolated structure somewhat away and isolated from the hustle and bustle of the city. It was a farm house of Mahesh. He opened the door and kept the luggage of the Writer in a cupboard. It was a rich farmhouse with all amenities. It pleased the Writer. "Mahesh you have a wonderful job. Thank You." "It is my pleasure." He showed them everything and handed over keys of two wheelers and four wheelers and said, "They can use them for enjoying outings. Looking at the wrist watch and said, "Sir it is already late. You take rest. Call me if I am needed. This is my phone number. Ring me whenever you require me." "You will be highly welcome." Mahesh left the farmhouse with a word to be back in their service. For some time they spoke about the nice management of Mahesh and they went to bed as it was about to dawn and they were tired also. When they woke it was noon around

12 o' clock. Sarojini entered the kitchen, had a look at it. She was happy with the availability of the household things. There was nothing that she needed to bring. She called Siddhartha, "Siddhartha, your coffee is ready. Come we will have it." They had coffee together. "Siddhartha, get ready, meanwhile I will prepare lunch for us."

In the evening, they had bike ride. They went to nearby place. Both were very happy to see beautiful landscapes of Manali. A period of a month passed like this visiting this and that place, taking diner in different hotels. It was an hour of dusk, Sarojini complained of stomach. The writer took her to nearby hospital. The doctor examined her and said, "It is good news. She is pregnant. Congratulations, Mr. Siddharth" Good news instead bringing smile, brought furrows on their faces. Siddhartha brought an artificial smile on the face and received the words "Thank You, sir." He looked at her, Sarojini looked troubled. Both return to the farmhouse. They looked at each other with troubled faces. Siddhartha asked, "What to do?" Without making a delay of a single moment Sarojini replied, "Let's abort. I don't want unnecessary trouble." The Writer thought it to be a decision of wisdom. "I think you are right. It would be a decision of wisdom." The next day they went to hospital. Siddhartha requested the doctor. "Sir, we don't want a child right now. We wish to abort it." "As you wish but before that let me check it out whether she is capable enough to bear its pains." Doctor examined her and said with grave face, "Siddhartha, the case has become quite complicated. It can do great harm to mother. If done, it can take life of mother. It will be more detrimental to the life of the mother. Decision is up to you." The assertion of the doctor put him in a great riddle which he could not solve. "Siddhartha, if it is so, I won't let it happen. I want my wife. Let's cancel it." He told the situation to Sarojini and she got scared. They returned to the farmhouse. Sarojini questioned in a serious tone, "What have you thought?" "You are very important to me. I think you should go for delivery." "How is it possible and here?" "Yes. Here only. I cannot take you back in such state." "Do you mean to stay here for next nine months?" "Yes. We have no other option." "What about your wife, my job and your friend." "Don't worry about all these. I will manage."

A period of nine month passed. One day Sarojini delivered a male child. The problem before the couple was what to do with the child. Taking it back to Bombay would put them in great trouble. They postponed their return and stayed there for next month. During this period, both tried to find a solution which would be suitable to both. Finally the writer put a suggestion before Sarojini, "Sarojini, if you don't mind, I have a suggestion. If it is not going to hurt you, I would suggest." "Don't hesitate. It is our problem. Not yours only." "We shall deliver our child to a cradle house and appoint a nurse who would look after it. I will pay her. Let the baby grow here only under her care. When he will be twenty, I will call him back to me." "It is not a bad idea." They visited nearby cradle house and delivered the child and completed the formality. He appointed a nurse and paid her hugely. "Nurse, please keep it in mind that you have to grow this child like your own. Don't worry about the payment. I will pay as you wish. I will come here of and on to enquire. They exchanged each other's number."

They returned to Bombay. Sarojini went to her company to join but the company refused to get her joined. When she enquired, she came to know that the Writer's friend who had offered her a job had been transferred and the new boss appointed someone else in her place. She called Siddhartha and told what happened. Siddhartha asked her to go back to flat he will be there soon. She went back to her flat. She was watching TV when the bell rang. Sarojini opened the door with the thought it would be Siddhartha but she got shocked to see a stranger. He told her that he was the Writer's friend and wanted the flat to be vacated as he had to bring his family in that flat. Sarojini got troubled with these rising troubles. He rang the Writer. Siddhartha had a talk with his friend. When conversation ended, Sarojini curiously asked him, "What did he say?" He told me that he would vacate the flat within two days." The gentleman left the flat. After an hour, Siddhartha came there. He asked her, "I think you should go back home till the things get managed." "Getting flat and job will take time. When the things will be managed, I will call you back." Sarojini accepted the option willy-nilly as staying there in such circumstances would be frustrating. She decided to return. The writer came to drop at the railway station. Standing at the window of the train, the Writer said to her, "Don't feel deceived. Let me manage the things here. It will take some time. When the situation will be in our favor, I will call you." Sarojini smiled at him. The Writer understood the meaning of the smile. But he preferred not to argue any further. The train whistled thrice and the train slowly left the station. They looked at each other as if it was their last meet.

The next day morning she reached to her native. She wore an artificial smile on her face to show her parents that she is happy in job. She was shocked to see her father at home, "Papa, you are at home? What about your job? Is it going well?" Mother intervened in the middle, "He left the job as he is not physically fit. Doctor has advised him to quit the job and rest as doing job is detrimental to health." Sarojini looked at her father and said, "Papa really you have grown very thin and pale" He looked at her with a frustrating smile and said, "I won't live long as I know how severe my illness is. Before I close my eyes, I want to perform a responsibility." "What responsibility are you talking about? Tell me I would do something worthwhile." "Without you, it is not possible." "What is that? Tell na, Papa. I am growing curious. Please don't stretch my curiosity and don't test my patience also." "We want to get you married off. We have seen a boy for you. He has good earning. You should say yes. If your affirmation comes; we will invite the boy here to see you." "Give me some time to think. I will give you decision very soon." One day she called the Writer and told the situation. He said to Sarojini, "I am trying to find a job for you but I don't think I will have it soon. Better you go with parent's decision to marry as it will be better to you. Since I married I can't give you status of a wife. Without that status, you won't like to continue your life. I don't want you should be disgraced with the status of a mistress, a kept woman." Sarojini disconnected the phone. The Writer tried to call her but he found it to be switched off. He stopped to call her as he knew it would disturb her. The boy came to see her. After seeing her, He gave his preference to her parents. As the bridegroom's party was in hurry, the engagement was done on the same day and within months time marriage was performed. The Writer's chapter was closed with the marriage of Sarojini.

A long period of twenty or more years had passed. The writer had grown old with great prestige as a Writer. In those years, the Writer had taken great care of his son. He financed his education and provided all that he wanted. He had paid hugely to the nurse who looked after him. One day he called the nurse along with her son. He warned her not to disclose his identity and tell him an excuse that there is a job as a writer with a good salary in Bombay. As per the suggestion of the Writer, the nurse did. She brought his son and left him at his flat in Bombay. She told him. Nandan, "He is your boss. He wants a Writer as his eyesight has grown weak and his hands are also not now working properly. You have to stay here and help him in his work. You will be paid a handsome salary." The boy nodded with affirmation. She took handsome amount and went back to Himachal Pradesh."

Years were passing rapidly. Nandan never doubted his relation with the Writer. The Writer also never let him know the reality. The Writer had created wonderful books one after the other. But his physique was not supporting him. His eyesight was growing poorer day by day and his hands were almost useless as it suffered from little shock of paralysis. Those years in the company of the Writer changed Nandan a lot. He aspired to be famous like the Writer. But he knew that he did not have that much caliber to acquire celebrity of the Writer. His mind began to work crookedly. The Writer grew old and he was not able to take trouble to go to publishing house and handover the manuscripts. So he shouldered the responsibility of it to Nandan who did it initially very sincerely. Never an evil idea touched his mind to misuse it. But the aspiration to be a big celebrity despite of the potential to have it made him restless. Slowly he stepped towards his destination without considering what is fair? And What is foul? When the Writer finished his work, he used to hand over it to Nandan to pass it to the publisher with a great trust that he would perform the task. But he never thought that his most trusted writer would change his mind. Nandan had great understanding of Master's limitation. He began to use them. He joined hands with the publishers and published Writer's work one after another after his name. The Writer never doubted. Once the Writer questioned Nandan, "Have you submitted all the manuscripts to the publisher?" "Yes! On the same day." When will the books be out?" "The moment they come, I will let you know. Don't worry."

One day the writer was sitting in front of the T.V. He could not watch but he could listen to the news, old songs and other programs of entertainment. One day a news captured his attention. He shocked to listen that the Nobel Prize for Literature of the year was honored to his book but there was no mention of his name but the book was associated with Nandan. He got shocked and felt deceived but later on he realized and understood it and did not blame Nandan for this fraud. When Nandan came to see him, he did not make him realize that he had caught his theft. He behaved very normally with him as if nothing happened. Just he asked, "Nandan, books are coming na?" Nandan as usually replied, "They will come shortly." "It is alright."

Nandan was scared with the thought, if the Writer came to know about his misdeed, what he would think of him. He was afraid that the Writer might be annoyed at and handover him to Police in the case of forgery. His mind entered the world of Macbeth where for the fulfillment one's dream, foul is fair and fair and foul. As Macbeth behaved with his Master old king Duncan in Shakespeare's Macbeth, Nandan too decided do it so that no proof of his misdeed would be left behind. One day the Writer told him, "Nandan, the work of completion of the manuscript of a new book was almost finished. Tomorrow he will have to handover the manuscript to the publisher. Nandan replied positively. The next day Nandan came at noon. The Writer had his lunch and desired to have nap as he was feeling lethargic due to heavy lunch. Nandan came and sat on the chair and greeted the Writer, "Hello! Sir, Good Noon. Have you had your lunch? "I have had it. I am feeling drowsy due to heavy lunch. I am going to take rest but I thought that I should handover the manuscript to you so that you can go to the publisher." "Where is it?" It is on my table." "It is ok I will take it. If you wish to have nap, you can proceed." The Writer entered his bed room to rest. After sometime, Nandan got up from his chair to get it confirmed that the Writer was asleep. He entered his bed room with mute steps. He picked up a pillow lying near and with a great force smothered the Writer in his bed. The Writer struggled hard but his old and paralyze power could do nothing before the young force of Nandan. Within a few seconds or minutes, the struggle of the Writer stopped. Nandan smiled at the Writer. He took out the handkerchief and wiped out the sweat on his face. He came out of the bedroom and rested for a while on the chair. When he got relaxed, he took a round in his bed to check it out that no proof of his crime should be left behind. He confirmed, came out and went to the table where the manuscript was kept. He took a look at it and just opened it to see what it was about and started turning pages. When he was turning the pages, he found a piece of paper which was folded. He opened it with great curiosity. He was shocked to see a line, "Well done my Son." The line on the piece of paper troubled him lot. He was restless to know the meaning of the line. He phoned the nurse and told her about the death of the Writer. By chance she opened her heart and told him that it was his father. He sat down in the chair with absolute frustration.

He informed the police and confessed his crime. He requested the police not to arrest him till he finished the rituals of his father's cremation. The cremation was done. Before submitting himself to the police, he conducted a press conference and told the truth it was the writer and not he who deserved the success. The next day Nandan's truth became great breaking news which shook all spheres. His Nobel Prize was withdrawn and conferred it on the Writer. All books were reprinted with the Writer's name. When all rituals were performed, he went to the police station to submit himself. Considering the severity of the case, the court announced lifelong imprisonment to Nandan on the charges of forgery and murder. When he heard the judgment, he gave a smile to the judge and happily came out of the doc.

Destiny

It was raining cat and dog. There was house at the end of a lane in Sethunagar. It was house but had an appearance of a hut. Its look was like that of a dilapidated hut. A small family lived in it. It was the family of Dinkar, a coolie at the railway station in Sethunagar. He sweated a lot but earned less. Too much struggle and less appreciation with this contrasting principle, Dinkar and his family was facing the blows of the destiny. As night grew darker, the rain also grew stronger. It was raining as heavily as if it was taking revenge on the poverty of Dinkar giving blows after blows to break the poor ceiling of the house. The blows were so powerful that it finally succeeded to enter and spread its rule. Mother along with a son was sleeping on the bed. It was as small as the house itself. The forceful rain attacked on mother and a son sleeping on the bed and disturbed their sound slumber. Dinkar who was sleeping down on the floor got disturbed as the water had spread under his bed and spoiled his sleep. When Dinkar looked up at the roof, the stream of rain attacked on his face as if it was slapping and spiting on his face and mocking at his poverty. The family looked everywhere and found that rain left none. Where to sleep, where to stand and where to step as not space of an inch was left dry. Dinkar looked up with great despair. Ceiling was almost broken. It had so many wholes which to be filled was the question before him. He shouted "Sharada, come here. See. Here water, there water, everywhere water and only water and not an inch space left to step. Why are you sitting idly? Put a vessel here, there and everywhere. Let not water spread." She collected a few pots and started keeping them under holes through which water was coming in. She brought whatever pots she had in the kitchen and began to put them. He shouted to bring more. She reacted ironically, "Vessel kept here and there but no vessels to be kept everywhere. How many holes will you fill? If they are one or two or you may fill but if your destiny has a hole how it will be filled. When it will be filled, no hole will bring rain in and we will have peace of mind and undisturbed sleep." It hurt him a lot. It made him realize his limitation and his poverty. He wanted to shout at her but realized that Sharada was right if his destiny mocked at him how he would bring a smile on his face. He looked into her eyes and the emotions of frustration and helplessness made him look down. He felt ashamed of himself that he was not able give a strong roof to his family.

Suraj a small boy of ten year was sitting half slept on the bed. He wished to sleep but no portion of the bed was left dry where he could rest. Suddenly his half opened eye saw a scene which moved his little heart. His father as well as his mother was struggling to prevent the rain to come in by pasting some sticky substance and putting empty pots wherever the tins leaked. The rain was so heavy that within a few seconds, the pots got filled. Mother hurried to vacant them by throwing water out. It continued till dawn when they realized that there was no use of it. He looked at his wife Sharada and said, "Stop. How long you will you do this

Kasarat? We will die but it won't end." Tired Sharada sat down with a big question mark on her forehead.

They looked at each other with absolute frustration. The frustration on their face made Suraj understood how much they suffered on account of poverty. He looked at them and muttered, "I will give them such a roof which will bring no rain in." With this determination he slept in sitting posture. When he got up next day he saw that there was a rangoli of pots everywhere. Mother was engaged in emptying them. She shouted, "Get up. Why are you sitting idly? If there is time for schooling then come and join me in emptying them. He looked at the old and broken watch hanging on the wall and found there was time. He joined his hands with his mother and did the job. He looked at his exhausted mother and said, "How much pain you have taken. Why are we not rich so that we would have holefree house?" "We don't have good fortune. We are not the favorite children of God. God gives them all to whom he loves. God's good eye has ignored us. It is because of this, winter, rain and summer have no sympathy for us. They won't stop blowing as they love to blow us." "Mother I will change the destiny." "Thank God at least you could say, but your father took years not said yet. Sweat my son and stop ours. Not God's but my blessings will be with you."

Years passed but the conditions of the family could not be improved. Suraj was a schoolboy studying in the eighth class. He was very diligent, intelligent and quiet boy. His good temperament, studious and industrious nature gave him good place in the book of his teachers. When he returned from school, he never wasted his time in unnecessary things. Much of the time, he spent either in reading or writing. He had a good passion for writing. He liked to read poems, short stories and variety of things. In the course of time, he cultivated a great inclination for creative writing. Once he wrote poem and told his mother, "See what I have written." "Show, what is written?" Looking at the black and white words on a piece of paper, she remarked, "You have written well but I am illiterate and I can't read. Better you read it out." Suraj recited the poem. "Very nice. Keep it up but by caring your studies." "Don't worry, study is my passion. It won't get divided. Whenever I have leisure, I will write." "Study is your passion. Why?" Looking at patched rusted teens he said, "These holes make me restless. It seems to me that these holes are nothing but wounds of ours. I have to cure them at any cost. For this I have to make money. I am wise enough to understand that money comes from study." "You are really clever boy. You think a step ahead of your time." It made him feel proud of himself. Mother left for her work and he buried himself in the world of books.

One day, there was a poetry writing competition in the school. He wrote a poem on the spot and showed it to his teacher. It became the talk of the town. It was great reading experience for the teacher. Everyone appreciated his talent. He participated in all creative activities and displayed his talent. His poems and short stories were displayed on the board. Every competition brought him trophy. He won so many trophies but irony was that they had no shelf or a space at home to keep them. His mother had managed a bag in which all trophies were kept. She wanted to display them in the carved shelf in the wall but she feared rain might damage them." Looking at those packed bag with holes here and there she exclaimed, "When these holes will stop accompanying us." Frustration of poverty dismayed her and she went back to kitchen to find if anything was there to cook.

Destiny had very ill eye on the family. As if it has abused it a number of times. Out of that it had left no chance to blow it. Dinkar was tired of routine arduous life. Dissatisfaction over limited earning and growing needs of the family made him restless. One day he sat in the company of drunkard friends knowingly or unknowingly tasted wine. Since then, he fell in love with it wherever he returned home; he carried it with him which became the cause of contention in the family. He did not want to leave it nor it too. Wife felt troubled and jealous over his excessive love for it. Since its arrival, there was a rivalry between wife and wine for the hold over Dinkar. Finally, Sharada accepted the defeat and let him live with it. He became habitual with it that it could not live it. When he had no money, he used to beat his wife. It became a routine contention. It disturbed the peace of the family. Suraj could do nothing but keep it watching. If there was a quarrel, he stood beside his mother and appealed his father, "Stop it. It scares me. It disturbs me and my studies. If you do it every day, how can we survive?" Drunkard father paid no attention to it. It became an everyday scene on the family canvas. Slowly, Suraj too started ignoring it. One day Dinkar fell ill. Wine's love made him weak, pale and almost paralyzed. Wine troubled not only him but his wife too. It enhanced the burden of the mother. It took her out of home and made her to work as a maid servant.

The family was too weak to bear the burden of a workless an ever sick father. Mother could not have financial ability to give her husband the best possible medical aid. One day she borrowed some money from her master and took her husband to the hospital. The doctor examined him and said, "It is useless to treat him. Wine has eaten him thoroughly. His liver is absolutely damaged. It is too late to amend and he won't live long." It was a great shock to her. They returned home with absolute disappointment.

Since then he caught the bed and never left it. One day mother made tea and went to offer him. She shouted, "Get up. I have tea for you." She shouted twice thrice but no response came from his side. She doubted something ominous. She kept the cup aside and began to move him and found him to be dead. Suddenly she screamed, "Suraj's father you can't do it with me. You can't leave me alone. Suraj, come here fast. Your father has left us alone." The crying sound of mother confused him. He came there and mixed his cry with his mother. Both cried which awoke the neighbors. Within a few minutes, there was the rush of the viewers and the watchers to console them. In a few hours, all relatives gathered and the cremation ritual was performed. For a few days the relatives and neighbors were there to accompany them that might be the reason why they did not experience the absence of Dinkar. But the moment the relatives and neighbors started vacating the house, the absence became striking for them.

It was night. Suraj was sleeping beside his mother. She was staring at rusted tins. Suddenly she remembered the scene of that night's torrential rain and their miserable and futile effort to stop the water from coming and spreading in. She looked at the patched holes on the teen and suddenly she saw a big hole which was caused by the departure of her husband. She thought, "She might fill all the holes but how she could fill the cavity caused by the departure of her husband. He was a support of the family. How to lead a support less family? What will be the future of hers and her son too?" These questions stole her sleep and when she left the bed it was almost dawn. It was the first day she had to begin without her husband. She was troubled with her heart. She made Tiffin for Suraj who had to attend the school. After sending him to school, she left for her work. She was growing weak to bear the burden of the family. As a woman there were limitations on her earning. She knew it that her limited earnings were not enough to run the family. It made her nervous at heart. The death of her husband and financial worries weakened her inwardly. Illness began to catch her. One day she fell seriously ill. The life got stopped. It was the year of matriculation for Suraj. He had to leave the school in the middle which spoiled his career. To support his family, he had to work as a labor on the nearby construction site.

Mother's illness grew slowly. One day he took her to the hospital. Doctor examined his mother and sent her out. A few minutes later, doctor called Suraj in and disclosed the illness. "I have diagnosed her illness and its asthma. I have given some medicine but it will give her relief but won't cure it as it has taken complete hold of it." The words discouraged him. He determined to fill the holes of poverty but destiny was vomiting fire on him. He thought that he had to prepare for one more holes. He muttered, "Holes after holes. When one filled other is ready to be filled. I fear that if they go on increasing like this, one day I will be trapped in them and won't come out. Everything may end but what about these holes. Will it end?" With this troubled question, he came home. He got shocked to hear that his mother had caught asthma. What made him disappointed was that doctor gave him no assurance of his mother's life.

Whole day he worked hard on the construction site. When he returned home exhausted and saw his ailing mother taking pains, he felt sorry. He questioned himself, "Why do you take trouble? Can't you keep quiet? It will harm you." "Then tell me who will do it." "I will do it." "When? At evening?" Suraj realized his disability and kept mum. "Why don't you get marry? You are earning. If wife comes, I will be free to go?" "Why do you speak of going? You won't go so early. Don't you want to see me the filling holes of the roofs?" "Life will go on like this but holes will never end. In poverty, it has long life. It goes on ceaselessly. I don't want to discourage you. If God wants, you may be rich and may fill some of these though not all. As life it is great hole in itself." That philosophical statement of the mother silenced his tongue.

One day a neighbor brought a marriage proposal for Suraj. Seeing the photograph of girl, Suraj's mother gave the confirmation. Within a few days, marriage was performed. JaMunna entered the family as the daughter in law. Her entry gave a relief to the ailing mother. For some time, life enjoyed smoothness. Suraj was earning good to meet the requirements of the family. Home was at peace as JaMunna was leaving no stone unturned in serving her mother in law.

One day Suraj was working on a construction site. It was a huge building. He was plastering the wall standing on a wooden plank. All of a sudden he lost his balance and fell down. Almost half of his body got injured. He was taken to the hospital by his fellow colleagues. Left hand and left leg was almost became useless. His whole body was plastered. It was the time of the sunset. His wife was waiting for him. Of and on, she peeped through the door to confirm her husband's arrival. The sun was almost disappeared and darkness was taking the town in its shell. A group of workers reached at the house. JaMunna was engaged in doing something. One of them said, "Is anybody there in?" Hearing a strange and new voice, she came to see who called. Seeing a stranger, she asked, "Who are you gentleman and what brings you here?" The gentleman kept quiet and indicated his group to bring Suraj in. The group of people carried the body in. When she saw the plastered body with face open, she shouted, "Suraj, what happened to you? How this happened?" One of the fellow colleagues narrated the incident. It was a great shock to her. When Sharada was informed about the happening with her son, Suraj, she could not bear this shock. Her illness grew and she lied on the bed like a silent creature staring and counting the holes on the roof. Her bed was arranged in one of the rooms.

For next few months, she cared him a lot. Tensions increased, burden troubled. JaMunna a poor fellow got confused with this jolt of the destiny. Earnings stopped. Ever sick mother in law always lying on the cot like a corpse and an injured husband blocked her mind. How to manage the household without Suraj's hands became a grave concern for her. For a few days, she could afford to be with him. Suraj had kept some money in a box which she utilized. Soon the money got finished. Suraj was lying on the cot and observing her confused state of mind and fear for future. He called, "JaMunna, come here. I know how much you are suffering on account of me. But I am helpless and never expected that this would be my situation. Tell me what should I do?" And he started crying. JaMunna too became emotional and said, "Don't weep. If you do it, I will be weakened. It is neither your fault nor mine. Perhaps destiny wants us to suffer. Lets accept the things as they come; this is how the life will go on."

She knew that sitting beside him whole day will worsen the situation. Having no option, she decided to cross the threshold of the house. Anyhow she managed a domestic job as a maid servant. Limited earning, limited needs, limited life that was how she had to continue. This pattern of life continued for some months. Plaster was removed. He was shocked that his left hand and left leg were become inactive. Now he could sit on the cot with his right hand he could do his activities. Whole day JaMunna was out of home, her absence pained him a lot. He was troubled with a question how to spend the time doing nothing. One day he asked JaMunna, "Whole day you are away from me. I feel bored and lonely. It eats me. Minutes pass like an hour and hour like a day and day better not to ask. I am really fed up with this life. How long one can be silent and remain isolated from the main stream of life?" "I can understand your situation. This is the worst period of your life. If you don't have control over your feelings, it may trouble you a lot." "You are right. It makes me restless and morbid thoughts disturb my mind. Sometimes I feel that I should end my life and lessen your burden. But on the next moment I think if I do it, how will you manage life without me." "Don't think like that. In such a period, mind acts negatively. If you don't control it, it will dominate you and make you act as it wants. So take care that your mind should think positively." "What should I do then?" "Why don't you do something?" "Read something. Read anything and engage your mind. Wait." She went in and opened the iron box and took out his old books and notebooks and handed them over to him and asked him, "Take this. These are your books. Engage your mind with them. This pen, if you wish to write something, you can do it." He looked at her and said, "Thank you. It will give me some relief."

It was afternoon. He woke from a nap and was lying on back. His eyes caught the holes on teen which reminded what he had committed to his mother, "I will fill these holes. I will change the destiny of the house." He took books and notebooks. For some days, he engaged his mind in reading books. A time came when he felt reading to be boring. A pen was lying near. It caught his attention. He picked up and made some marks on blank notebook. Suddenly he remembered that it was the notebook in which he had written his stories and poems. He started turning the pages and got engaged in the world of stories. Suddenly an idea hit his mind and he picked up the pen and began to write. He wrote for months and his months' rigorous work brought out a wonderful book which he named 'Destiny.' He called his wife and said, "See what I have done in your absence. He opened his notebook and showed what he has written." JaMunna asked him, "What is this?" "It is a novel". "How nice it is!" She took a look at it and read some lines and said, "It looks worth reading." It brought a smile on his face. He felt very happy over the compliment of his wife and expressed his desire to get it published. "Jamuna, I am sure that the book will be a great success. What we need is a publisher who would publish it. But problem is how to reach to the right publisher." Suddenly JaMunna remembers

Mr. Bhatiya. "I know Mr. Bhatiya in whose house I work as maid servant. He is a renowned journalist who has good contacts in the market. I am sure that he would help us in this connection. If I get the chance, I will talk to him and I will let you know."

One day Mr. Bhatiya was taking breakfast along with his wife. Seeing them in jubilant mood, JaMunna asked her master. Masterji, I have a work with you. "Speak JaMunna. What is the problem? If possible I will help you." "Actually my husband has written a novel or something like that. He has sure if it is published, it will be undoubtedly a success. I want you to help us in getting it published." "Why not? I will do it. Bring the manuscript tomorrow." JaMunna was excited with these words. "Thank you, Masterji. I will bring it tomorrow." She went home and told her husband that she had a meeting with her Master about his book. Seeing a smile on her face, he guessed something positive she has to share with him. Before she opens her mouth he said, "What happened?" "My master has said yes. He has told me to bring the manuscript tomorrow." "Thank you Jamuna you have done a good job for me. You take it with you tomorrow without fail." Next day she took the manuscript with her. She showed it to Mr. Bhatiya. He had a serious look at it. He read a para or two and found it be to interesting. He said Jamuna, "I have read a few lines. It seems to be interesting. I will handover it to my publishing friend. I know a little about novel writing. Let's see what does he say?" "As you wish, Masterji. Please give it to your publisher friend. Please do this favor to your maid servant." "Don't worry, Jamuna. I will give it to him. If he says yes, I will let you know. But it will take some time." "Let him take his own time. But get it published." "Sure! Have patience." The next day Mr. Bhatiya took the manuscript and directly reached to his publisher friend. "Good morning, Vilas." "Good morning. How you remembered this poor fellow?" Laughing at this humorous remark he said, "I have not forgotten you. Only thing is that we are so engaged that we don't get time to see each other. "Don't take my words very seriously. I was just joking. Let's come to the point." "I have an urgent work with you. I have a maid servant at home. Her husband has written something like a novel as she said. I personally request you to see it seriously and if possible and if it is worth publishing, please do justice with it. I would be happy if you publish it." "There is no question of saying no. There is an editing committee which takes decision about publishing. If the committee likes it, then there is no problem. It will be surely published. But if it dislikes it, I can't do anything in that regard" "You are right. Let the committee takes it own time. I won't force you to do it. But let me know at the earliest." "Have patience. The moment I get the committee's decision, I will call you on phone." "It's good." One day JaMunna and Mr. Bhatiya came face to face. He had her face reading. Before she opened her mouth he told her, "Don't worry. It has been given to the publisher. The result will come within a week or two. Have patience."

Almost a month passed, no result came. Suraj was anxious and disappointed as the result had not come. JaMunna too had not opened her mouth on the issue. One day he could not control his patience in a disappointing tone he asked, "Has result come?" "No. He has not spoken anything. I have also asked him. Perhaps it has not come yet. Otherwise he would have told me. Better we think it has been rejected. It will give us pain for sometime but the pain that we have due to curious waiting would come to an end. We will engage our mind in something else." Suraj realized that there was no meaning in waiting for it. The more he waited for, the more it would pain him. Better he should give up the hope of something positive will come out." Both were trying to console each other. But despair in some corner of the heart was still there which dismayed the homely atmosphere. Suraj was almost hopeless, extremely bored and unease. What to do next? How to spend time with silent interiors? How long to give trouble to his wife? All these questions made him restless. Jamna too was nervous at heart but she deliberately did not show it to him as she knew his state of mind.

Mr. Bhatiya was watching television. JaMunna was busy in helping his mistress in the kitchen. Suddenly the mobile on the tea table rang. Mr. Bhatiya hurriedly picked it up and was shocked and surprised with the call from the publishing house. "Hello! It is Vilas. I am very glad to inform you that the editorial board has given green signal to publish the novel. The work of publishing will start from the next week" "What! What a surprise! I will talk to you later. Let me give this happiest news to the maid servant who has been long waiting for it." He called JaMunna, "Where are you? Come out? I have good news for you." JaMunna came out, "What happened?" "I have received a call from the publishing house and feel very happy to tell you that the book has been accepted and it will be published very soon." JaMunna was about to faint in happiness. She was not getting words to express her happiness and celebrate the occasion." "Thank you very much Masterji. You have done a great job for me. I shall ever be in your debt. Will you let me go early today? I am dying to share this good news with my husband." "You go now. Your request has been granted. Don't waste time. Hurry up!" JaMunna left the house for home." She was hurriedly walking towards home. She was so eager to share the news with her husband that she could not step properly. When she reached home, Suraj was hopelessly looking at the holes of the roof. She called with excitement, "Suraj what are you doing? I am dying to share something with you." The words animated him. He asked out of curiosity, "What thing you want to share with me?" "Your book is going to be published." "Really!" Yes. Mr. Bhatiya broke the news. He had a call from the publishing house." "It is really amazing. I can't believe it was unexpected and doubtful. Is it really a dream or reality? Please touch me it will confirm the news." JaMunna touched him and it took it to be a confirmation.

Very soon book came out. The publisher sent the first copy on the address of Suraj. Seeing the cover of first book, he found himself in the seventh heaven. Mr. Bhatia took the initiative and organized unveiling ceremony of the book. Every one appreciated Suraj and his wife's struggle in making it reality. In short span of time, the book made record breaking sale enriching the poor couple. A ceaseless flow of money started which changed the destiny of the couple. The couple accumulated such amount that JaMunna did not need to work as a maid servant. Suraj understood his ability. He did not let the air go in his head. He continued his writing giving hits after hit. Publishers and Mr. Bhatia supported the family and gave the best possible treatment to Suraj which removed his disability. It gave him new vigor and enthusiasm.

When he became financially strong, he told his wife, "JaMunna, we have earned a lot through book writing. I am very happy but what disappoints and troubles me are the holes of the roof. I think the time has come to fill the holes." "What do you mean by refilling the holes of the roof?" "We need to renovate our house." "Go ahead. It is the right time to do it. After all you are a great writer. Every now and then, your followers, fans and your colleagues visit us. For our and their comforts, we need to have a capacious house. I like the idea. Please don't have rethought over it." His mother was suffering from asthma. She was given a separate room to rest. She was very happy with the changed destiny of her son. All possible treatment was given to her but her body had grown too weak to respond to it.

The renovation work was undertaken. It took a few months time. Within a few months a new bungalow took the place of the dilapidated house. A grand house warming ceremony was arranged. People from various fields attended it and made one of the most memorable events in the couple's life. It was a hectic day as the guests were ceaselessly coming and going. It was late in the evening; silence was restored in the home. Suraj was sitting at mother's feet. JaMunna was sitting down to serve the diners. He looked at his mother proudly. He caught happiness in her eyes. Suddenly the memory of holes of roof revived. He looked at the new ceiling of the house and asked his mother, "See at the roof, its holes have been filled. I have changed the destiny." He looked at his mother. She did nothing but gave him a serene smile and embraced him.

Falling Star

Bilaspur was a small village having population not more than a thousand. It was far from the charm of the city life. Many facilities such as education, electricity and others were yet to reach there. People were happy in following their heritage of their predecessors. Heritage of traditions, rituals customs was honestly inherited and enshrined by the people. The impact of it on their minds was so strong and powerful that they never dared to go against it and introduce any undesirable change in their lives. Its influence on them was so dominating that they shaped their lives as per the guidelines of their culture. The people were god-fearing and believed that any revolting action would spoil their lives. Accidentally or coincidentally anyone dared to reject it or object to it perished or a suffered a lot. So it strengthened their faith that their culture and its traditions and superstitions were for their betterment.

There were many superstitions which cursed their lives. They believed that if they don't trust them, it will perish them. So they very strictly followed the superstitions such as avoiding seeing the face of an owl, twittering of a specific bird during night hours, crying of dogs and above all and the most important was the falling star. It was strongly believed that seeing them would cause something ominous to their lives. Seeing a falling star meant inviting danger to the lives. It was strongly believed by the innocent rustics there because their ancestors told many stories related to people who saw the falling star and consequently died. So it became the firm conviction of the people that if they wish to avoid the death or any other undesirable disaster, they avoid watching a falling star. Out of the fear of the falling star, the rustics never came out of their house during night hours or hours at the dawn where there was possibility of watching a falling star. They never slept on the cot or bed kept in the front yard or open space. So they preferred to be inside their houses. No one reached home late in the evening or left the house during the early hours of the morning. If anyone did it knowingly or unknowingly, he caught illness which took his life and thus innocent people believed that he might have seen the falling star which took his life. Thus the fear for falling star became widespread and life influencing among the poor rustics.

In such superstitious conditions lived a family of a peasant, Shrimant. His wife Meera was pregnant and was strictly instructed not to go out during night times or early hours of the morning. One day she delivered a child. It was a son. The family was very happy with the arrival of a son. Naming ceremony was arranged at grand level. The boy was named as Narendra. One day Meera was giving a bath to her son. There came a stranger having appearance of a sage. She lifted the baby and welcomed the sage. Meera offered him bread and butter and cup of tea. The sage got pleased and blessed her long life. Suddenly the baby caught his attention. He smiled at baby took his palm in his hand and seeing at the lines on it he predicted, "This son would be a great star in whatever field he would be." It excited Meera, "Really!

My son will be a great star." "Yes, the lines on his palm show that." But suddenly he stopped in the middle and his face turned grave. Meera got scared with sudden disappearance of earlier smile on his face and anxiously questioned, "Why are you so silent and have you seen anything ominous?" The sage opened his mouth after a brief silence, "Don't take it to your heart, if I disclose to you a bitter truth of his life." Meera taking breath with great concern said, "Please proceed not to hesitate. Don't stretch it any further. It will kill me." Sage replied, "There is no doubt that your son will be a star of his field but watching a falling star will be dangerous to his life. Perhaps it may the cause of his death. So you see how you can save him from the curse of a falling star." The sage departed but left behind a never ending concern for Meera. She was confused with a contrasting prediction; happiness of success on one side and fear of end on the other. It was evening she was feeding her son with concerned mood and waiting for her husband. Sometimes later, her husband came. She made her son sleep in the cradle. They sat for dinner. Her husband Devendra read her concerned and silent face and questioned her, "Why are you silent? What is the reason? When I left the house in the morning, you bid me a happy farewell. Then what happened in my absence that made you so melancholic? Please share." She opened her mouth and tears began to fall. "A stranger had been to our house early in the morning and made a strange prediction." "What he predicted?" you said to me, "my son will be a star of his field but the moment he sees a falling star, he will die." It brought furrows on his face and made him silent for a sometime. He encouraged her, "It is good thing that our son is going to be a star of his field. As

Parents, we shall take care that he should not come under spell of a falling star." "But how long we will do it? We won't be there with him through out of his life and if it happened in our absence, then? If he did not know that watching a falling star would be dangerous to his life and accidently he saw it then?" He tried to remove her concern by saying, "Let him grow and become mature. We shall let him know this secret of his life. He is baby. Let him grow. It is not the time to shade tears and feel concerned over the prediction of the future." Thus he silenced the crying Meera.

Time passed rapidly. Bilaspur extended a lot. It was on the verge of becoming a town. All the facilities of the city were availed by the people there. Schools, colleges and hospital were being introduced there. But the people with old approach were still under the influence of the inherited culture. The hold of old superstitions was still there. Narendra also grew with the growing time. He looked very fair and smart like a child actor of a Hindi Cinema. He attended school there at Bilaspur. He was very sincere and good at studies. Teachers appreciated him for his virtues. Parents were very happy with the way he was growing. But the prediction of the stranger was till alive in their minds. When they found him to be mature enough to understand the concepts of life, death and prediction, father opened his mouth one day. "Narendra come here, I wish to disclose a secret to you and it is very important." "What secret, Pappa?" "When you were born, a stranger had been to our house and predicted that it is dangerous for you to watch a falling star." "What will happen if I do it?" "It is not good for your life. It may take your life. So avoid looking at the sky especially during night time when there are more possibilities of falling star." Innocent Narendra took it seriously and said, "Pappa, watching a falling star is so dangerous to me then I would never have look at it."

Narendra took to this prediction to his heart. It had an adverse impact on his psyche. He never preferred to go out in the night. When his friends came to him to take him out, his mother warned him, "Narendra, you can go but take care that you should return before it gets too dark and the stars came out to decorate the sky with their glittery and take care when the stars start appearing in the sky, avoid their beauty." "Don't worry. I will take utmost care. I won't fall prey to the beauty of the stars in the sky." Narendra went out with his friends but never looked above. It developed a great fear in his innocent mind for a falling star. So this fear prevented him going out during night times. There was no question of getting up earlier in the morning as he was not in habit of getting up earlier.

Bilaspur was growing day by day introducing a new amenity to its people. For the entertainment of the people, a theater was introduced which became the talk of the town. To watch a movie at the theater, whole Bilaspur made the crowd there at all hours of the day and evening. Naredra was in his tenth. His friend used to come to him to take him to watch a movie at least one Sunday in the month. He too liked to watch a movie. Slowly it became his weakness. He was greatly impressed by the character of the hero in the movie and started imagining being a hero in a cinema. So it became his dream to be a hero in Hindi cinema. In the course of the time, there was appreciable physical change in him. His fairness grew and with built body. But in his madness of film and making a career as a hero, he never neglected his studies. He completed his H.S.C. with good marks which gave him admission in a medical college in Mumbai.

Actually his father was not in a position to pay for his admission. But he managed anyhow and finally he got admitted in a medical college. He was very happy to go to Mumbai as he knew that it would fulfill his long cherished dream to be a hero. College began and Narendra got involved in his studies. He read the news paper without fail as he thought it would bring him the opportunity that he wished. One day he came across an advertisement of audition for a new face to be introduced in Hindi Cinema. Narendra had a very good personality but didn't have the knowledge of acting. But he was confident, if opportunity given he would shine. So hopefully he went there. There was a long queue of the aspiring candidates. Looking at the long queue of the interested candidates, he imagined that how struggling it was to get the work in cinema. He had to wait till evening. At 8:00 pm, he was called in. Selection committee got impressed by his built body and fair look and offered him a role to play which he could not. He was disappointed but the selection committee encouraged him saying, "Narendra, you have everything only thing is that you need to work upon your acting skills. For this you join some acting classes. Come in our next audition, we shall give you a chance." Narendra thanked the selection committee and hopefully left the hall. It raised his hopes to be in cinema. He joined art classes. But he never ignored his studies. He studied hard and in leisure, he cherished this hobby of acting. He joined acting classes work hard to acquire every skill of acting.

Time passed, he finished his M.B.B.S. and tried his luck in the field of acting. It might be a coincidence that he happened to see an advertisement of audition. He went there and it was his luck that he got selected. In his debut film he succeeded in catching attention of the industry and of course the audience. Soon he started getting roles in different movies. Slowly his celebrity reached to its peak. One day he returned to his town. When his car entered the town, people shouted in his praise and were running after his motor car to take his autograph. When the car stood in front of a small house, someone ran in hurriedly saying "See your son, a great actor has come." Parents came out to receive their darling son. They became emotional and there was a proud smile on their face which showed how happy they were to see their son at a prestigious position. Father asked, "How is your life going on there. You have become a great artist. We watch your movies on television. We feel proud of it." "Narendra felt proud of himself. Looking at old and dilapidated house he said, "Pappa, our house has become very old now. It needs to be reconstructed." Looking at the man who was staring him, asked him, "Do you know any contractor who builds the house? Please send him to me urgently." The man left the place and within a few minutes a builder came there. Narendra instructed him to reconstruct the house make it huge one." Parents became very happy. While taking dinner father asked him, "Narendra, you are a great actor and so you might have lot of fans of yours especially girls. Haven't you chosen anyone for you?" Giving a blushed smile he said, "It is just beginning of my career. Whole day I am engaged. I don't get the time to think of it also. Let the time come I will tell you to do it." All laughed.

Before going to bed his mother called him and reminded, "Narendra, you have become a great star. But keep in mind watching falling star is dangerous for you." "Mummy I am so engaged that I don't get the time to think of it. But I will take care of it." The next day giving necessary instructions to the contractor, he left for Mumbai.

He started giving hits after hits. His popularity as a star was at its peak. He was fondly called Narendra Kumar. He earned a lot. Financially and professionally he was secured but still a sense of insecurity was there in his mind. It was the uncertainty of life. The fear of falling star was still there and sometimes he had nightmares that he had seen a falling star and died. He had posh bungalow and he took care that the outside sky should not appear. He had curtained all the windows. He opened the curtains in day time but took utmost care that no window should remain open so that eye could catch a falling star. Many times he had nightmares that he saw a falling star and died consequently. The superstition had such strong hold on his mind that he could not come out of it. Whenever darkness fell, he tried to be as secure as possible and avoided looking at the sky especially during starlit nights.

Once it happened that a premier of big budget movie was arranged in the theater. Many actors and actresses had been to the premier. They were sitting in the front row along with Narendra Kumar. The movie was so thrilling and exciting that all were absolutely engrossed in watching. Narendra Kumar too was watching with great interest. But he was feeling somewhat restless and uncomfortable. A death scene was being presented. A man was lying on the cot in the front yard of the house. He was staring at the sky as if he was waiting for the call from the heaven. His kinsmen were around him with grave faces. All the audience in the theater had become one with the scene. The people around the dying man were questioning each other why the old man was consistently looking at the sky. One of them said that he might be counting the stars in the sky. Other told that he might be seeing the god coming out of the sky. Third one said he might be looking at his favorite star. Suddenly the old man started raising his hand pointing his finger at the star. The audience too became curious what the old man wanted to show. Narendra was also watching with full concentration. The last breath of the old man was about to leave him, he pointed his index finger towards a star and shouted, "See my star is falling" The star fell down and with that the soul of the old man left him. The moment Narendra Kumar watched it; he received a severe heart attack and died in the chair.

Butcher

Cut! Cut! Cut! Bya! Bya! It was the sound of a departing male goat which survived the cutter and his family. A wooden log was bathed with blood of male goat whose head was separated from remaining body. Its head was lying there on the piece of a wood with open eyes as if the animal was reluctant to leave this world. But it was its lot that it had to go to leave someone back to see this world at its cost. Flies, insects and dogs were waiting for its death. The moment it was killed, all get ready to attack upon it. Flies began to hover on it as if they were dancing to celebrate its death. Dogs were waiting there outside with half tongue out to see what would come to their lot. The spots of blood had colored everything which came within its coverage area. It was the most trusted mutton shop of Liyaquat who had inherited this business from his ancestors. It was his regular business to kill the animals to survive his family. He had become so flint hearted to emotions of the living animals that he took it to be a game or a fun. He wanted that his son Tajuddin should also continue it. So he always took him to his mutton shop to make him acquire the skills of his business. Everyday little Tajuddin accompanied his father and began to observe how his father ran the business. Initially, he was immensely scared to see his father cutting animals with a sharp knife. The struggle of the pressed animal to get escape from the strong hold of the cutter moved his merciful heart. He could not bear this scene of bloodshed and murder of a poor and innocent animal. Closing his eyes to the scene and bringing tears in his eyes he said to his father, "Abba! Don't kill it. Let it live." Looking at horrified and moved little Tajuddin, Liyaquat said, "Don't be an emotional fool. It is our business. If I don't do it, we all will be starved. Its existence is our death, it is better to let it die. Don't shade tears. You are a son of a butcher. Tears don't suit to you. Do you know who is a butcher? Butcher is one who loves to take life to save life. It is our heritage and we have to preserve it and continue it." Tajuddin nodded his head.

The scene in the mutton shop had a great impact on the innocent mind of Tajuddin who could not bear the innocent animals being murdered mercilessly for their no fault. The next day when his father asked him to accompany him to the shop, he modestly denied. "Abba I don't wish to accompany you to the shop." "Why? What happened?" "Abba, I can't tolerate innocent animals being mercilessly killed. The scenes at the mutton shops terrify me. I had nightmares in the night which made me restless." "Come on, Tajuddin. You have taken their deaths to your heart. Act and think like me you would find to be a great fun." "Killing animals that were reluctant to die is great fun for you. How can you be so inhuman?" Liyaquat got annoyed at him. "Don't teach me lesson of humanity and mercy. I know very well what is human and inhuman. I do it that is why you are survived. If you don't like it don't come. At least don't feel disgusted at me and name me." Seeing angry face of his father, little Tajuddin preferred to keep quite. He knew better too much talk would punish his tongue.

Liyaquat was shocked with this sudden change in his son. But he overlooked it. Since then Tajuddin never accompanied his father to Mutton shop. The scene of murder of the innocent animals for making money and surviving people had changed his mind. He disliked it and gave up eating mutton of all types at home. He transformed into a pure vegetarian. Everyone in the family got shocked at this sudden change in him. When Liyaquat insisted on him to have it, Tajuddin refused to do so which arose Liyaquat's anger. He scolded him for going against the family traditions. Little Tajuddin answered very bodly, "I won't accept such traditions which victimize innocent animals to satisfy the demands of the tongues. Why can't you forget that one can survive without having meat? There are people who don't look at it. Yet they survive. Why don't you and I?" Liyaquat got annoyed at this too much wisdom coming out of the little brain of little Tajuddin. "Keep your philosophy with you. Don't spoil my life and our family with that. It is disloyalty to our profession. I can't tolerate anyone who name my profession and disturbs my profession. Doesn't matter let it be my own son."

Disharmony between father and son began to disturb the peace of mind of the family. Disgust towards father's profession was growing. One day he asked his father, "Abba, I wish to continue my studies. I want to do something different which would please me and give me social recognition." "None in our family has interest in studies. What will you do by doing studies? It will be wastage of money. Instead of that why don't you take interest in my business it will give you bread and butter? Why do you kill your time in reading books?" "I told you Abba that I am really not interested in your business. I don't like it. I can't tolerate to play games with the lives of animals who can't protest because they can't protest." Finally Liyaquat bent before obstinate Tajuddin and permeated him to go to Madarsa. Liyaquat realized that he won't succeed in convincing his son to accept his profession and decided to let him live the life he wished. The schooling brought about a great change in him. He did not like the teaching in Madarsa as it was absolutely religion based. His mind was trying to go beyond the religion. He took great interest in reading books. He didn't want to confine his reading to his own religion as he knew that it will make him fanatic. The books in Madarsa were religion based. His passion to know about the other religions took him out of Madarsa. So he joined libraries and spent his leisure in reading those books. He read all the books and took the best from them. The books in the libraries exposed to the goodness in different religions. He read books of Jainism, Buddhism, Hinduism and many more. It shaped his inclination and made him great humanitarian who loved all religions appreciated the best in them. He began to think going beyond his religion. He knew that the people in his religion are extremely fanatic and won't accept this new pattern of life. They will oppose him one day or the other. One day he took a book of some other religion to home. Liyaquat's eye caught it. He was literate enough to understand that the book was of some religion and not belonged to his own. It hurt him. He called Tajuddin, "What the book is about? Is it about our religion?" "No, Abba. It is not of our religion. It is of Buddhism." "It is too much. Water is going over head. Going to school and getting education, I can understand it, but I can't tolerate a son of through Muslim reading books of other religions." "What is wrong in that? I believe in reading the best if it is of other's religion I won't object. Knowledge is knowledge and it has no religion.""It is disloyalty to our own religion. I won't let it happen. It will spoil you and me also. Do you know ours is religion loving community and it never tolerates anyone going against it? Reading books of other religion is stepping towards that revolt which would disturb the harmony in the society and no member of its community would tolerate it. Better you stop doing all these foolish adventures. If you don't do it I will stop your schooling." "No Abba you can't do it?" "Why not? If you are going against the family values and social taboos; I will have to think of it. I have to live in the society and I don't want it should be hostile to me. If you have to be in this house, then you have to listen to me. I won't tolerate anyone challenging my authority and my religion." Tajuddin realized too much argument with the father would stop his schooling which he can't tolerate it. He said to him, "Abba, if you don't like my books, I won't bring them home. But don't stop my schooling."

For a few days he took interest in the teaching in Madarsa, but human mind in him took him out of it and he clandestinely visited libraries to read books. It continued for years. He took precaution not to bring any book home which would disturb the harmony and peace of the family. Years passed rapidly. It had made him wise and conscious to the good and evils in the society. He completed his matriculation from Madarsa. There was no facility of higher education in Madarsa so the boys and girls joined the colleges run by other religions.

Tajuddin joined one of the colleges in Shripatnam. In such colleges majority of the students belonged to other religions and a few were Muslims. Being so these students felt isolated and they did not easily join other groups. They formed their own groups and lived among them only. Tajuddin too had undergone this racial indiscrimination but he did not bother it. He focused on his studies and in leisure he buried himself in the books.

One day he was reading a book sitting in the library. Suddenly his eyes met the eyes of a girl who was reading on the other side. It was their first meeting. Tajuddin had been the member of that library from very initial days but never saw that girl previously. The next day when he came in the library and sat on chair, again he saw the girl on the same chair. When they looked at each other, he found a smile in the eyes of the girl. Both smiled at each other. Slowly this smile brought them together. The girl dared and broke the long ruling silence in their relationship. "Hello! I am Reshma." It disturbed all there. The library attendant made a sound, "shooook! Silence please. If you wish to speak, please go out. Don't disturb others." It made them shut their mouths. Reshma got up from the chair and left the library indicating Tajuddin to follow. Tajuddin followed the gestures of Reshama and followed her. He saw her going towards the canteen. He saw her sitting in the corner. When their eyes met each other, Reshma shouted, "Hello! I am here." Tajuddin acquired the seat staring ceaselessly at her. She reintroduced herself, "Hello! I am Reshma Zangiyani." May I know your name, please? "Tajuddin. Tajuddin Ali."

"Nice to meet you. Have you been a regular member of the library?" "Yes. I have been a member of it since my first day here." "What do you read?" "I like all kinds of reading." "Especially what type?" "Religious." "Do you read books of your religion?" "No like that but books of all religions." "How can a Muslim take interest in reading books of other religions?" "Why not? All Muslims are not equal." "But Majority is of them?" "Majority may be of them but a few are there who respect other religions and follow the best from them." "I am from those a few." Reshma got impressed by the non-secular and philanthropic approach of Tajuddin. They had tea together and dispersed.

It was a love at first sight. That night Tajuddin thought of the face of Reshma. Her face had occupied the canvas of his memory. Her gestures, postures and facial expressions and all traits of her personality touched the right chord of Tajuddin's heart. He was sleepless till late hours of the night. He got up quite late. When he looked at the wall clock, he shocked to see that it was10 O'clock. He had already missed the first lecture. He left the bed and hurriedly did all activities. Without taking the breakfast, he left the house telling his mother, "Amma it is already late. I will have the breakfast in the canteen. Don't take pain to make it." Amma shouted, "I am making it. Please have it." "No! No! Not possible. No time. I will have it later." Tajuddin left the home for the college. By the time he had reached there, first lecture was finished. While entering the class, he took a look at the girls section and was pleased to see Reshma sitting and busy in whispering something with her friend. Tajuddin was little disturbed. His mind was not there in the teaching. Whenever he got the chance, he took a look at her. She too did it in return. Eagerness of Tajuddin to meet her was at apex. He was waiting for the end of lecture. The bell rang and Tajuddin felt relaxed. Both looked at each other gave the indication to meet. It was recess for lunch. Both met in the canteen. Reshma asked him, "Have you brought your tiffin?" "No. I got up late. In hurry to attend the lecture, I forgot it." "It's not a problem. You can share mine." "It won't be enough. You will be half-fed. Better I order something." Tajuddin ordered something. Tajuddin questioned, "Are you coming in the library after final lecture." "Yeah, I will surely be there." It was late hour of the afternoon. Both met in the library. They took books and sat on their chairs. For the first time it happened that a voracious reader in Tajuddin got disturbed. He was ceaselessly staring at her. Reshma too realized it. She had realization of growing interest of him in her. She too knowingly or unknowingly was responding to his gestures. Almost half an hour was spent; the restlessness of Tajuddin did not let him take interest in the book. He looked at her and indicated to go out. He kept book there on the table and went out. Instantly, Reshma too followed him. They met in the canteen.

Tajuddin ordered coffee for them. While sipping coffee, they were looking at each other. But this time their look had different touch. When Tajuddin looked at her with that feel, she looked down with smile or tries to avoid having eye contact with him. Reading and understanding the emotions in her eyes, Tajuddin put his hand on hers. She little shrunk but she too wished the same. Thus their friendship turned into love relationship. Gradually they were become rare at the canteen and libraries. They preferred to meet at their clandestine places. Their relationship did not remain a secret for a long time. Everyone in the class knew it. Gradually it reached to their teachers and Principal.

On account of poor attendance, the institute wrote their families. Liyaquat showed no interest in it but Reshma's father came and got shocked to see that his daughter was absent on the roll call. He was informed by the Principal about her relationship with a Muslim. He felt ashamed of her. He went back home and waited for her. Reshma came home at the usual timing. Father was sitting in the swing taking it forward and backward. He felt the presence of her. He called her. "Where had you beenReshma?" "I had been to college attending lectures and reading books in the library." He turned red and angrily threw the letter on her. "See it. Tell me what is this?" Reshma got terrified and with trembling hand began to read the letter. Her body began to sweat. She realized that her theft has been caught and no meaning in giving any justification which would be false. Like a traditional father he told her, "No more college now. Help your Mother in her work." "She wanted to protest it but red face of her father prevented her from doing so. Like a mute animal she took the orders and disappeared from the eyes of the father."

Tajuddin was shocked at the absence of Reshma in the college. During off time, he visited library but he could not tolerate the presence of someone else in the seat of Reshma. It went on for some days. Tajuddin was sad at heart. He had lost his mind in everything. He disliked the company of the books and gradually showed his back to the library. One day he got her address from his friend. Every day he took round in the lane of Reshma with the hope that she would meet him. One day Reshma peeped through her window on the road luckily she found him in the street. She wanted to call him but she shut her mouth realizing the danger of it. When Tajuddin came in front of the house of Reshma, he looked up and their eyes met each other. It happened after a long time. It was not long time but in love when lovers are separated every moment passes like a year. Tajuddin smiled after long time. He was so excited that he could not understand how to respond to this situation. She smiled at him and indicated him to come tomorrow." Tajuddin was very happy he could see her face after a long time. What made him the most happiest was her gesture of meeting tomorrow.

Dressing himself richly and with a delightful mood he entered the lane of Reshma. There was a small tea stall where he stood and was waiting for her to come out. After some time he found a tall man with kurta and payjama coming out of the house. He went to other end of the road. Tajuddin guessed that she would come out now. Half an hour passed yet she had not come. He was looking at the balcony of her house with great expectation that she would come. His patience and eagerness came to an end with an expected entry of Reshma in balcony. Both looked at each other and felt happy at hearts. Reshma indicated him that she was coming down. Within a few minutes, she came down passed from the tea stall indicating Tajuddin to follow. At the end of road, there was an isolated and dilapidated house where she stood. As it was the end of the lane, there was no possibility of anybody's coming there. She stood in such a corner that no one could catch her. Tajuddin followed her keeping his eyes back and front. Tajuddin could not control himself and embraced her. They lost in each other's arms.

With tearful eyes she said to Tajuddin, "My father is looking a boy for me. Perhaps he would get me married this year. I am afraid. Do something. I don't want to marry anybody else except you. She began to cry." Tajuddin was moved. He was not able to handle situation. His hands were trembling and tears were rolling down from his cheeks. He encouraged her, "Reshma have patience. I will do something. Would you like to elope with me? She conveyed her affirmation with nodding head." Suddenly someone shouted Reshma what are you doing here? Reshma scared and ran away towards her house. Realizing the hazard of the situation, Tajuddin too left the place. The man who caught them there was the close friend of the family. Reshma was sure that he would intimate her father. She was scared. It happened exactly what she thought. The man reported to her father. Father reached home with angry face asked his wife, "Where is Reshma? Present her before me." Reshma was absolutely frightened with the consequence of her adventure came with a rabbits heart and trembling steps. Father spoke not a single word, slapped her, dragged her to a room and confined her in a room and warned her mother not to let her come out of her room. Dreams shattered. Hopes killed. Union was killed by separation. Once again history repeated itself and true lovers separated permanently. Tajuddin stopped entering in the lane of Reshma realizing the danger of being caught and punished. But the separation made him restless and eagerness to see Reshma was at its peak. Mustering courage, he entered the lane of Reshma but no use. The door of Reshma's house which opened to gallery was closed and the window beside too was closed. He waited there at the canteen but only frustration came to his way. He waited and waited with hungry stomach but his hope that door would be opened and his Reshma would come to give him *darshan* became bleak. The canteen owner knew that he came there for Reshma but he never let it know that he knew it. He asked him, "How long will you wait for her? She won't come. Go now." Tajuddin felt somewhat awkward and he left the place reluctantly.

The next day he came there stood for some time. But the situation was not changed. The doors and the window of Reshma's house were in the same state with grave silence. The canteen owner informed Tajuddin, "If you don't mind I have the information that she has been sent to her relative and no one keeps the information where they live. Perhaps she might be forcefully sent there for the purpose of marriage. I think better not to wait for her and waste your time. I can understand how difficult it is to accept it but whatever I have heard, I shared with you. Considering your interest and your state of mind I have advised. If you don't trust it you can wait here as long as you want." Tajuddin kept silent with great frustration and said, "I trust you. I think the same." His eyes were tearful. The canteen owner felt very sorry. "If you are hurt I say sorry." "It is not the matter. You advised well. You are not wrong. Thank you." Tajuddin took a last look at the house and its gloomy balcony and despaired window and with tearful eyes left the lane. The canteen owner stared at him till that point where he got disappeared and exclaimed, "Love makes man mad."

Tajuddin went home and found it to be hot for him. He entered the bed room shut the door informing his mother that he was taking rest as he was tired and told her not to disturb him. He lay down on the bed, took a pillow pressed it against the mouth cried loudly so that no one outside hear it. He cried and cried as long as he wished and gave rest to his troubled eyes. Mother knocked the door and called, "Tajuddin get up. You haven't taken anything since morning." Hearing the sound of knock, Tajuddin came out so that she should not feel that he is disturbed.

He rejoined the college after a long interval. He sat in the class but his eyes moved towards the girl section trying to find Reshma. In recess he went to the canteen to have his Tiffin sat on the same chair where they used to sit. Seeing the front vacant chair, Tajuddin felt broken at heart. He imagined the meeting with Reshma and her blushed and smiling face the way he touched her hand. Imagining that she was sitting there, he moved his hand to keep on her. He felt hardness of the table in place of the smoothness of that delicate and beautiful hand realized the present. He feared at heart and withdrew his hand and closed his eyes. Tears made the table wet. Nowhere had he found his mind. Every place troubled him what left was library. He entered there. The serene silence of the library made him more silent. He went to the counter gave his ID and took a book. He took a look all over the library and found his chair to be vacant. He occupied it and took a look at the front chair found someone sitting there. The absence of Reshma on the front chair hurt him but anyhow he controlled his emotions. He opened the book and started reading some religious book. It impressed him so much that he forgot everything. He wanted peace of mind and the book gave him. He took the book home to read it. The next day was Sunday. He used it for finishing the book. Since morning till evening he had been reading it. It made him silent and somewhat mature enough to accept the life in its real form. He took dinner and without thinking anything he gave whole night rest to his eyes, his mind too. The next day when he got up he was absolutely fresh and looked to be hopeful. He began his routine as he had it when Rehshma was not there in his life. He got a source to be free from the painful memories of Reshma. He spent hours in reading books.

One day he was taking a look at the newspaper. A news heading caught his attention. It was about violence caused due to eating beef. He read the news with dedicated heart and soul and got disturbed. It made him think on this issue and put him in a question, "How can people be inhuman to humans and animals who mercilessly slaughter them?" He thought that he needed to do something against this evil practice which killed enumerable innocent animals and making their slaughter as issues killing innocent people and damaging public property. Suddenly an idea clicked his mind to form a forum where likeminded people would gather and to do something concrete which would save innumerable animals being slaughtered. Initially he was alone. As the youths and people came to know about his organization they began to join his hands. A few likeminded people joined hands with him which strengthened his will. He visited various schools and colleges and delivered lectures against eating meat which kills thousands of animals a day. The group visited various cities and villages to create awareness among the people. His work gave him great popularity and a few friends but lot of foes. Gradually his own people and people from other community came forward to oppose his mission. He had anticipated it when he had to take a step to save lives. He bothered least of that opposition.

At home things were not peaceful when Liyaquat came to know about his son's adventure he scolded him, "Keep your philosophy with you. Don't try to shine the world with it. No one would like to walk in its brightness. Your cause will put my bread in danger better you stop naming my bread." It made him angry. He replied in an angry tone, "I won't. I have to do it let anything happen." "If you are so committed to your mission, here after you and I can't live under the same roof. Better you search a new roof for yourself. I may afford to lose you but on account of your foolishness not my bread and butter. I am not educated like you. If don't do it, my family will starve and die of hunger. So for my bread and butter I can lose you." The moment these words fell on his ears, Tajuddin realized that he had lost his place in his home. He felt better no to stay with such family and people who stopped him and weaken his determination for great cause. He bid farewell to his family, "Abba if it is your wish, I don't make lose your bread and butter. But I won't prefer that bread and butter which smells the blood of an innocent animal. You don't wish to share your roof with me, I should not force you." He went into his bedroom took half an hour to pack his bag came out and saw his mother engaged in doing something in the kitchen. He approached her found her to be weeping. He embraced her said, "Ammi, I can understand you and Abba but Abba can't understand me. Family runs on understanding. If it is not there what meaning is there in sharing reluctant roof? I can understand your motherly feelings but understand me. Let me go otherwise your emotions would weaken my determination." He came out looked at his father and said, "Abba, I am going. I don't know when I will be back. If you miss me and wish to meet me please call without hesitation I would come." Abba preferred not to respond him and meet his eyes pretending paying no attention to him and engaged himself in his work.

He joined Madarsa as a teacher and continued his mission. Madarsa provided him free accommodation. But extremely fanatic people of his community took objection to his presence in the Madarsa fearing that he would change the minds of the children which would ultimately put their religion in danger. He had to leave the job. He came to stay in a room offered by one of the members of the organization. He determined to dedicate his life to his mission. Conducting meeting and chats and conferences and lectures enhancing his organization by making people join his organization. He had found good results of his efforts. He knew overnight change was not possible. The cause demanded patience which he had.

It was around 9 PM he was just coming from attending a meeting. At a particular stop all his friends dispersed. He was on his way finding way to his room in the darkness. Suddenly someone overtook him shouting cow has been slaughtered in the mutton shop. It set the entire place on fire. People of both communities came out on the road and began to set each other's property on fire. People began to slaughter each other as the animals are slaughtered in the slaughter house. Tajuddin felt sad to see everywhere, the streams of blood and butchered bodies of humans. His ears were hurt hearing the screaming women who were being victimized by some lusty and sensuous falcons. He wanted to save them and stop the bloodshed but he found his strength to be paralyzed as the destructive hands were overpowered him. He took a shelter in a corner where he could not be seen. He was shocked to see thousands of people coming on the road on an issue. Suddenly someone from the angry crowd saw him shouted, "He is there lets attack. Tajuddin smelt the danger and he ran to save his life.

It was darkness he was finding way through the lights of the street lights which were scattered at distance. Accidently he entered the lane where his house was located. He shouted loudly so that somebody would come out to save him from the murdering hands. Suddenly he saw his house at distance and shouted loudly, "Abba, *bachav!*" Hearing the sound, Abba came out to see his Tajuddin running and shouting for help. Seeing an angry crowd of hundreds, he stopped still and saw his son being caught by the angry crowd as if a group of tiger attacks on a lonely deer like that hundred or doubles hands with sharp weapon fall on him and fountains of blood came out it.

Liyaquat could do nothing but to see the slaughtering scene of his own son helplessly. He sat down absolutely sunk in despair. Within moment a shouting body was cut into pieces as an animal was cut in a slaughter house or a mutton shop. The mob did its job and within twinkling of eyes dispersed from the place. Liyaquat absolutely broken and with tearful eyes began to collect the pieces of his darling son's body.

For next month or two, there was *matam* in the house. The crowd of relatives was coming and going out disturbing silence of the interiors joining the broken hearts of the Liyquat's family. His shop had been close for a month. It put him a financial concerns. So he reopened his business. While going to shop he stopped for a while at the bazaar and bought a goat for sale. He was pulling it towards his shop. When he was pulling that mute animal, he found the string to be heavy as the goat was dragging him backward. He realized it that the goat was reluctant to accompany him. But it was question of his bread and butter so he cared a least for his reluctance and took him forcefully.

There was a queue of the customers to have fresh meat. He took the goat in a shade and lifted a sharp knife to cut it, suddenly he remembered his son shouting for help, "Abba, *bachav!*" He got disturbed and looked at the goat. Its struggle to save its life remembered how Tajuddin was trying to escape from butchering hands. A true human being in him awoke. He took away the knife and left the goat. The goat left the shop speedily jumping up and down and moving this and that side. When he saw the goat, smile sprung on his face.

He told the customer not to wait. They won't get mutton. He came out of his shop with knife and locked it permanently and walked towards his destination throwing the knife high up in the air.

Jasmine

There was an eye-catching bungalow at the midst of the city. It was the bungalow of a rich businessman Balwant Singh. His prosperity knew no bound. There was ceaseless flow of money as he had number of businesses. Most important thing was that he had spread the roots of his business overseas especially in U.S.A. So he had to go to U.S.A. every now and then. His younger brother looked after his business in America. It was the hobby of Balwant Singh to collect beautiful artifacts of the world. His bungalow was well decorated with the worlds' costly and beautiful artifacts. His bungalow was so nicely built and colored that anyone who passed by fell prey to its beauty and unknowingly took a deliberate pause at it enjoyed its beauty walked away saying 'How beautiful and splendid it is! Like the exteriors, the interiors of the bungalow too were marvelous. It was wonderful experience to get the inner look of the Bungalow. Very costly artifacts accumulated from the different parts of the world were there which showed the aesthetic sense of Mr. Balwant. At an earlier age, he had visited half of the world and at every meet to a different country in connection with some business brought some artifacts. The presence of the artifacts was so enhancing day by day that the huge bungalow was growing small. Everyone who lived near wished to have a darshan of the interiors of the bungalow but the entry into the bungalow was strictly prohibited. Bungalow had a huge gate and there was a security to prohibit the entry of the unnecessary elements.

Balwant Singh was one of the wealthiest persons of the town. With his money power, he bought and brought thing which liked him and gave him happiness. But this wealthiest merchant was sad at heart as he had no son but he had only a daughter Rupa to whom he loved more than himself. For her sake he did all that was possible. He took his wife to the world's best gynecologist but his riches could not bring him a son who could inherit his property. The couple was little despaired but happiest as they had a very beautiful girl to whom they treated as their son and loved not less than their lives.

There was huge garden and lawn in front of the bungalow. Beautifully carved swing was fixed which showed the aesthetic sense of its master. Every morning and evening, the family used to sit there to have morning and evening coffee. Rupa was just ten years old. From very childhood, she was fascinated towards the plants specially which had flowers. Much of her time she spent in the garden watching and observing every flower. Softly touching and smelling them pleased her. What she liked the most was watching the flowers. So he warned the Gardner whatever may happen, never pluck the flowers and never let the plant grow dry. She warned him to water the plant sufficiently and take care no plant should be unnoticed.

She was in the third standard of a convent school. Whenever she returned from the school, she took her book and went towards the garden. Finding a huge tree having sufficient shadow, she sat there to study till evening. In the evening after finishing her studies, she took water can and began to water each and every plant. Touched, kissed and smelled every flower which bloomed on them. Whenever she accompanied her parents to their relatives or acquaintances, the first thing she did was that she took a round around the garden and saw new flower tree which she did not have. If she found any new one, she asked the families to give the seed of the flower or plant and introduced that plant in her garden. Thus she had accumulated a good number of plants. When her father was going to overseas, she asked him to bring new plants or seeds of them so that her garden could be enriched with them. One day Balwant jokingly asked Rupa, "What will you do with all these flower trees. If they grow like this, one day there won't be a place for us to live." Rupa laughed and said, "Papa, you know how much I like the flowers. I have fallen in their love. I can't live without them." "This is your love for the flowers and trees make me concerned." "Don't worry, Pappa. I won't die." Balwant Singh asked, "Which flower you want this time?" "Any flower which we don't have?" "How can I guess which flower tree is not there in our garden?" "You have seen our garden and each and every flower tree. It is you who has brought most of them. So a single look would be enough for you to bring the desired flower." She held his hand and lovingly dragged him towards the garden.

One day she accompanied her mother to her maternal uncle's house who shared the same city. He too had a very posh and grand bungalow. While loitering in the garden, her eyes fell on a small plant which was not the part of the garden actually was growing secretly in a niche of the garden. There was only one flower. She liked the flower so much that she fell in love with it. It was her first time to see the flower and remembered that her presence was not there in her garden. She hurriedly went in and took both her mummy and her maternal aunty to the garden. They came along with her at the spot. Pointing towards the plant, she asked her aunty, "Aunty Do you know which flower is this? I have seen it for the first time." "I don't have any idea of it. I know the names of almost all the trees in the garden. It is not planted. It has grown naturally. Perhaps your uncle will tell you." Her curiosity to know the flower was at apex. Out of that curiosity she questioned, "When will he come?" "He will come for lunch shortly."

Rupa's mother and aunty left the garden but Rupa did not accompany them she stood at the plant started watching it. She remained there till her uncle came in the garden to call her for the lunch. He came there shouting, "Rupa, it is growing hotter. What are you doing here? All are waiting for you for the lunch. Come on!" Rupa asked, "Uncle, you come here first and tell me what flower is this?" Uncle said, "You mad flower girl. What flower you are talking about." Pointing her index finger she said, "This one. How lovely flower it is! What a color combination and what a structure! Simply marvelous! Please tell me its name." "It is Jasmine. What is special about it? There are more beautiful flowers there." "Uncle, I liked it very much. Can I have it?" He called the Gardner who was late that day. He asked him to dig out the plant and keep it in the motor car of Rupa and take care that the plant should not die. Gardner did the job. Rupa was very happy that she got a very beautiful flower that day.

Her car entered her bungalow. Without going in, she directly entered the garden. She called the Gardner and asked him to dig a ditch for the plant. She very carefully and delicately handed over the plant to Gardner. She herself watered the plant after planting. Since then an attachment developed between them. Her fascination for the plant grew so much that she started taking special care of it. With every season, she grew and thus grew the plant. Day by day the plant was growing beautiful as lot of flowers were blooming on them. Rupa became almost mad in her love for the plant. Balwant and his wife were worried about this too much love of their daughter for the flower. They scared if anything wrong happen with the tree, what will happen to their daughter. Balwant Singh warned his wife, "See. Rupa is growing too much emotional with the new plant. Her love for it is appreciable but such an attachment would be dangerous. You know I don't get the time to spend with her. She is the only child of us and the mistress of our property. If anything wrong happens to her, we will be perished. What will be the use of this Tajmahal none is there to look after it? So you have to take care that too much love for the plant should not harm her." She understood his seriousness about Rupa. Mrs. Singh says, "Don't worry. I will take care of it."

It became a hobby for Rupa that whenever she returned from the school and after having lunch, she took her book and went straight to the plant. There was tree quite close to the plant under the shade of it she sat and studied. As soon as he had finished her studies, she went close to the Jasmine plant and observed as a mother observed a change in her baby. Psychologically she was attached with the plant. She could not digest any undesirable change in the plant.

She started taking it to her heart. The plant was growing sufficiently huge and created its own existence like other flowers. Previously a flower here or there came and then the flowers were spread everywhere and it was excelling every beauty. Its beautiful existence began to please Rupa. It was the spring; the tree which was fully grown began to drop its leaves. Everyday Rupa was observing this change in the tree. She took it to her heart. The change in the tree was psychologically affecting her. When the tree turned yellow and becoming leafless as a psychological reaction of it, beautiful and white Rupa turned little black and pale, dull and energy less. She grew physically weak and unable to walk. When the tree became completely leafless, she became almost paralyzed. Balwant and his wife observed this change. They were almost disturbed. They initially took it to be seasonal variation in body. He showed her to the best doctor there but no medicine could do magic. No doctor could find out the reason behind her illness. The Singh family became helpless before the strange illness of Rupa. They performed pooja and path and did that was told to them but no worship could do the magic.

As the season came to an end and new leaves began to grow on the tree, Rupa started getting energy back. When the tree became fresh and green as it was, Rupa got revived, turned fresh and full of energy. She ran towards Jasmine plant and began to smile and laugh at it. She was so happy that she forgot that she had been ill for several months. Balwant sing and his wife got shocked and surprised with this sudden change. But they realized that her love and attachment for the Jasmine was really dangerous. If the life of the plant which had the power to exercise its influence on her, it could be problematic. As long as the tree survived, Rupa would breath. The moment something wrong happened with the tree, better not to imagine the plight of Rupa. The Singh's fear grew. They became very serious about the tree because they knew that the life of their darling daughter depended on the tree. So they started taking special care of Jasmine. Balwant Singh ordered the Gardner to take special care of Jasmine.

Whenever Balwant Singh was free, he visited the plant checked its growth. If anything wrong he noticed, immediately he brought it to the notice of Gardner. Jasmine became the cause of tension for the family. All the time there was talk of care among the family members. Sometimes the family ignored Rupa but enquired about the Jasmine. Gardner was extremely troubled with this routine enquiry. He too realized that if anything wrong happened to the tree, his master will kick him. He understood wrong with the tree meant wrong with Rupa so he became very cautious about the plant. Whenever he came to the garden the first thing he did was that he visited the plant after confirming that the tree was absolutely alright, then he started doing other works. Even at the time of going, he came near the plant, took a serious note of it and confirming its good health he left. But Gardner was so afraid that at home he talked and talked about the Jasmine. One day his wife asked, "Was there only one tree that was Jasmine? No other tree is there? Was the garden of your master was so small?" The Gardner smiled at this humorous question of his wife and replied, "Jasmine is not an ordinary plant. It is the life of the garden. It is the life of mine and yours and of course the master's too. "How?" When the Gardner told her about the relationship between Rupa and the tree, she shocked and exclaimed, "Can it be possible? Can someone love a tree to such an extent?" She too felt concerned and advised him, "Love and care me less but take care of the plant if it is the life of so many." The gardener laughed and said, "Not required telling. I have focused on it I water it and fertilize it whenever required.

Once it was hot summer. Too much heat started causing great damage to the plants and trees which were sensitive to the growing heat, they were harmed. The leaves got burnt. When Rupa observed it that a leaf or two were burnt, her body began to sweat. She came running and said to her father, "Pappa! Pappa! Jasmine has received burn injury. Come on hurry up! Seeing the streams of sweat on her face, Balwant Singh felt worried. He touched her forehead that Rupa was burning with fever. "Rupa you have a fever. Let's go to the doctor or I will call him here." "Call him later. That is not important. Let's go to Jasmine first. It is in trouble. Balwant scared he ran with Rupa towards garden. He called the Gardner and shouted at him, "What do you do whole day? Haven't you seen the leaves of the Jasmine are being burnt you are sitting idly there. If you don't take care of it or how to take it better you stop coming from tomorrow. I don't need your careless service." The Gardner got terrified with this angry mood of his master. He watered the plant and fertilized it. Then he made a shade of some transplant cloth over it so that the heat of the sun should not harm it. The Gardner got scared. While making shade over the tree, his hands were trembling and his body was sweating. He realized the worth of the plant. He begged his master, "Better you free me from this responsibility otherwise this plant would take my life one day." Master angrily said, "If you had taken care of it and took precaution, heat would not have harmed the plant." "I am really sorry. I won't let it occur again." Balwant Singh said, "It is alright now. Take care that nothing wrong should happen to the plant. You know that wrong with the tree means wrong with our lives. And you too."

Jasmine became the cause of worry. It stole his sleep. Balwant Singh too took it to his heart felt very much concerned about the future of the tree and of course Rupa too. One day the gardener was shaping the trees in the garden. Suddenly he missed Jasmine; he hurriedly reached there and got shocked to see the tree got infected. He realized that Jasmine won't survive and he will have to face his angry master. On the next day he called his master and informed him that he left the job. It caused further tension to the Singhs. Balwant got busy in getting a new Gardner for his garden. He called his friends and asked them to send anyone they knew. Rupa came from the school had her lunch and hurriedly reached to Jasmine. When she noticed some spots on it, she scared. She came shouting "Pappa, Pappa what happened to Jasmine. I found some spots on its leaves. I am scared something wrong is happening to the tree. Let's hurry." Perspiring Balwant reached there with Rupa. He observed and realized that Jasmine was infected. If not noticed now, it will invite the unnecessary disaster to the family.

He called the experts in the field and treated the plant. But no magic could happen. Infection of the tree grew and it started infecting Rupa. Slowly Rupa started showing symptoms of illness. As the tree was turning dry and leafless, Rupa too was responding to its change and within few days the tree turned leafless and Rupa almost lifeless. She was lying on the bed. One day she expressed her wish to her father to shift her cot near to Jasmine. Father did it instantly. The Singhs were worried over the sudden happenings. There was the last leaf left on Jasmine which was still fresh and green. It was because of this Rupa was till surviving. Balwant Singh understood it and realized he had to do whatever he could before that green leaf turned yellow and ultimately die. He called everyone he knew but none could do anything hope rising. He thought a lot over it and finally reached to the conclusion that nothing was in his hand. He left it to Almighty.

He informed his younger brother, Siddhu, who was abroad about the poor health of Rupa. He came there in a few days. When Balwant Singh told him the reason behind the illness of Rupa, he got shocked over the strange relation. He knew that as long as the tree will be there, Rupa will be there. An idea clicked Sidhu's mind. He shared it with Balwant Singh. It gave him a hope and brought a smile on his face. He managed Jasmine tree which resembled like the real Jasmine. When Rupa was asleep, they covered Original Jasmine with some canvas and exactly in front of it, they fixed this new plant. They knew that if they fixed tree with a lot flower and leaves, Rupa would get doubt so they did one thing, they fixed the stem first with a single leaf. When Rupa got up and saw the tree with a single leaf was there, she looked at her and gave a smile. Balwant Singh became emotional. He sat near her and said, "My dear too much love for this tree is not good. It will take your life. It is good thing that you love it but you have become so mad in its love that you forget the people who love you more than themselves. Why don't you think that if you can't live without Jasmine, how do you expect us to live without you. As you are committed to Jasmine, you are committed to us. If we love you and live for you then you should do the same for us. If anything wrong happened to the tree, your life will be in danger and if you are in danger not to imagine about us we will be no more. I don't say that you should not love Jasmine. But it is dumb. If you have such an attachment with a dumb object then why don't you feel for us who are living and living for you?" Rupa smiled at her father and turned her eyes towards the tree and took a corpse like posture. Balwant Singh realized his words went in vain.

Siddhu started adding leaves after leaves and flower after flower. Every day when she got up from her sleep and saw new leaves and flowers bloomed on the dead Jasmine, she felt revived. She started making movements of hands and legs and spoke some words. One day she said to her father, "Papa, see my Jasmine is coming to life. When it will be complete with leaves and flowers, I wish to leave this bed and kiss its flowers. For long I have not touched my jasmine. I am eager to be with it." He was moved and tears wet his eyes but hiding them he said, "Yes my dear Rupa, your Jasmine is coming to life and very soon it will be perfectly bloomed." "When that day would come? I am growing curious." "Very soon your Jasmine will be as you wanted it to be. Then touch and care as much as you want. Don't speak. Be silent. Get ready for your wish." Rupa smiled at her father and slept.

Balwant Singh asked Siddhu, "Don't you think that we are deceiving Rupa. I am afraid if she came to know the reality, what could she do? It will be shock to her and I fear that she won't be able to bear it." "I can understand it but what can we do now. If we stop doing it, then Jasmine will die and ultimately we will have lost our Rupa. Better we should do something which will save her. Leave rest up to God." Balwant nodded his head helplessly with affirmation.

Improvement in the health of the tree caused the improvement in the health of Rupa. She started taking enough food and could get up and sit on cot but unable to step as weakness was still there. A few flowers were left to be added. Assuming that Rupa is asleep, Siddhu and Balwant began to fix the flowers and the leaves on the tree and became happy to see that the tree was fully bloomed. They waited for tomorrow's morning to see how Rupa reacted to the change in the tree. It was a sleepless night for them as thought of tomorrow could not let them sleep. The sun came up the rays of the sun fell on the face of Rupa which made her awake. Both Balwant and Siddhu were eagerly waiting for the response. Rupa opened her eyes and looked at the tree. She exclaimed with joy, "Papa my jasmine is turned alive. See it is perfectly bloomed." Both reached to her and said, "Yes! Rupa, your Jasmine has come alive. Come and touch it yourself." Like Jasmine, Rupa too became perfectly fit and energetic as if the life in Jasmine had been transferred into her. She excitedly got up and steeped hurriedly towards Jasmine and shouted, "Oh my dear Jasmine you're returned to me. I was sure that you won't leave me alone here. I am dying to touch you." She touched its flower and felt it to be strange and not of her Jasmine. She looked at her father and fell down never to wake up. Rupa became silent with that everything around. Father exclaimed, "What a love and commitment as if they were made for each other."

Chillum

The python of darkness was gradually engulfing the town, Belapur. The street lights and electricity bulbs in the houses were giving tough fight to stop the aggression of darkness. It was city which always remained in limelight due to its controversial temperament. Every now and then a case of violence of all sorts was registered in the local police station. The city was very sensitive and cursed with casticism. It had claimed many lives and spoiled many families of the town. Perhaps it might be the reason why the town is where it was in the past. The town was divided between two communities such as Dalits and rest of the castes. Dalits were leading the lives of slaves and were deprived of their place in the main stream of the society. It is said that time is solution for the problems but in Belapur it seemed that its clock might be stopped. Dalits were till Dalits and Orthodox was growing Orthodox. None could bridge the gap between these two communities. It was growing and expanding and strengthening its roots as the python of darkness in night.

It was around 10 O'clock of the evening. A cacophonous shouting of a person grabbed the interior silence of the town. Suddenly, the town which was to go for rest became alert and active. Dragon like fire of the news spread so quickly that entire town which about to be inactive due to hectic schedule of the day suddenly got alert. The people, who were just entered in the bed, threw away their blanket came out curiously and hurriedly to know what the shout was about. When the orthodox community came to know that a girl of their community eloped with the Harijan boy, they became ferocious and they came with whatever they had to take revenge of this disgracing act. One of ardent orthodox laid them and the angry mob marched towards the *Harijan vasti* which was ostracized and marooned from the rest of the community.

Harijan Vasti was completely ignorant of this coming disaster. When the community heard the human roaring, it took it to be the matter of inner dispute of the orthodox and disassociated itself with echoes of these detrimental roaring. Within a few minutes the angry mob entered the Harijan Vasti and crushed it under its merciless feet. They set their houses and huts on the fire and beat the people black and blue. Some sensuous and lustful elements grabbed this chance and entered the houses molested and raped the women without bothering of their ages. Some old men who could not bear this attack died on the spot. The women who were raped either gone mad or committed suicide by jumping into the wells. The angry mob was moving through every lane of the Harijan leaving no hut, no house and none in the family. The scene of devastation was so terrific that if anyone had seen ithe would have closed his eyes and ears as it hurt him a lot. The fire was spread everywhere and the pythonic smoke was seen attacking the sky. The last house at the end of the vasti was still to be unharmed. The angry mob marched towards it. The house was in sound slumber as it was little bit away from the Harijan community. It was the house of a *bhangi* staying with wife, daughter and a son. Suddenly the huge thumbing at the door terrified them. The family was absolutely scared with this unexpected thumbing. He was marching towards the door to open suddenly a gush of angry faces entered and hit the *bhangi* with an iron rod. The hit was so powerful that he died on the spot. Mother shouted "Munna, Bhag." The little boy ran in one of the rooms. The daughter clung to her mother. Senusous eyes fall on them and within minute sensuous and lusty python engulfed their existence. Munna was unfortunate to see his mother and sister being raped and looted before his open eyes. Their loud shouts and cries, their naked and wounded bodies with the scratching marks of human hurt him a lot. The scene was so tragic that it left its permanent mark on his mind.

He wanted to protest but he was helpless as his power was that of rabbit before dainasoric human force. He did nothing but shut his mouth and shed tears. One of them saw him and the angry mob laid its *morcha* towards the bedroom. All of a sudden the electricity in the house got disturbed and Munna who was about to fall in the hands of the merciless crowd got escaped. The angry crowd searched him but they failed. One of the annoyed mouth exclaimed, "Bhag gaya sala, Harijan ki avladh". Munna, finding his way through dark passage of the night fully scared and following all possible ways to save himself from the angry hunter reached at the railway station. Without bothering where the train was bound to go, he boarded on it and sat beside the toilet. He was so tired of running that he went into realm of sleep. When he got up he found himself at Dadar. He got down from the train got totally confused and bewildered seeing ants like people running ceaselessly. He saw a big question mark in the crowd asking him where to go? He came at the washroom sat there for a very long time unfed and thirsty waiting someone to give him helping hand. His mind was engrossed to solve the riddle of the survival. He checked his pockets and found not a coin. It scared him a lot. He sat there and being tired slept there. The sweeper came and woke him up. "Hello! Who are you? Why are you sleeping here? Don't you know it is not the place to rest? Go out of the station otherwise the police will punish you?" The moment the sweeper uttered the name of Police, Munna began to cry loudly. The sweeper doubted something in his cry. He sat beside him and pitied with him by moving his human hand over his head questioned him, who are you and how you came here?" Munna with tearful eyes narrated how he lost everything and became orphan. The sweeper took pity on him and asked him, "Did you have anything? Munna replied, "Nothing since last night. My pockets are empty. Take pity on me and give me something to eat. I am really hungry." Munna began to cry. The sweeper was really moved. He took him to the canteen and offered him some snacks and a cup of tea. The sweeper was ceaselessly looking at the innocent face of Munna. He found a scare and uncertainty of life on Munna's face. When Munna finished his breakfast, the sweeper asked him, "Where will you go? Do you know anyone here?" Munna nodded negatively and began to cry. The sweeper asked him, "Will you come to stay with me?" Munna became so happy that he clang him and began to cry." The sweeper lifted him and took him home in slums.

Life here in slum was not new to him as he belonged to Dalit Vasti where the conditions were almost like the slums. So he accepted that life also. He felt fortunate enough that he got an umbrella of love and care in an alien area. Sweeper's wife was very happy with arrival of Munna in the family. As they were very poor they could not afford to educate Munna. They nurtured him in all possible ways and gave him whatever they could. Whenever night came, he got scared as the memory of devastation of that night made him restless and kept him awake for a very long time. When he got extremely terrified, he clung to the sweeper who slept near him. Whenever the scene came on the canvas of his memory and reminded him how his family was brutally treated, his anger ignited him to take revenge on that orthodox society which murdered his family so heinously and brutally. Whenever he woke from that nightmare, his body turned wet with sweat. The seed of revenge slowly was getting sown in the innocent soil of his mind.

The Sweeper was very poor. His income was so meager that it was very difficult to meet expenses of his family and the presence of Munna enhanced his difficulty. So the troubles began. Finally the sweeper decided to send Munna for a job. The sweeper had good acquaintances there. So he managed a job for Munna. Munna never wanted himself to be a burden on the family. He was waiting for the opportunity to serve the family for their shelter. Luckily it came to him. When the sweeper asked him, "Munna, would you like do a job? It would give you money and you won't be troubled by the boredom at home." Munna replied, "Of course why not! I will do it? Tell me where to go and work?" "No need to go too far. It is there in *beedi* making factory which is at a calling distance from our hut." "There! It is great thing." On the next morning he got up early and with the sweeper he went to the factory." When he entered the factory he was very happy to see many children like him making *beedi*, Cigar and chillum. He felt it to be a pleasant thing as he after a long time got exposed to new friends and new surroundings. What made him happy was that he was going to earn and support the family which spread an umbrella of love over him. It made him happy because he was going to be an earning boy and not dependent. So he was really happy at heart. When the sweeper left him with the other boys and asked him, "Will you be happy here?" Munna replied cheerfully "Uncle, don't worry. I will manage. You go on your duty." "Come home carefully after finishing your job." Munna nodded positively and gave a smile and began to work.

Initially Munna felt bored and marooned in new conditions but soon he befriended with some children there which became the cause of happiness. It was a two storied building and had many rooms. The interiors of the building had doubtful appearance as if it had been carrying some clandestine activities. The first floor of the building was reserved for the children where they made *beedies* and other tobacco carrying products. On the second story, some elderly men did the same work. But the entrance of the second floor was always locked from inside. The children were never allowed to know what was going on there. A note in red letters was displayed there, "Children are not allowed upstairs." The warning was so strict that no one dared to go upstairs and poke his nose in the matter which made noise in a closed door. When Munna joined the factory, he was warned at the very outset about this prohibited entry. So he never threw his eyes on the steps which went to the upstairs. The secret behind the closed door of upstairs always stroke his mind and developed an interest to see the picture behind the closed door. But he was afraid to go up and do it as he was fully aware of its consequences.

Once it happened that the entrance of the upstairs was slightly open and Munna saw some middle aged labors were coming and going. Some of them came and went out. After sometime they came with heavy boxes without speaking with the children who were in making cigars. Munna was observing the behavior of the labors that deliberately preferred to be away. Munna smelt something mysterious and doubtful. The seed of disclosing the secret was sprouting in his mind. When Munna came to work, he ceaselessly kept watch on the closed door. He observed that once the labor reported on the duty, they entered the room and closed it till the evening time when the labors of the night shift came on the duty. If they had to bring something from outside, they came silently and carried whatever they wanted. Munna wanted to get acquainted with them but he was not getting way. One day he was filling a cigar, suddenly his eyes met a middle aged person. Their eyes met. Munna gave such a smile, that labor could not prevent himself from giving a smile back. It became Munna's habit to wait for that particular labor and try to befriend with him. One day it happened that the labor came down looked at Munna. Munna did it in return and said, "Uncle! Good afternoon. May I know your name please?" The labor smiled at him and replied, "I am Shantaram. I am going out. Would you like to come with me?" it was the chance Munna eagerly waiting for. He replied, "Why not uncle? Where will you take me?" Shantaram replied, "I am going out to have cup of tea. Would you like to have something with me?' "It is my pleasure to be with you." They went out sat at a small tea stall. Shantaram offered him some snacks and a cup of tea. Munna spoke so sweetly with him that Shatraram knowingly or unknowingly opened his mouth. "Our's is very old factory. When I was of your age, I joined this company. Since that day the factory has been going on ceaselessly. Initially I used to work down as you do. When the owner of the factory realized my cigar making skills, he promoted me and asked to work upstairs." Munna interfered him in the middle and asked, "What do you do up?" "Nothing special my friend, I make cigar with my colleagues?" If you make cigar like us then why do you shut the door. I smell something secret in it, if I am not wrong." Shantaram in scolding voice says, "Your mind taking too much interest in it. Better you do your business. If the owner of the factory smells it he will sack you. Better you be do your work and not to take interest in the activities going on upstairs." "I am not taking interest. I have no interest in it. Out of curiosity, I asked. If you are hurt, I won't ask you" "it is not the matter of hurting. I am not at all hurt by your questions. There are some secrets which I can't disclose to you." "Shantaram uncle, can I get a chance to work with you up?" He replied, "You need to grow first and display your cigar making skills you may be promoted up." Munna's eagerness got ignited. His wish to know the things behind the closed door got aggravated. He began his work of cigar with a great interest and became mad to achieve excellence.

His nights were troubled one as the memories of injustice done to his family made him restless. He was finding way to take revenge on the society which looted him. As soon as he entered the factory, the memory of the nightmare lessens his spell and Munna got one with his work. 'Excellence in cigar making' became his target. Time passed and with passing time maturity eclipsed his mind. Slowly Munna was coming in limelight with his excellent skill in cigar making. Everyone took a note of his skill. He was promoted as a leader of cigar making labor working downstairs. His salary was enhanced which enhanced his interest and he became more responsible employee. Gradually his contacts with owner increased and soon he succeeded in making a good place for himself in his book. The owner of the company started looking at him with a great hope and expectation that Munna would enhance the recognition of the factory. One day the factory owner called him up in his cabin asked him, "Munna, you have been in this company for many years. These years are not the years of service but honest and dedicated service. I want that you should take the charge of both stairs and control activities going on here." Munna became happy with this favour of the factory owner. He replied, "It is honour of mine that you considered me to be worthy for this position. I will do my level best but never offer you a chance to complain about my work." The owner became happy with affirmation and began to take him in his confidence so that he should not open his mouth elsewhere which will put him in trouble. Till now he was completely unaware of the things going behind the closed door. Now he was in charge of the both the chairs and nothing could be hid from him. One day he was taking a round, he got shocked to see that the labor was adding some white powder in cigars and *beedi*s. He asked the labor, "Hello! Gentleman what are you mixing in? What is this powder about? Who told you to do it?" The labor kept mum. When Munna got annoyed he shouted, "Tell me, who told you to do it?" The labor answered, "The boss." Munna became silent with this answer. Munna questioned further, "How long you have been doing it?" The labor looking down answered, "It is regular practice here. It is being done for years and being on the order of the boss and requested Munna not to trouble him any more on this issue." That remark of the labor shut the mouth of Munna. He wanted to meet his boss and wanted to convince that the practice being conducted was not good and if exposed and came out it would spoil all of them. But that day his boss was out of station. He went home had his dinner and went to bed in his room. His mind got engaged in a philosophical thinking that practice being conducted in factory is malpractice and it was fraud with the human life. Outwardly the boss seemed to be a gentleman then how could he promote such practice. Suddenly his mind took him back to the incident and heart breaking cries of his mother, sister and almost dead father counting last breath overpowered him. His anger for that racist and inhuman society which mercilessly and brutally finished his family and his community got aggravated. Suddenly idea of revenge clicked his mind and he began to ponder over it. When he again closed his eyes to sleep he smiled as if he got something which he was long waiting for.

The next day he went to his office and went upstairs to meet his boss. But he found him not there. He asked one of the labors, "Husain, haven't boss come yet? It was urgent to meet him" Hussain replied, "There was a call from him that he would come late." It is ok. I would wait for him." He went back to his work. Sometime later he heard the sound of the footsteps of his boss going upstairs. He wanted to meet him immediately but he stopped and thought he has just come, let him rest in his chair. After half an hour, he went to meet him. "Good after noon sir. As a responsible employee of the factory I wish to make you known with the things happening here." What is the matter? Is anything worth concerning?" the boss questioned. "Yes. Yesterday when I was taking round upstairs to see how labors worked, I got shocked to see that they were filling chillum with drugs. I felt it strange." "See Munna, better you ignore it. It would be better for you. It is my business and I don't like anyone taking unnecessary interest in it. As you are close to me, I advise you better you overlook and let it go on as it was." "Sorry sir, if I hurt you." "It is ok. You may go now." Feeling disheartened Munna left the cabin and buried himself in his work. In the evening he left home but the words of the boss were making chaos in his mind. He was thinking to quite the job as he knew what will be the future? Since he had no job in his hands, he decided to continue it for some days." It was at the mid night, the nightmare began to trouble him and provoking him to do justice with the family which was victimized for other's fault. When the nightmare left its hold on his mind the idea of chillum began. Before he closed his eyes to sleep, he determined to have a talk with the boss."

The next day he met his boss and said, "I wish to quit the job and to go back to my town." The boss got surprised with this abrupt decision. "Have you been hurt by my word? If it is so, I would take my words back. But don't quit the job. I won't get an employee like you." "No it is not matter. I wish to take your business to my town. "You want to take my business to your. How is it possible? And for why?" Munna narrated the whole story behind the tragedy of his family. The boss got moved with the way Munna's family was brutally raped and murdered due to sheer racism and assured him full support in his mission." But he questioned, "How are you going to expand my business there. You will come to know about it very soon." "You just do one favor to me. Manage to make delivery of the Cigars, chillums and tobacco carrying products to my native." "Don't worry. You will get all that you want." Shaking hand with him, he left the cabin conveying him that he would call him within a week or two."

Munna returned his hometown after a long period of almost fifteen years. Appearance of the town had adopted a lot of change. Children were turned youths the people who harmed his family were almost middle of their age. No one could identify him as Munna had changed a lot in that long period. He went to his Harijan vasti and became emotional to see his old dilapidated hut was locked. After the incident, someone from the Harijan vasti locked it. He took the key from the neighbor and opened the door. He felt restless to see the things at the mess. They were as they had been on the night of the tragedy. He began to keep all the things in a proper order. Soon, his hut took its old form. He missed the presence of his family members. The hanging photographs of parents stuck to the wall took him in his childhood. When he came out of the memories of the childhood, he found tears were rolling down from his cheeks. For him his hut became a symbol of the memory of that night's tragedy.

He determined to begin to work on his plan and to give justice to his murdered parents.

He took a round in the Harijan vasti revived some old acquaintances and befriended with some youths of his age. People who had seen in his childhood curiously asked him about his whereabouts and sympathized with him for whatever happened. Soon he became known to his vasti and now he took round in the town to see what change had been brought about the orthodox society. He observed that society was the same only appearance had changed. The hold of racism had not let lose its hold on the mind of the people. Nothing could bridge the gap between the two communities. Munna realized none could do it. His eyes were searching for a space where he could start something for his survival. He fixed a spot which was on the boundary where Orthodox community came to end and started the Harijan vasti. He had a very good friend. He managed that space with the help of his friend. There he started a pan shop. Soon it became a crowded place. Gradually people from the Harijan vasti started gathering there. Munna knew each and every one of them. Rarely people from orthodox vasti stopped there for chewing tobacco or taking pan or smoking a cigar. Munna brought about a change in his conduct. He became a sweet talker which gradually attracted the people from orthodox community. Munna decided to take absolute advantage for his revenge. Meanwhile he contacted his boss and ordered drug loaded chillums, *beedies* and cigars. When a chain smoker from orthodox community visited his shop he used to offer him that drug loaded chillum or *beedi* or a cigar as per the requirement of the chain smoker. He knew it once it was consumed; the customer was bound to be back to his pan shop. In this way he started spreading poison of drug. Gradually, people of all categories began to visit his pan stall. Almost half of the population of orthodox community became drug addict. He had some glimpses of the faces that attacked his house and robbed his family. When those men came to him, he used to give them heavy doses. They grew so addict that they could not live for a single moment from it. The moment their chillums or *beedies* were finished, they grew uneasy and naturally they moved towards his shop. The people could not bear it they began to die. Some had caught the bed and the young men grew mad for chillums and cigars. The pan shop was remained crowded till late in the night. Munna had earned lot. But he took precautions that no Harijan should consume it. It was his fortune that none from his community could be addicted.

When the old people to whom he knew as the culprit of his family disgusted a lot and when they came to him begging, "Munnasheth, give us chillum. We don't have money. We will pay you later." Munna with a stone heart refused them to see and enjoy their helplessness. When such black face begged before him either he scolded him or kicked him out. When he saw that the entire orthodox community had been affected and paid a good price for their misdeed, he decided to leave the place. As he knew that one day or the other his deeds would be exposed and he would be behind the bar. Once it happened a young boy got fainted due to overdose of drugs. He was admitted in nearby hospital. The doctor made the diagnosis and reported the parents that drugs caused his death. The matter was reported to the police station. The police came there and began to investigate people. The police got informed by the parents that he was chain smoker. The police started their raids on the pan shops in the town. The news of police raid reached to Munna. He took the shutter down and hurriedly came home. He took whatever he had and ran towards the railway station. Luckily, the train bound to Mumbai was ready to leave. He boarded on it and hid in the toilet and did not come till the train left the platform. In the morning he reached to Dadar and hired an autorikshaw and reached to his factory.

Meanwhile, the police raided his pan shop. When they found it to be shut down, their doubt became strong. They went to Harijan vasti collected all the details of Munna. A team of Police visited Bombay. The team met the local police officials and with their support they began to raid the slums where the culprits generally preferred to hide. Almost all the slums in Bombay were raided unsuccessfully except the slum of Dadar. As a final effort to reach to Munna, the police moved their *morcha* towards the slums of Dadar. When the news of the arrival of the police spread in the slum, entire vasti got alert. The police raided various places there but no success could come to their hands. When the news reached to the factory where Munna was hidden, the labor working upstairs began to vacate the factory with fright. The police doubted sudden flight and raided the factory. Police caught one of them and asked him angrily, "Do you know Munna? Where is he?" The labor being absolutely frightened opened his mouth and the secret of Munna came out. The labor with scare replied by pointing his finger towards the upstairs of the building, "Saheb, he is there up!" One of policemen asked him bossingly, "Why are you running as if you are criminal?" The labor said, "It is not the matter. We were running to see to whom police are arresting." The police left him and entered the building. Munna was sitting in the cabin and waiting for the arrival of Police. When he heard the stepping sound of the police coming towards him upstairs, he sat in his boss' chair who was out of station on that day and was waiting for the Police. When the police reached upstairs, they saw a man was sitting in the chair. They confirmed him to be Munna. They approached to hunt him as the hunter did when the prey came within his reach. When the police entered the cabin they looked at him and found him smiling at them. When they went close to hold him, Munna left his body. It banged on the table. Police got shocked to see it. One of them found a bottle labeled cyanide on the table.

Scientist

It was one of the pleasant mornings in the African town Texas. Newly born sun with golden appearance and eye catching costume was shining over the town reaching to each and every corner and niche of the houses in the colonies. It was the time when slavery was just banned in Africa but still some landlords were carrying this practice clandestinely by abducting black Negros from various parts of Africa. The black Africans were still to come out of the influence of long lasted slavery. It was on one of the cottages in a colony; the sun penetrated its warm rays through the broken ceilings and awoke the slept soul. When the light fell on the eyes of the mother, she got up and opened the door of the cottage to make a smooth passage for the entry of the sunrays. Looking at the marching sun, she shouted, "Thomas, get up, the sun is going to school. Don't you want to go with him?" Lingering Thomas in the warm bed deliberately took silent stance as he was overpowered by the sweet magic of the sound slumber. But as the sun was hastily stepping towards school, the mother angrily shouted, "Hurry up! You are getting late. Teacher will punish you. Don't you listen? You vagabond?" When the word punishment of the teacher pierced though his ears, it hurt his timid heart and the injury and its fear got him up and made him leave the bed frightfully. Within half an hour, Thomas got ready for school. Mother offered him his school bag with the Tiffin and bid him farewell. Merry had lost her husband after the birth of Thomas. Since then, she had been working in a grocery shop as an assistant. At home she had been accompanied by her mother. She was sufficiently old but proved to be a great support. When Merry was engaged with her work and came late home, grandmother did all the responsibilities of feeding and caring of Thomas. Thomas was very smart boy. At school, he had been greatly appreciated by his teachers for his industry and his inclination towards the study of science. At home he never kept himself free always engaged in doing this and that related to science. When he was free from his studies, he used to visit various shops and nearby industries and collect some bottles, chemicals, some electric circuits and other electrical and scientific components and stored them in his study. There were some selves which he used for keeping bottles.

When the teachers in the school realized his inclination and his interest in science and his scientific temperament, they provided him all sorts of help such as providing chemicals test tubes and other glass made objects with which he could perform practical. Every day after meal, he entered in his small laboratory began to perform experiments and played with some electric circuits. He had made some electric appliances and some weapons which were displayed in science exhibition held in the school which gave a pat on his back. This appreciation became the origin of his indomitable will to be a scientist. One day teacher asked everyone present over there about their dream for future. When the turn of Thomas came, he answered with full confidence that he aspired to be a scientist and serve the nation. Teacher was immensely impressed and astonished to see such magnified and idealistic thought came out from a little mind of Thomas.

It was on one dark night; Thomas was having meal with his mother and grandmother. Suddenly some veiled faces entered the house. They were as dark as the night and too horrible that the interiors of the house seemed to be terrified with their presence. Suddenly two of them came forward and put a knife at the throat of grandmother and little Thomas who felt almost dead with their appearance and terrific presence of these veiled faces. When the mother saw a knife at the throat of little Thomas, her motherly affection aroused and she shouted, "Don't be inhuman to him. He is little like a lamb. Give me whatever trouble you want to give to him." One of the sturdy veiled faces came forward and lifted Merry and within a few second they became one with the darkness. Tears began to wet fleshy cheeks of little Thomas. Grandmother was almost paralyzed as the scenario was unexpected and so terrific that she forgot to speak. When the marks of the veiled visages melted with darkness, little Thomas cried, "Don't take my mother away. Leave her and send her back. I can't live without her. I beg to you, veiled faces. Have mercy on me and give me mamma back." He sunk in despair when his appeal was unheard by the cruel and deaf ears of inhuman veiled faces. Grandmother looked at crying and disappointed Thomas imprisoned her tears, strengthened her old bones to support little Thomas. It was the most critical moment in his life. He found himself to be like a fish out of water. His education was about to stop as there was none to finance his education. Fortune smiled and his maternal uncle came to support him. Education continued and the hopes of survival survived. Years were passing as the clouds got engaged in athletics bringing maturity in little Thomas. He overgrew excelling age. Now Thomas turned tall, thin and with dense curly hair. Eyes were looked watery as if his eyes were still buried in the painful memory of that night of abduction of his Mother Merry. His face seemed to have forgotten smile as the event had eclipsed it with its dark shadow.

Thomas was in his S.S.C. Keeping his studies on side by side he continued his interest in the experimentation and creation, invention of many scientific things which were appreciated highly at school level. In the class he shared his bench with a white girl, Gema, Gema Furnandis. She had been accidently there in his school due to unexpected transfer of her father in the collector's office. Sharing the bench, having tiffin together chatting a lot whole day strengthened their friendship. Once curious and observant Thomas questioned Gema, "What have you planned for your future?" Little beat naughty and funny Gema answered, I wish to be an internationally known T.V. journalist and make the whole world mad with my anchoring skills." "How ideal and different you think of your future." Taking interest in Thomas, she asked him, "I have been informed by many in the school that you have your laboratory and you made instruments. And you aspire to be a scientist." Thomas nodded and replied, "Yes! Gema, what you have heard is true. I wish to be an internationally acclaimed scientist." "How great and commendable it is!" These aspiring minds spent a lot of hours together discussing this and that. They were so emotionally involved in each other that they could not spend a single moment in isolation.

If any one of them remained absent on some excuse, the other felt isolated and eagerly waiting for his or her arrival. Their friendship became an ideal for the school children. Everyone in the school loved this couple and what made them curious was the black and white combination. They took their examination. Gema went for summer vacation to her native along with her mother. Thomas buried himself in the world of inventions and experimentations. When there was nothing to experiment in his laboratory, he visited nearby places collected material required for his future work. In his laboratory he had kept everything perfectly and neatly. All the bottles were properly labeled. Hazardous chemicals were kept at separate place so that it could provide no harm to anyone. As there was none in his house except his grandmother, there was no question of any stranger's entry in his laboratory.

Whole day and till late hours of the night, he had been engaged in the world of chemicals. One day he received a letter from Gema that she is coming to school to receive the result. There he realized that the summer vacation was round in the corner. It was the day of result; Gema had been there earlier than Thomas. Richly dressed, looking bold and confident stood in the gallery and waited for Thomas to arrive. When she saw Thomas entering the gate of the school, a smile came on her face and wished to go quickly to shake hand with him. She hastily came down and started running towards Thomas. When Thomas's eyes caught her coming towards him, he hurriedly stepped towards her. They came close, exchanged smile, and gave a tight handshake holding each other's hands walked towards the school. They entered the crowd of the students who were engrossed in seeing their numbers in the merit list. As it was crowded, Thomas preferred to be away and wait patiently till the last one got moved from that. Suddenly his eyes caught writing on the board. He was astonished to see the writing; "Congratulations to Thomas" Thomas began to guess about the success. He called Gema who was standing at edge of the crowd and showed the writing on the board. Gema embraced him and congratulated him. When the crowd of the students saw Thomas at some distance, they approached and in one vice congratulated him. When the crowd dispersed, both came towards the notice boards where the result had been displayed. Both were surprised to see the name Thomas was at the top. Gema had secured distinction. Both happily congratulated each other. They spent a lot of hours together discussing a lot about their future prospectus. When the time came to part, both wept and embraced each other and promised to be in touch with each other wherever they go and wherever they will be in their future.

Thomas continued his education in a local college where he completed his H.S.C. During these two years acquired ample knowledge of science, developed a good reading habit. He spent a lot of hours together reading scientific books of various authors. Thomas read biographies and autobiographies of world acclaimed scientists and collected a lot of information about their scientific accomplishments. On holidays he continued his search for material required for his small laboratory and engaged himself in doing this and that experiment. He had made good electric appliances and scientific projects. Once there was a science exhibition in his institute where he presented his scientific project. It brought a great applause to Thomas. When the teachers came to know about this scientific talent of Thomas, they gave all possible support to get his talent exposed. He continued his education till B.Sc. in chemistry which was special subject.

He wished to continue higher education which was not possible as there were no institutions furnishing higher studies in Texas. So he decided to take admission in a university which was some kilometers away from his native. During this period of education, his maternal uncle supported him a lot and fulfilled his financial needs. When the time to take admission in University for higher studies came, the problem of money raised its head up. Maternal uncle came forward paid all his fees and motivated his studies. Luckily he got a room in the hostel. The problem was what to do with his grandmother who was grown old and she was beyond bearing the trouble to traveling to the place and staying there. So he asked his maternal uncle to take the responsibility of the grandmother. She went to stay with him. It gave a great relief to Thomas who loved his grandmother the most. It was she who took absolute care of him and never let him miss for motherly affection. When the time came to leave his native, he went near to his grandmother and resting his head on her shoulder, Thomas wept a lot. Grandmother said, "My dear Thomas, don't weep. If you weep, your tears will weaken my determination and perhaps I won't let you go. You are a genius. I want that genius should come out for the betterment of the world. You are a god gifted child and I am sure one day you will shine on the canvas of the world of science. If I stop you now, it will be an injustice to your talent and the world won't pardon me and blame me for being selfish. So my conscience tells me that I should not do any such thing which would stop you from going. Go my son, take care of yourself. We are capable to take care of ourselves. Take care of yourself as I won't be there. Remember you have to shine and shine the world. The world has to be decorated by your knowledge and inventions. Think beautiful and make beautiful. I am sure with your inventions and the world will look more beautiful. Now don't stop here go and come to meet me wherever you wish. My blessings are with you." Thomas took out a handkerchief drying up his eyes replied, "Grandma I won't ignore your teachings. They will be with me and guide me wherever I required. You have dreamed big for me. I promise you that I won't shatter it. I live for it." He clung to her and began his journey for the university. Throughout the journey, his eyes were shading tears. His mind went back to the past remembered all that had happened. The memory of the abduction of his mother and that dark night made a great wound to his innocent mind. The moment that scene came before the eyes of his mind, he got disturbed. It was the bitterest memory in his life. As journey in the past marched, some golden moments he recollected which he spent with his best friend Gema. As the journey was coming to an end, he missed Gema a lot wished to know where she could be and what she could be doing. He wished to write her and to know how was her life going on there wherever she was.

The journey came to an end and Thomas along with his maternal uncle got down at the university. After completing the formality of admission, both went to the hostel where he had to stay. They kept the luggage and went to the canteen where they had something. When the time of Uncle's departure came, Thomas became emotional. Uncle supported him and said, "You are a grown up now. Tears do not suit to you. Be strong not in body but in will. Remember your determination and our dream. You have to be a scientist." Remembering his dream, he left Thomas. Thomas stared at him till he got vanished from his eyes. He experienced same seclusion which he had on the night of the abduction of his mother. There was a boy in his room who too had come there a few hours earlier than Thomas. His name was John. Both had chat and soon they became good friends. John too was a Negro perhaps it might be the reason that they came easily together. In the evening both went to have a round in the campus of the university. Thomas had never seen such huge campus in his life. His observant eyes were watching and staring at everything with great curiosity. It pleased him a lot.

The next day he went along with John to attend the lectures. It was all together a different experience for him. He was greatly impressed by the teaching and scholarly professor there. What impressed him was a huge library there and the students buried in the world of books. Seeing the scenario in the library especially the books in the shelf, his passion for reading enhanced and became a regular member of the library studying a lot till the late hours of the night. It was his good fortune that he had a very nice Professor who appreciated his industrious and enterprising nature. With his dedication and devotion for study, he succeeded in acquiring a place for himself in the good books of his teachers who supported his research spirit in every possible way. Library and laboratories were his favorite places in the University. One day it was the time when the old and tired sun was going for rest, Thomas remembered his friend Gema. He was too moved by her memory that he sat down to write a letter to her. When he was writing a letter, he felt that the innocent face of Gema was there on the paper and giving a smile to him. Giving smile back in return, he colored his paper with his feelings. One day he went along with his roommate John to the letter box hung at a tree and posted the letter.

Life was going very smoothly. Thomas' studies were full in swing securing good marks in every exam. Every day was an enlightening experience for him. His scientific mind was absorbing as much knowledge as possible from wherever he got. It enriched the faculties of his mind. Thomas was growing mature day by day. He grew so popular that there was none who did not know Thomas. Everyone from the library and laboratory and teaching staff knew him personally. One day when he returned to his hostel and opened the door of his room and found a letter pushed in. He looked back of the letter and became extremely delighted to see the name of Gema there. He got engrossed in reading the letter and felt delighted to know that she had been pursuing her studies in Journalism in different university. Since then, the communication went on ceaselessly which brought them together.

Every now and then Thomas received a letter from Gema which became a source of happiness for him. Once, Gema came to see Thomas in university. As she did not know his address, she came directly to his class. A Professor was conducting the class. She asked the Professor, "Hello! Good morning. I am Gema, a student of journalism. I am interested to see my childhood friend M. Thomas who is in your class." Professor took a look at the class and found him to be sitting on the last bench. Professor said to Thomas, "There is someone who wishes to see you." Thomas got up from his seat and went out. He was really surprised to see Gema standing in front of him. He felt excited. They embraced each other. Thomas left the class and took Gema to the canteen. "What a surprise! Your visit is really unexpected and pleasant and what change in you. You are turned woman. Gema in the tenth is almost vanished." "You too have changed Thomas. You too have lost your past. See, you have grown tall and thin. See your face it has been changed a lot. Initially I was confused with it whether it is really Thomas or someone else." "Gema how is your study?" "It is going on smoothly and expectedly and I am in the last year of journalism." "Did you have any other purpose of visit?" "Yes. I had to interview a leader of labor here. I had his interview and came to see you." "Tell me something about yourself, Thomas. I would be delighted to listen to your achievements." "Nothing special. Studies are going satisfactorily. It is the last semester of Post-graduation and probably next I will go to research." "What about your new inventions and I would like to know about your grandma?" "They are going on. There is nothing worth noticing and admiring. Grandma is fine. I left her with my maternal uncle as she has grown old and unable to make quick movement." Looking at her wrist watch, Gema said, "Thomas, I need to go now. I had train at 5:00pm. It is already 4:30pm." "Won't you stay here for a day? You have just come." "No Thomas. Next time confirm." "I won't stop you. As you wish" Both walked towards the railway station on foot. When they reached on the railway station, Train was ready to depart. Gema boarded on the train caught a sit at the window. Thomas stood outside and had a chat till the train left the station. Giving her a smiling farewell he returned to the hostel. When he spread on the bed and tried to sleep, the memories of the Gema troubled him. He remained awake till late in the evening.

The womb of time was giving birth to new moments with the growth of the moments, Thomas too was growing. He finished his studies of PG and took admission for research in the university. Once he received a letter from Gema informing that she had been appointed as a journalist in an international newspaper. He wrote her a letter of congratulations. She too sent him note of gratitude and best wishes for his research.

Here in the university Thomas spent whole day in the laboratory doing this reaction and that reaction. Once he found a new chemical which could be used in making nuclear bombs. The news spread everywhere. It also reached to the ears of Gema. Once she came to university to interview Thomas. It was the most memorable interview for both as both friends were doing well on their frontiers. Before the interview, they embraced each other and gave smile of success. Interview began, "Hello! Mr. Thomas. The world is interested to know a lot about your achievement." "It is concerned with a chemical which can be used in reducing the effects of nuclear bombs in case of blast." The interview continued for half an hour. After interview, both had lunch together. The next day the photographs and entire interview of Thomas published on the front page of the international news papers. This gave him recognition as Thomas the scientist. His invention was given publicity at international level. The interview consolidated the emotional tie between Gema and Thomas. Previously they used to meet occasionally now their meetings became frequent. Gradually they got fascinated towards each other. Clandestinely, they met where they had time. Someone caught in a hotel which became breaking news of that day. Both had no objection over their relation and happy with the relationship being popularized.

Once, Gema came to see him in the university. At that time, Thomas was busy in doing some reaction in the laboratory. Gema questioned, "What is going on, dear Thomas?" Thomas disclosed to her, "Gema, this is going to be the most ambitious research project of mine and if I succeed in it, it will be the greatest scientific invention in my life." "What the research is about?" "I am preparing such chemical if it is placed in surrounding, it will act as a protective cover for the people in case there would be atomic blast. When there will be an atomic blast, the gama rays will be released in the surrounding at the same time the sensor in the protective cover will be active and it will absorb the most detrimental gamma rays and active neutrons and will reduce its ability to harm human beings. It is life saving chemical and I am sure I will find it out soon." "Commendable! God bless thee." They had a brief talk and had some amorous moments. Before leaving, she informed Thomas that she was going to some distant town of Africa to write the articles on the life of tribes living there. So she won't be able to meet him for the next few months. Bidding him farewell, she went with a promise that she would come to see him soon.

One day, Thomas was doing his experiment in the laboratory till late in the night. There was a confident smile on his face. The smile was there because he had reached very close to the formula of the chemical. Suddenly a blasting sound shook the laboratory and Thomas got severely injured in that mishap. There was fire everywhere. Luckily he had had a narrow escape but he had received severe burn injuries and his hands were almost dead. The university management took him to hospital gave him a primary aids and after that he was sent to his native place. When Grandma and maternal uncle looked at his condition, they got moved. He was almost like a corpse helpless and movement less. It was a great shock and an irrevocable damage to them. Maternal uncle took him to various doctors but no miracle could occur. Thomas's condition grew critical. A world known scientist laid an isolated life. He became unnoticed. None came to see him. He was lying in his bedroom like a corpse. Even the media gave little importance to his mishap and a small news having caption, 'A scientist injured' was published which fell to catch the attention of the world. Thus he got overlooked by the world's eyes.

One day Gema visited the university and there she came to know about the mishap occurred with Thomas. She felt extremely sad with the destiny of her friend. The next day she went to Thomas's native. She got shocked to see the condition of Thomas. She went near to him and put her palm on his forehead. When Thomas looked at her, he could not control his emotions and he began to weep. "Thomas, don't weep. It was inevitable. Perhaps it was for your betterment. Don't worry. Everything would be alright soon. I am with you. Get ready I will take you to the topmost doctor in Africa." Thomas felt encouraged and gave her a smile. Gema admitted him in the topmost hospital in Africa where he underwent long treatment for more than six months period. After six month much of his injuries are recovered but hands which had received severe damage during blast did not response to the treatment. The caring doctor told Gema that his hands had received severe damages and it was very difficult to say how much time it will take to get recovered. But the hopes are less. It sunk her despair but she did not display this disappointment on her face so that Thomas would not get disheartened. After six month's treatment, Thomas returned to the native. Gema went back to her job as she had some important engagements and appointments. Some days later she came to Thomas. Looking at her he said, "Gema I fell restless." "What is reason my friend?" "My research is left incomplete which I wish to finish." "How you are going to have it?" I wish to go back to the university laboratory and continue." "How can I help you in your mission?" "Be there with me till I finish my work." "What I will have done there?" "As you know I can't move my hands and without hands it is just impossible. So you have to be a helping hand. Since you were the science graduate, you know experimentation all the things, I would tell you and you have to do it accordingly." "Surely I will do it. It will be a pleasure of mine if I could come to your help."

Encouraging words of Gema revived the dead hopes of Thomas. The next day he along with Gema went to university laboratory. They stayed there in the hostel. Gema managed a room in a girl's hostel. The university management assured him all possible support in his research work. Within a two weeks time, Thomas managed all the material and equipments and began his research. Gema stood with him as a helping hand and she acted as she was told. It was a wonderful chemistry which resulted in a great wonder. They work day and night over the research. It was the last day of the month and it was around 11: pm Thomas and Gema were deeply engrossed in taking the last reaction. Reaction took place as Thomas desired and his experiment proved to be a successful. It brought a smile on the face of Thomas. He was so delighted with his success that he embraced Gema and kissed her hands a number of times. Everyone there congratulated Thomas. Gema gave him special congratulation. Both embraced each other and exchanged a serene smile.

The research accomplishment was appreciated all over the world. The fortune smiled upon the hard work of Thomas and the Nobel Prize for the scientific contribution was declared to the research accomplishment of Thomas. He was invited to Philippines for prize distribution ceremony. Thomas along with Gema reached to the ceremony. There was a huge auditorium where the ceremony was held. All the Nobel Prize Winners representing different areas were there. Thomas and Gema were sitting in the front row. When the name of Thomas was announced, it received a huge applause from the audience. Some officials came down from the dais to take him up with honor. Thomas went up. He was given a chair as he was not capable to stand. The anchor gave him a mike and Thomas gave an outlet to his feelings. "Mine is not an individual accomplishment. It is the success of the helping hands. I felt proud to tell you that those helping hands are of my loving friend Gema. I wish to share this honour with her as she equally deserves it." The anchor cordially invited Gema on the stage. When she was being taken by receptionist on the dais, as torrential rain falls, there was a huge round of applause for Gema. It was the proudest moment for her. She looked at Thomas and exchanged a loving smile and embraced him. They stood together and received the honor. When they looked at the smiling innumerable faces in the auditorium, they felt that they were the special children of the destiny born for this great cause.

Anchor gave a mike to Thomas and said, "Congratulations Sir!" "Thank you, Gentleman." "There is no doubt that this might be one of the most pleasant moments in your life. What pleasant thing would you like do the next?" Hopefully, looking at Gema he replied, "I wish to be a life partner of my Gema. In presence of you all I propose her, "Gema, my dear friend. You have blessed my life. Will you accept me as your life partner?" Gema hurriedly and excitedly took away mike from Thomas and said, "It is honor, happiness and pride for me." All the audience gave them a standing ovation saluted to the human goodness which was rarely find in these days. When they came down everyone present over there rushed to congratulate them. The warm shake hands took them to world of euphoria.

Window

It is the time when the various king dynasties ruled Rajasthan and its various parts. It was the month of May. The month of May in Ranthumbore in Rajsthan may be ever remembered by the people there as they had never burning experience like this earlier. It is hot morning as the sun is spitting out fire earlier than yesterday as if the sun is burning with revenge. Entire Ranthumbore has turned into a harness baking the lives. The place has become quite hot for the people. There is a temple of Lord Shankar in one of the corners of the town. There is holy water tank just beside the temple where the devotees are taking holy bath before entering the temple. Some who have bathed are climbing up the steps of the temple as the temple is at a huge height. Their climbing posture makes one feel that they are pilgrims on the way to heaven. Suddenly a sweeping sound falls on the ears. A sweeper is engaged in cleaning the road. As it is very hot outside, the streams of sweat are gliding down on his robust body. The sweeper has tied a cloth around his head and with a strong grip on his broom; he is cleaning the road that leads to the temple. Due to sweat, his body shines as his body is turned into an endless fountain releasing shining streams of water. Seeing his standing postures and the cuts in his body, every passerby imagines him to be a well carved sculpture. He is man with great built which is always a talk of the town. If he is sweeping the road, and if any woman or a girl passes cannot ignore the cuts of his built body. They clandestinely have a look at his fascinating body and engaged in self mutter, "Who will be that fortunate girl who will have him" Giving a blushed smile they pass from there. He is the appointed sweeper of Ranthumbore. Since morning he is busy in sweeping every nook and corner of the town. His racial restriction leads him to the steps of the temple and he cannot go in. When he sweeps all the steps of the temple, there are people in the temple who wash it off with water and without forget to add some holy water in it to remove the Dalit touch.

His honest service and his approach towards people makes all love him. Everyone fondly calls him Raju. He belongs to the Dalit community. As the community is inferior in status prefer to stay in outside area of the town. Sweeping is a heritage which he has inherited from his ancestors. His ancestors have been doing the work of sweeping and enjoying the grace of dynasties. There is a temple of lord Ganesha at walking distance from Ranthumbore where people gather on every Monday. Every day Raju goes there and cleans the front yard and back yard of the temple and waters the trees. He has cultivated a beautiful garden there where the people sit for a while get lost in enjoying the smiling flowers on the tree. The common men, the wealthiest merchant and the ministers in the court of the king comes riding over the chariot. Occasionally the king comes to perform puja.

It is one fine morning, Raju is cleaning the road towards the temple, and suddenly a steeping sound of the horse carrying a chariot falls on his ears. As a part of respect he moves aside stopping sweeping and giving a passage to the chariot. A girl whiter than snow and softer than a rabbit, richly dressed and wearing diamonds and fairy like costumes is riding over the chariot. Raju seeing the chariot is about to bow down as it is tradition to bow before the people representing the court before he closes his eyes takes the glimpse at the court and meets the eyes of the girl. Both stare at each other for a while and the chariot rapidly passes away. For the first time in his life, he gets attracted towards a human beauty. The face of girl is so enchanting that Raju helplessly falls in her love. After having dinner, Raju goes to bed but the face of the girl starts appearing on the canvas of his mind and he feels restless as the charm of the beauty steals away his sleep. Whole night he troubled for the sleep. No way has it come. He hurriedly wakes up takes the broom and leads towards the temple. Sweeping the road he reaches at the point at the same portion of the road where he saw her yesterday. Suddenly like a blowing wind the chariot comes and takes brief pause. Raju musters his courage to see the face. The fairy like girl takes a glance at his carved body and gives a smiling face the chariot leaves towards the temple. Raju is so overwhelmed by the smiling face that he stares the chariot till it reaches to the temple. He wishes to run after the chariot to have one more enchanting look of fairy like girl but he gets conscious of what he imagines withdraws in his determination as he knows what could be the aftermaths of his thoughtless action. Whole day he spends waiting for tomorrow morning as she comes riding over the chariot.

Fascination for fairy face of the girl makes him turn his nights into days. When he is lying on the wooden cot, a twinkling star catches him. Raju is so much under the charm of the face that he imagines that the star is nothing but the face of the girl and is smiling at him. Staring at the charming star, how night turns into the dawn he does not understand. The star slowly begins to disappear and the sleep takes the charge over Raju. In his slumber he mutters addressing his fairy girl,

"You sleep closing eyes
And I with wide open.
You think of yourself and I all the time yours."

The sun rises and the first rays of the sun fall on the face of Raju. The warmth of the sun awakes him. He hurriedly picks up the broom and runs towards the meeting point but it is too late to reach there. He feels frustrated that he has missed the opportunity to have her look. He stands still staring at the temple and gets pleased that the chariot is standing there. He breathlessly runs towards the temple and start cleaning the steps. One of the security guard asks him, "Raju everyday you come early but today you are late. What is the problem? Why your face is so dull as if you haven't sleep for days?" Raju gets confused what to reply because inwardly he realizes that his theft has been caught. Without looking at him, very humbly he replies, "it is not like that. I had a sound slumber last night. The slumber was so powerful that I could not understand how night passed and when I woke up the sun had become brighter. Realizing it is late to begin the work so I have here without washing my face." Poojari listens to him and says, "It is alright. Do come early tomorrow. He informs him without fail that there is a girl performing the pooja in the temple. She may come at any moment. I warn you not to look at her. If you do it you will be severely punished. After finishing your sweeping go away, don't stand here meanwhile I bring water to clean the steps" Raju nods head mutely. Grabbing the opportunity he stands pretending to be sweeping. Poojari comes there shortly and starts sprinkling water on the steps. After doing it Poojari goes in. Raju stands still secretly waiting for the girl. Suddenly she comes out and eyes of both meet each other. She comes climbing down the steps and stands at safer distance. She looks at Raju's physique and gets impressed. She asks, "What is your name?" Raju gets baffled. His mouth gets watered. Heart begins to beat and gets troubled with question how to talk with this girl. With trembling body and more vibrating lips, he answers, "I am Raju the sweeper of the town" "Hello! I am Radha the daughter of the chief minister in the court of the king. Why do you get scared? Don't worry nobody is here to get scared off." Raju dares to raise his head up to and his eyes gets blind with the white beauty of her face. Half closing his eyes and with absolute respect he says, "How magnanimous you are that you have a talk with a trivial creature like me! What to speak is really a problem. I don't understand whether it is dream or a reality. Please, don't talk too much. Go away from here. If someone sees us talking here I will be in trouble." Radha says, "As you wish but don't forget to meet me tomorrow." Raju gets baffled and not in position to believe that his dream girl has asked him to meet her tomorrow. He returns home. Whole day he spends in waiting for tomorrow. After dinner he goes to stare at the sky and gets engrossed in the beauty of the twinkling star and imagines that she has come to meet him. He mutters,

**"How happy to be with you.
How painful to be away from you.
How sweet to miss you.
How painful to forget you."**

With these words he goes to sleep with disappearing star."

Raju grows mad in her love. For days he doesn't sleep. With their increasing meeting, increase their love. Slowly their love is caught in the eyes of the passersby. They clandestinely meet in the Lord Ganesha temple excluding on Monday as it is the day when entire town comes to take darshan. It is after noon, Radha and Raju are sitting under a tree behind the temple. Someone comes there and catches them. The news spread like a wild fire in entire kingdom. Radha's father comes to know about the affair of his daughter and he feels disgraced. When she returns home father asks her, "where have you been so long?" Radha replies, "I have been to the temple" Father gets annoyed and says," "at this odd hour" Radha prefers to keep quiet" Father understands the meaning of her silence. "Rumours are spread in the kingdom that you are flirting with the sweeper" Radha tries to lie, "it is not true, father" Father angrily says, "Shut your dirty mouth. Yours going to the temple at this odd hour of the day is evidence of your misdeed." Radha understands that she has been caught <u>red-hand</u> and there is no meaning in making any concoction. Father understands affirmation behind the silence and he starts shouting, "Radha, you have disgraced my entire family and the dynasty we belong. Rumours are spread in the kingdom about your affair with that dirty sweeper. How to go out and with what face? It is not just a disgrace but a death. You have punished us for our no fault. Now you bear for what you have done" He calls to the security and asks them to take Radha in the old haveli and confine her in a room." The security takes Radha in an old haveli outside the town. The haveli has a single window. When she peeps through it she finds a small stream gently a moving and a small temple beside.

Meanwhile angry father calls Raju and says, "You dirty sweeper how you dared to think of my daughter. It is because of you she has gone astray. As she is responsible for the disgrace you too are equally responsible. If you want to save your life leave this place at the earliest possible. Otherwise you will have to lose your life. He orders the security guards to take him out of the kingdom. As per the instruction of the Minister the security takes him out of the kingdom and throws him into the desert.

A period of six months or more is passed. Raju clandestinely returns to the kingdom. He has totally changed his look. He looks like a true beggar. His dress is turned shabby torn at a lot of places. His hairs have turned brownish full of dust. His face is turned black and have grown long but dirty beard on it. Due to starvation or other reasons he has lost his good physique and looks rather pale and thin. His outward appearance is absolutely changed that no one can identity him to be Raju. He takes a round around the town.

During his round he always sings these lines;

Blind are those eyes which do not see you.
Futile are the dreams which don't dream of you.
In vain is that breath, which does not breathe for you.

**Useless is that life which does not hope for you.
Thoughtless is that thought which does not think of you.
In vain is that song which does not sing of you.**

He begs for food. As he is very much tired, he retires to one of the temples in the town. Slowly he takes round in every nook and corner of the town. Seeing him begging is a regular practice for people. So being beggar no one objects for his presence. As he is totally changed no one knows him that he is Raju, the sweeper. One day while begging through the city he reaches to the old haveli. Seeing the stream there he rests and opens his alms and begins to take food. When he finishes his food he takes some water drinks and some water sprinkles on his face. He rests there for some time. When he gets up takes his dirty bag and is about to move suddenly his eyes meet a standing woman at the window. He gets shocked as her face resembled to Radha. He stands there for long time.

Radha has seen a man like figure after a long time as it is a dense forest area no one comes there. When the man stares at her, she feels strange and questions to her, "who could be this fellow? Why is he staring at me as if he knows me?" She withdraws herself from the window. Raju felt very happy that he has retained his love. He leaves the place and takes a round in the town. After collecting his alms he returns to the place. There is a Bunyan tree in a jungle under which he makes his bed. After collecting alms he returns to his place and sits under the tree stares at the window and turns glad to see the face again. It becomes their daily practice. One day Radha is sleeping. Raju sits under the tree waiting for Radha to come. He waits for a long time but she does not come at the window. Raju cannot control himself and he shouts Radha. When the words fall on Radha's ears, she gets up and feels surprised as a familiar sound falls on her ear after a long time and she whispers, "From where the sound comes? Why it seems to me that I have heard this sound previously? Who could be this fellow taking my name. Is it not of Raju?" Instantly she comes at the window and sees that it is the beggar sitting under the tree is calling her. Raju looks at her makes some familiar gestures. Radha slowly realizes that the person who is calling and making gestures knows her. She carefully watches his physical traits and understands that his facial traits resemble to that of her lover Raju. When she gets it confirmed that the mad man is nobody else but it is her Raju in disguise of a mad man. She feels at the top of the air. As the window is at a huge height she can't speak loudly as she is afraid that someone may get the wind of it and she will be in trouble. She does not want to miss her Raju again.

Slowly their communication begins. Both are happy in staring at each other. Beggar is the most happy because his fiancé is in front of him. Every day he goes in the town and collects some eatables. He manages a stick which is made long enough by joining many sticks and ties a bag in which he puts some eatables and lifts it up to the window. Radha standing at the window enjoys the food. Thus their romance begins. One day Radha asks, "Where had you been for the last so many days." Raju replies, "It was your father who banished me from the kingdom. I spent the months in the hot desert burning with double fire of hunger. Your memory was my food which survived me. If it had not been there I would have been a mere a Skelton. He recites some poetic lines,

You were my savoir in that hot deserted desert.
Your memory was my food and your love my support.
How barren were those days, when we were apart.
I willed for thee and you prayed for me.
Both made magic and once again we became a part."

This is how my life passed in that hot desert. I never hoped that we would be togetheragain. But who can change the writing of the destiny." He asks Radha,"You have suffered more than me at least I was free in that deserted desert. I lived both in light and in darkness. But you have been in darkness of the room. You have suffered more than me. Tell me please how you bore it." Radha opens her heart. "I was just dead when we became part. I had given up the hope that we shall be together again.

Soul died long back what remains is body.
Unwilling to leave as it pied for you.
Dark confinements took away the soul
What left behind is this body fool.
It died not as it hoped for thee.
The ray of light which peeped through the window
Brought hope for me.
It was with that I waited for thee.
With dead soul and body alive I prayed for thee.

Listening to the record of Radha's miseries tears roll down from Raju's cheek and asks Radha better you discontinue your suffering otherwise I will die hearing them. Radha stops in the middle and withdraws from the window as someone brings food for her. Raju pretends to sleep and lay down there under the shade of the tree till Radha returns to window.

Their romance continues for years exchanging feels of romance and waiting to be free. Once Radha asks, "Don't you feel nervous that we could not get physically united?" Raju answers, "of course I feel broken at heart but what is important and not less for me that for years we have been face to face. At least we can see each other smile at each other asks about happiness and miseries. Imagine if we had not been together. Better we should be happy with whatever we have and should not expect more. Union of body gives less pleasure than the union of the souls. Now we are united spiritually and this is the achievement of our love." Radha smiles at him and withdraws herself from the window.

Once, the neighboring royal dynasty attacks on Ranthomber. The troops take the hold of Ranthomber. Soldiers enter the haveli and in a locked room find a woman that is Radha. They release her from the dark confinement. She walks down and comes back at the Haveil. Raju is resting there. She wakes him up. "Get up! Get up my dear! The time to unite has come near. Hurry up. Raju gets baffled seeing Radha near him. For a moment Raju fails to understand whether it is a dream or reality. When he sees that it is Radha and nobody else. Raju takes his bag starts walking out of the town so that they should not get recaptured again by the army. It is evening time. The sun is about to set. Holding each other's hands move through the desert leaving their separate foot prints behind which slowly become one with falling darkness and setting sun.

Passion

Somewhat murky and colorful with faded colored cottage like house perfectly named 'Kalasangam' was standing with great pride in one of the lanes of 'Kalanagari'. The place was appropriately named as it produced many artists but none could attain national or international stature and write the name of "Kalanagari" in golden letters in the history of art. 'Kalangari' was still waiting for that moment when an artist of it would fulfill her ever enshrined will with its desired acclamation land of the art. The Kalasangam seemed to be set on the fire of artistic voices as the voices of the amateur artists performing some dramatic rehearsal in one of the rooms of Kalasangam come out through the gaps of the ever decaying red roof of the cottage. The Kalasangam had great artistic background as the family living in it has received great heritage of the art from their unsuccessful stage artist. The cottage had produced many artists but none of them could become what one popularly callsNatsamrat. Kalasangam and Kalanagari have been in long waiting for that great artist who would quench their thirst for being a center of excellent art.

On entering the cottage the picture became quite clear. Some amateur artists were engaged in doing some dramatic rehearsal in the closed room. All of a sudden, motherly woman gave a call. "Shantaram, what are you

doing? Stop your doings and join me as I need you urgently."
The rehearsal got disturbed all the amateur artists came
out one by one and started leaving the house. Shantaram
lets loose his tongue and questions, "Aai, you remembered
me?" Looking surprisingly at him, mother continued her
talk. "What is going on in the room?" Shantaram a boy
studying in matriculation humbly replied, "Nothing special,
doing drama rehearsal to be staged at the annual social
gathering of the school. What business is there for me?"
Mother replies, "Nothing special. I want you to go to nearby
grocery shop to bring some groceries" Shantaram takes the
order and departs.

Sounds of rehearsals continued in the closed room of
Kalasangam. The day of stage performance came. It was the
time of dusk. The front yard of the school was full of crowd.
A sufficiently big stage was established. Performances came
in sequence and enjoyed good applause from the audience.
It was the time of Shantaram and his group to present. As
per the outline of the script, Shantaram took the charge of
the stage and briefly introduced the theme and characters.
"All my dear audience, we are going to stage a drama on
mythological episode in the great epic, "Mahabharata'
entitled *Draupadi Vastraharan* and expect your blessing
to please you this night." After introducing the characters
in the script, Shantaram departed for further preparation.
The drama began as per the demand of the script. The
characters came and played their roles. The presentation
was so humorous that laughter roaring of the audience
transformed the front yard of the school into a laughter club.
Of and on clapping sound accompanied by never ending
clapping applause and delightful whistling enhanced the

moral of the artists on the dais. The performance turned out to be an outlandish success and became the talk of the town. What audience remembered the most was Shantaram in the role of 'DharmarajYudhistir'

The performance brought great acclamation for Shantaram who became very popular for his heart stealing performance. This performance proved to be a turning point in Shantaram's life as it ignited a hidden artist in him. He took oath that hereafter I would live for the sake of art and art only. Soon his school life came to end and he joined college. The life at college gave a greater exposure to his art. He participated and staged various dramas and became a very popular student of everyone there. With increasing stage performances, improved his art and his passion to be a great artist became further ignited. He always looked here and there in search of such opportunity which would give him a chance to be the world elevated and honored actor. When he was in his final year of graduation, he got the opportunity to represent his college in state level Drama competition. A well known director and producer in Marathi cinema had been there to judge the talent of performance. Performances of the young stage artistsbegan; suddenly the judge stopped to use his ink and paid his ears, heart and soul catching dialogues on the stage. It was a dialogue from the immortal drama, 'Natsamrat'. The drama was being staged By Shanataram and his school. When the performance was going on in, the entire auditorium had a pin drop silence. Entire crowd was almost dead with the emotions with which Shantaram was adding colors in the role of Natsamarat.

The audience in the stage was habitual to excellent performances but for the first time after a long interval of years, they had such performance made them act like a corpse almost dead in enjoying silence as if silence too preferred to be dumb while enjoying the performance. The entire auditorium had never such pin drop silence it seemed to them that the pin too was enjoying the feel and artistry of Shantaram forgotten its falling. The last scene was being staged. It was the scene in which Shantaram had to pay the debt of Nature. The audience was just watching with their talking eyes and talking breath with almost bodies dead at the way Shantaram hurriedly spoke final words in his dialogue. Slowly the intensity of his voice started taking pauses and a moment came when it took a never ending long pause. Shantaram a great artistic soul with wide open eyes leaves. Whole auditorium was drowned in the crying tears over the death of their loving artist. The walls and ceilings of the auditorium had rarely seen such unique combination talking silence and talking tears. Suddenly the bell rang which brought back the dead audience in the world of life. It was the mark of ending Shantaram's performance and coming of the next. Shantaram got up and paid his departing adieu to his appreciative audience. The auditorium stood up and paid a standing ovation to the artistic talent of Shantaram and his entire team. Shantaram and his entire team got overwhelmed by this titanic reciprocation.

The Prize distribution began at the hands of the judge. The anchor gave the honor to the judge to declare the best dramatic performance of the night. The judge took the mike and loudly announced "The prize for the best dramatic performance goes to "Shantaram and his group" There was jubilation everywhere. The crowd was also happy with the way the justice was done to the talent of Shantaram. The excited and thrilled with pleasantly feared Shantaram and his group came up on the stage and received the honour.

After giving away the honour, the judge took the mike made his tongue speak a few words of commendation for the artistry of Shantaram. He said, "As a director and producer of the stage, I had been serving the stage art by directing and producing many hit and super hit dramas in Marathi language. I had an opportunity to direct many vetran Marathi artists. Of course their artistry was very impressive. But when I was watching this emerging artist 'Shantaram' I was engaged in dialogue with myself which said to me that this emerging star in Marathi drama would create a great havoc on the Marathi stage." Being absolutely under the spell of charismatic and conscious stealing artistry, the director producer made an announcement, "My dear and loving audience hereafter you will see Shantaram enacting in almost all the dramas which I would produce in the times to come." It was a delicious feast of rapture for Shantaram and his entire team and of course to the audience. At the end of the function, the director producer called Shantaram and gave him his address card and asked him to come to Mumbai to join his drama school.

The news of Shantaram's unbelievable accomplishment spread through each and every nook and corner of the state. Kalanagari could not remain untouched by the fragrance of the success of Shantaram. When Shantaram came to Kalanagari, the people in Kalanagari organized a great and grand procession in which entire family of Shantaram was honoured. For the first time, Kalasangam was set on the fire of pleasure. The Kalasangam and Kalanagari were very happy to see that their son was being promoted. It was the night before Shanataram's departure to Mumbai. Shantaram had had the departing dinner together with his family. After dinner his father came out in the front yard and lied down on the wooden cot. It was moonlit light. The moon was shining with greater might fading the darkness. Shantaram's father rested his body and got caught by the shining stars in the sky imagining his son to be that ever shining star.

It was a moonlit light. The moon was in her full form as if she was displaying her ever hidden beauty. The stars were shining with their fullest brightness and trying to over perform the blackest darkness. It seemed that the Moon, the stars and the blackest darkness are competing in mad race on the ramp of beauty peasant. It seemed that they are engaged in conversation teasing each other. The moon and star say," We are beautiful than you. We are whiter than you. We give a new hope to the world in the moments of frustration and unhappiness. With somewhat teasing intentions, they added, "What do you give to the world just darkness and enhances their troubles." The darkness gets annoyed at the teasing remark and angrily argues, "It is just because of me, you exist. IfI am not there, who will ask you? If white has its beauty then black too has. It is because of my presence, you are signified. You make them awake and lead them to work. It is me who make them stop their work and rest sometime in my bed." They were about to continue theirargument; suddenly they heard the voice of conversation between Shantaram and his parents. It seemed that they were little bent taking overhearing posture.

Shantaram came out in the front yard drying up his wet hands with some cloth; he sat down and rested his head on his mother Narmada's thigh. Narmada caressing and moving her delicate fingers through the dense forest of his hair showering on him mother's affection and care said, "Shantaram, you are leaving us and Kalanagari tomorrow. The house will be hot to all of us. We cannot imagine staying here without your talking presence. You will go and we will get in troubled question with whom to talk? We are like those bird couples who want their kids should be alwayswith them but cannot forget they are growing and with that their wings too. As they cannot cut their wings to keep their kids forever with them like that Shantaram we too cannot cut your ambitions to fly in the realm of art." Narmada's eyes turn watery and with one of the corners of her sari, she tries to dry up her eyes pretending to be removing some dust particle from eyes. With a little beat mourning tone, she said, "Shanta, you are going to Mumbai, won't you forget us after going and becoming a great artist." "Shantaram understands and experiences the grief of her mother. Wiping her tears with one hand and supporting her with the other he says, "What nonsense you are talking about? Going to Mumbai does not mean that I am going permanently. My dear mother, how this question troubles your mind that I would forget you. The mother answers, "Can a flower forgets its smell. No! No! Like that I also. You are the flower and I am the smell. I am born to spread your fragrance. So don't worry. When I will be financially strong I will take both to stay with me permanently. Stop eating your mind and don't let any evil flower to bloom in the garden of your mind and spoil its beauty and any other word of advice for me?" Controlling and suppressing her insuppressible stream of tears pregnant with mourning moisture she said, "Shanta, you are going to be artist. Remember hereafter "Art" is your mother. Love her, respect her and spend your every breath of life for the sake of art. Don't commit any misdeed which would disgrace her because remember it's defame is mine. Let the success come and touch your feet don't go crazy after money and fame. It is your dedication and adherence and love to it would force them come to you on their own feet. Remember; don't let your success make you mad. Keep your foot always on the ground. Let there be frustration but don't get carried away by that morbid emotions. Let it be there, perchance it might be the taste of your adherence to the art. I assure you that it will make you a hardcore artist." Shanta tries to rein her advising tongue saying, "Aai, stop na. How much you advise me?" Look the beautiful moon is at the mid of the sky. She is hurrying towards her bed. Come on! We shall go with the moon. Locking her mouth with the palm says "One more word. Let the passion of art would be your prime love and please yourself by pleasing the world of art by giving them feast of outlandish artistry which their eyes and senses never had had it. Shanta locks her mother's tongue in the cell of his palm and gives rest to his eyes.

A never ending flow of crowd gathered in front of Kalasangam. Shantaram is very much pleased to see that the entire Kalasangam was there to bid him a farewell. Shantaram took his bag touched his parents' feet and kissed them on their forehead. When he peeped into the eyes of the crowd he saw the flood of tears carrying a load of enormous expectations for him. Shantaram left for Mumbai saying final word of farewell to all those who came there at the bus stop.

After reaching Mumbai, he hired the taxi and reached to residence of the Director Producer to whom he had already intimated about his coming to Mumbai. Shantaram met the security guard at the gate and told him about his whereabouts. Already informed the security guard hurriedly took him in. The director producer became very happy to see Shantaram. On the very next day he took him to his school of drama and introduced him to other stage artists. For six months, Shantaram engrossed himself in acquiring skills of dramatics. The director came up with new theme to be staged offering Shantraram the lead role. The way Shantaram enacted the role during the rehearsal caught every one's admiring eyes. Soon he became very popular among his colleagues. The first dramatic endeavor was staged which received a tremendous response. The director producer got greatly impressed by the performance of Shantaram. Every one fondly started calling him 'Master Shantaram'. Soon his popularity as a great actor started reaching to the climax with every hit dramatic performance. His friend circle increased. Late night parties after every successful and hit stage show began. Gradually, Master Shantararm fell in deep love with the taste of wine.

One day his parents called him back to Kalangari and performed his marriage. The marriage was really a grand one. People in an around Kalangari had been there to attend marriage ceremony of their favorite actor. It was great feast for children. The children were dancing with great enthusiasm as if someone from their own family was getting married. Many famous stage actors and actresses and eminent people had been there. For the first time after a long interval, Kalangari had witnessed fair like appearance. It was most memorable day for entire Kalanagari which it preserved in its memory as shell preserves a pearl. Hustle and bustle of marriage was getting silent with departing guests and slowly departing son towards horizon. Almost all the guestswere dispersed. A few were there resting in the pendal.

After staying a few days with his parents, One day Shantaram asked his old and somewhat thin growing mother "Mother get ready you and Anna have to accompany us to Mumbai. Narmada questioned with some concern. "Who will look after this house? Offering her some sigh of relief Shantaram says "Aai don't worry we shall lock it. Nobody will do damage to it." Shantaram insisted on them to accompany him. "Aai! Why don't you come to my house in Mumbai? I had huge and capacious flat. We can stay over there. Fondly calling him sliding his palm over his muscular chin Narmada said, "You have just married. These moments never come again. Enjoy yourselves. We are just like those old utensils which make only sound and serves no purpose. If your carry them; they will steal the peace from your life. Let them trouble with cacophonous sounds to these dark and decaying walls and ceilings." Shanta got annoyed at the way mother compared them with old and useless utensils." "Stop belittling yourself and tell me full and final of your coming with me." Narmada said, "There are many more days of festival. I will come on one of the occasions and garnish your home with our old presence." Shantaram without stretching the matter any further left his mother there and got involved in the leaving preparation for

Mumbai. The next day morning the couple left Kalanagari for Mumbai.

Shantaram enjoyed some blissful moments of matrimonial life with his wife Yamuna. She also felt proud over her husband's status in Mumbai and limelight which he enjoyed in the realm of art. She was very happy and satisfied. Shantaram's career as an artist was flourishing with every hit drama. With that was flourishing his habit for wine. Parties of celebration of success of the drama were turning nights into days. In the next few years, his dramas made such havoc on the stage; it made Master Shantaram the most demanding stage artists. Years passed. The consistent presence of Shantaram was ever felt in the house. Yammuna had become almost solitary creature always eagerly waiting for rarely coming husband. Shantaram's busy schedule and his consistent visits to various parts of the state in connection with stage rarely bring wife and husband together. Whenever they came together, they rarely talked with each other. Almost all the time Shantaram was fully drunk. He deprived *Yamuna* from matrimonial pleasure which caused irrevocable gap in their relation. Previously he had come after a few days interval. Now he came once in a two week or some times after months. It disturbed *Yamuna*. Whole day she had to spend talking to herself and luxurious artifacts in the house. Her solitariness and suffocation was at its extreme state. She felt that if that corroding silence and loneliness continued for some more days, she would go insane. When it became too much she decided that she would settle the issue with Shantaram and if he did not respond as per expectation then she would be free to take whatever the decision possible.

One day Yamuna was standing at the window of her kitchen got engrossed in enjoying the beauty of the lonely Moon in the sky. Suddenly the sound of the horn of a car of Shantaram disturbed her lonely silence and saw that the security guard is opening the gate to give entry to the car of Shantaram. She saw Shantaram in the car and got herself engaged in keeping the dishes on the dining table. The bell rang and she hurriedly ran towards the door to open. While running towards the door she happily muttered to herself, "At least they will have dinner together after a long time" She opened the door and got shocked to see that the driver of the car came up controlling and supporting the fully drunkard Shantaram." She asked the driver, "What happened?" The driver said, "*Malkin* there was celebration of Saheb's hit drama and he carried away in the emotions of wine". Yamuna looked at the driver with a despairing gesture "It's ok! You rest him on the sofa and go and I will do the rest." The driver left room. Yamuna looked at unconscious Shantaram and entered in her world of soliloquy. "What I dreamed of and what is happening. I never thought my dreams would be so horrible nightmare. At the time of the wedding ceremony, when I was garlanding my husband I had thought that he would give me all that I had ever aspired for but he made me beggar. He looted my happiness and spoiled my dream. I thought how lucky I was that I got married with an actor with glamour and limelight. But never thought that his glamour and limelight would suck me as a leech sucks the blood of helpless cattle and don't let them die by give them eternal suffering. I am like that dumb and helpless creature who wants to speak but no one can listen to her, always hungry, miserable and deprived." Shantaram lying unconscious makes a louder snoring sound and mutters something which brings Yamuna back to the reality of the bitter world. It was sleepless night for Yamuna. For the first time she was feeling somewhat restless as if it was going to be her last night on that solitary bed. Yamuna slept with her wide open eyes till the moment the moon breathed the last with the birth of burning sun. Yamuna came out of ever brooding world with the knock of milkman at the door. She opened the door took the milk went back with the determination that she would restore her peace of mind with a decisive dialogue with Shantaram.

Shantaram woke up. After finishing his morning ritual sat for tea face to face with Yamuna. For the first the first time after a long interval they had face to face contact. Shantaramdid not dare to have healthy eye contact with her as a sinful thought was torturing his conscience. He knew that he was answerable to the sufferings of Yamuna. Perchance it was that guilty conscious which locked his tongue in the cage of injustice. Yamuna began conversation with somewhat uncertain tone, *"Kase ahhat? Khup divsani alat. Kasakay chalaya Natak tumche."* Realizing the gravity of her tone, Shantaram preferred to answer with silent tone, *"Nehamisarakha, Ka, Asa kavicharta?"* Yamuna somewhat absurdly answers, *"aasach, khup divwasani gharchi athawan ali. Mahiti aahena ghari tumchi kunitari wat baghata. Anni shewatcha prashana. Me thambu ki jau?"* Absolutely confused and little beat scared with her question? A little sweat cold his face and the vein turn hot with sudden rise of blood pressure. Foam in his mouth made him stammer and with gush of voice conveyed his feltshock. "What?! *He bagh aasa kahi karunako. Me khup busy aahe. Malathoda wail de. Sagala kahi thik hoil."* Already irritated Yamuna shouted. *"Kiti kal hawai aahe tumahala. Anni tumhala wata to paryant me ya jagat aasel Ka? Samajat Ka nahi tumahala. Hal keleye ho tu me maje. Tumcha hey alishan ghar mazasathi kali kothadi zali aahey. Sahan hot nahi aata. Bas kara sahan hot nahi atta. Shakyazale tar vichar kara mazya manacha. Shakyazale tar thodas aanand dya jagnacha. Nahitari aata shilak rahilatari kay?"* Shantaram sat like a corpse in his chair. That day Shantaram spent the whole day within the locked door enjoyed some matrimonial moment with Yamuna. That was the first and the last happiest day in Yamuna's life.

The next day Shantaram left rather early in the morning. He went on his mission of stage shows entertaining the world and confining his lonely wife in the most boring and monotonous family theater to remain unappreciated and unnoticed. He wenton a long tour leaving Yamuna in the Tajmahal of miseries and uncertainties. Giving up hope of matrimonial bliss and return of her most busy husband, she started packing her bags. Before leaving she sprinkled the moisture of her feelings on the blank life of piece of paper and quenched its thirst. She locked the door and kept the key at a secret niche known to her husband. Shantaram returned home at the time of dusk as if a lost gentleman returned home trying to identify the marks of his habitation in the past. It was the first time, Shantaram was not drunk perhaps he might had had but now its spell was not there. He was fully conscious. He came up climbing up disturbing the dismay corridors. He shocked to see the door locked. Before taking the key he enquired the neighbor about Yamuna. He knocked the door of the neighboring flat. A middle aged woman came out. "Hello! Sir. What is the matter?" Shantaram spoke with shocked, doubted and scared tongue. "Mam, Do you keep knowledge of my wife's whereabouts? "The woman answered "A few days back she had been to me and told me that she was going to her father's house and will take uncertain time to return."

Shantaram came back took out the key from the secret niche and entered. For the first time the house seemed him to be a hollow. She strikingly experienced the presence of his dumb wife. Suddenly his eyes fell on the talking piece of paper. He hurriedly picked up the piece of paper buried himself in the book. The feeling of the paper and its current was powerful that Shantaram sat on the chair almost paralyzed. For a moment he thought that he had lost everything. Suddenly he entered in the world of monologue. "Yamuna, My darling, my care taker and my devotee and my soul of body, you left me alone here to die in the eating silence. What is use of this dead body if his soul is not there? I whole heartedly acknowledge that I did a great injustice to you that I did not pay heed to you and not cared what always wanted. Your sudden going made me realize your worth. A moment without you in this solitary room made me think how much you might have suffered in my absence. I beg your pardon come back if possible. Your Shanta wants to say sorry to you and be with you forever. I can't bear this Shajahan'slonliness in this dismayed Tajmahal. I am coming to you. Get ready to come back." Suddenly the pendulum disturbed the silence and took out Shantaram from the world monologue. He took a glance at wall clock which talked to him.? "How much you think and think? Stop thinking and please your bed as it is feeling lonely. If possible go back to wife's town and bring her back. We all are feeling bored." Gradually the sound of the pendulum silenced with that restlessness and troubled mind of Shantaram too. He woke up and began to prepare for going. He packed the bag and about to lock the door. Suddenly he stopped and spoke to himself. "What am I doing? Why I am going? What is its use? I won't fill the gap between the two minds. I have severely hurt her? I am murderer of her feelings? I have deprived her of what she ever wanted from me? I am criminal and my going won't serve her anyway. On the contrary, It would aggravate the matter and repentance won't do any magic. Let her be there in the company of human beings. What is here? All the times she has to communicate with dumb interiors of the house. There atleast her tongues get companions. Her heart will be open; her mind would be free from morbid fills. If I bring her back and if the past repeated, she would never forgive me and I too. Instead falling rather down in her esteem, it is better to keep her there. At least I would get some space to hide my face. With what face I should go to take her back. I am sure she won't come as she knows chameleon never change their habit." He reopens the door with great frustration and a relief that at least he won't hereafter aggravate Yamuna's feel."

Since then, there was no communication between Yamuna and Shantaram. For days he remained out rarely returns home. Whenever he returned, he found the house to be an enchanted as if the ghost of murdered feels of Yamuna hovers around. Whenever he slept on the bed where Yamuna used to sleep, he felt that the bed was thorny and trouble him for what he had done to Yamuna. The pendulum of the wall clock made cacophonous sound as if he was shouting at him for ill-treating Yamuna. There was a grave silence which scared him made the house hot for him. It might be the reason why he preferred to be out from the silence which tortured him a lot consistently reminded him of his injustice to Yamuna.

Unexpected departure of Yamuna and personal loneliness corroded and weakened him only. He tried to overcome that corroding silence of his interiors with hot and cool influence of the wine. Previously Shantaram was occasional drunkard. Then he began his day with the taste of the wine and slept with that. Surprising thing was that the more he drank, the more his art flourished. The interest with which poured his wine into his body, with the same interest and he added his heart and soul in making every role given to him a great success. His art and wine became passion for him without which he could not live. Every drama in which he acted celebrated silver and golden jubilee. His every stage performance and the drama became a great feast of pleasure and entertainment for audience that is why every show was overcrowded with roaring smiles and sweet and cacophonous whistling sounds.

His artistry was greatly appreciated at state level and national level. The state gave him great honors. His room got full of mementos but they seemed to have forgotten their smile as none was there to appreciate them. His dramatic artistry was at climax now. The art and wine took absolute hold of his mind and body. His blood veins carried nothing but blood of art and wine. He began to lose his consciousness in such conditions he gave outstanding performance of art. All the times he thought that he was enacting some role and muttered some dialogues. Rarely did he come in his real world as most of the time he was under the spell of wine. The world of art started dominating his real life and he began to act like an actor performing some role. Every now and then he muttered some words and imagined that he was in some role and doing it in front of the audience. One day he returned at the very late hour of the night. He tried to sleep but he could not as suffocated spirits of murdered emotions of Yamuna stole his sleep. With that restlessness, he spent his half night with sleep absolutely with fully opened eyes. The pendulum did not let him sleep and gave him a severe blow of sound which brought back in the world of consciousness. With half dead eyes he took a look at the wall clock which showed it was 6 O' clock in the morning. The spell of wine departed with murky and winy darkness of dawn. For a moment he forgot the departure of Yamuna and unconsciously called, "Yamuna! Where are you? I am ready. Bring my cup of tea" He waited for some time as his mind was engaged in some private thought. But when no response came, he entered the kitchen the dumb utensils and widow walls and mourning spiders with their hot cobwebs made him known with tragic lot of the kitchen as their Yamuna, their mistress, their caretaker was not there. The things at the mess made him restlessly remember his truth that the mistress of the house was not there. Suddenly a log ailing lizard counting her last breath fell on the shoulder of Shantaram and fell dawn and died. It was supposed to be a bad omen indicating of some ominous event. An ill thought of some ominous event stroke the mind of Shantaram.

With the help of his friend, he managed a maid servant to keep the house neat. The maid servant came every day cleaned the house and went. One day he came at late hours of the morning home absolutely hypnotized by his passion for art imaging that he hadto play some different role. When he entered the kitchen, he found that maid servant was washing 'Kitchen watta'. The villain in him got awoke. The world of art strengthened his hold around the real world. Shantaram imagined that now he had to be in the role of a villain. His passion for wine and passion for art began to play a game on him as if they wanted to convey him the message "Too much love of them would be hazardous". The woman's body of the maid servant made him to change the colors of his eyes and intentions of innocent mind. As like a hungry tiger with watering mouth jumps on his prey, Shantaram attacked the maid servant and began what his role demanded. The inattentive maid servant got confused and frightened with that unexpected attack of an inhuman human being. Suddenly she screamed and ran out of the house chasing her Shantaram too came as if he was reluctant to let escape the prey. The screaming sound of the maid servant disturbed the silent interiors of the household of the neighbors. As the confused and shocked herd of wild animals ran after smelling some disastrous situation like that the neighbors rushed towards Shantaram's flat and began to beat him black and blue. Finally he was taken to the nearby police station. Crime of molestation got registered against him. The police put him behind the bar. Consciousness of Shantaram was restored with severe beating of the crowd. He realized that how foolishly he acted and blamed his art and his wine for this disgrace.

The news of the event spread like a wild fire. It was a great shock to his fans and colleagues and the directors and the producers trusted him and invested in him. The crowd rushed towards the police station to make their favorite actor free. Most of the directors have invested their money in Shantaram and wanted to complete their pending shows. All the directors and producers decidedto free him. They took the bail ofShantarm. Shantraram returned to his world of drama. The event of molestation of maid servant had deep impact on his mind. He determined that hereafter he would not love wine and drown him in the taste of art. He returned on the stage started his art but he could not as he used to do under the spell of wine. The director producer expressed dissatisfaction over the shots given and dryness in his acting. Suddenly his body began to demand wine. The determination of Shantaram not to touch wine melted like solid candle turns into liquid. He asked the director producers for wine. The director producer offered him a pack and the moment the stream of wine entered his body the dead artist revived and started giving appreciable shots one after other. Shantaram completed almost all dramas. Only last scene in the drama of the director producer was to be performed. It was scheduled on the next day. He returned to his house quite late around 1 O' clock.

He tried to sleep but restless room did not let him enjoy sound slumber. He was growing restless for sleep and accordingly he was changing sides. But bed gave him no slumber as if it was being touched by some sinner. He got up from the bed and started ceiling fan. Suddenly a thought deeply buried in some corner came up breaking the embryo of memory. It was the thought of Yamuna. The moment he thought of Yamuna, it seemed to him that all senses were happily dancing. When he came out of the thought took a look at the surrounding, he thought the interiors were emotionally appealing him to bring back Yamuna without whom they were lonely. It was early hours of the dawn, his eyes were wide open and the mind was tired of thinking ceaselessly. Before he goes to bed he gives him last thought to bring Yamuna back. Shantaram accepted the thought of mind and muttered abruptly, "Yamuna, my Darling get ready wherever you are, I am coming tomorrow to take you with me." All the inanimate things overheard it began to dance and the bed took him in her arm forgetting what he had done to Yamuna. That day he woke up quite late in the afternoon. After taking lunch, Shantaram reached to the studio where the last scene of the play was to be performed. He took pack of wine tried to understand the scene from the director producer. The director produced said to Shantaram, "It is the last scene of the play in which the major character dies. Master, remember, it is the death scene and I want that you should give it in such way that not only the spectators but the death itself feel happy how painfully and sublimely it died. Let her cry and shade tears on her death. Shantaram I want such death that the audience should feel that the actor is really died and not pretending." Shantaram nodded rather positively. He took two three packs of wine and lied down on the bed throwing his dialogue in such way that it was not Shantaram but that imaginary actor was dying. There was a pin drop silence as if the silence was absorbing every word of Shantaram. All the men were engrossed in watching the way Shantaram died. The director producer was catching every minute gestures, postures, eye contact and facial expressions which showed dying Shantaram. The silence in the studio grew. All became serious, Shantaram uttered the last word of the dialogue and he took the last breath keeping his eyes wide open. Suddenly the clapping sound of studio men asked the grave silence get lost of their way. The director producer suddenly exclaimed, "Hands up to you and to your art Shantaram. What a real and noble presentation of death. Even the death would not have done it. You are simply genius. With an appreciative gestures and postures he reached to Shantaram to get him up but he could not. The studio enjoyed thundering sounds and floods of tears which engulfed the entire studio. The wide open eyes of Shantaram seemed as if they were waiting for someone. The director producer closed his eyes but their desire to see that face was remained unfulfilled.

Lajvanti

It was a foggy morning in the winter. The fog had spread its white carpet all over the town. The winter was so cold that no one wanted to leave their beds. Housewives were sprinkling water mixed with the cowdung in their front yard. Some were engaged in drawing a column in the front yard of the house as it was supposed to be good sign of a good house wife. Suddenly a voice was heard from a cottage and it was a cottage of a shepherd who looked after the cattle of the entire village which was situated at the bank of the river Yashodhara. As the Shepherd was not getting his black blanket, he called his wife, "Vaishali I'm not getting my blanket. Will you come and help me in getting it. I am getting late." Suddenly a soft and melodious echo pierced through the soft stream of air mixed with the sweet smell of the cowdung fell on the ear of the shepherd, "Just a minute, I will find it out for you meanwhile you have your tea. Shepherd was recently married with Vaishali a daughter of a milkman from a nearby place. Vaishali hurriedly came out with blanket and humorously said, "You always make the mess of the things. No thing you keep at its place. You enhance my trouble. But I like to do it. It was a sweet job for me." Shepherd gave her a loving smile spread his blanket on one of his shoulders and with his stick he left for green lush meadows spread around the river Yashodhara.

He took his own cattle along with him and on the way other cattle joined him. Though he was shepherd, he was little educated. He had taken some lessons of reading and writing. He had to leave his education due to sudden demise of his father who was also a shepherd. He carried a flute with him and played wonderful and heart stealing melodies on his flute. They were so wonderful and melodious that all the aspects of the nature seemed to be engrossed in it. When a word or a line touched to the mute heart of the cattle, they conveyed their appreciation by moving their bells tied around their necks. The processions of the cloud took pause for a while in the musical hut of the shepherd and slowly and helplessly started departing. The stream passing by took a stop as if it was confused with meaning of the melody and when understood started running noisily as if it was beating the drums of the musical talent of shepherd. Blowing wind preferred to linger happily for a while in the musical celebration of the shepherd reluctantly passed ahead to carry on his duty. The green crops in the field took exciting and thrilling gestural and postural steps on melody of the song. His melody was so powerful that any passerby caught his melody, he stood still listening. His melodies charmed both animate and inanimate objects.

This was how a happy and delightful life of the shepherd was going on. One day he was taking lunch under the shade of the tree. All of a sudden his eyes fell on the beautiful girl who came there to collect the cowdung. She was so beautiful that she took out a flute and started playing a melody in praise of her beauty. When that beautiful girl heard the melody, she stood still got engrossed in it. After some time, the shepherd stopped the flute. The girl came out of the melodious world of the shepherd. She was so much impressed that before leaving she looked at the Shepherd and gave him such a stealing smile that he felt mesmerized with the smile. As the dusk started spreading its bed, the shepherd collected the cattle and moved towards his home. For the first time it seemed to him that his mind was engaged in the thought of the smile.

He had his dinner with his wife and drying up his hands he came out to rest on the wooden cot. When he closed his eyes he saw the smiling face in front of his eyes which invited him in meadows. The face was so beautiful that he could not ignore. For some time he got allured in enjoying the sweet smile of the face that he forgot that his wife was sitting beside him. Seeing her husband staring somewhere and engrossed in something, she moved him with her hand. "Where are you my man? I am here? I have been here from last ten to fifteen minutes. You are not paying any heed to me. Where is your mind? And what is that which takes you out of here." Closing his sinned face with his palm he said, "Nothing serious just busy in thinking about future of the family." Vaishali anxiously questions, "What is there to get troubled with? Everything is alright. Things are happening as expectedly. Then why do you trouble yourself by falling in unnecessary questions. Stop brooding over future and let's sleep. You will be late to morning work." The night passed sleeplessly as the smiling face in his eyes was obstinate to be there where the staring of Shepherd was fixed. Smiling face troubled a lot to him throughout the night it seemed to him that it was calling him on the meadows.

Dark hours of the night got engulfed in the mouth of the past giving passage to dim rays of the twilight. Shepherd who was till awake closing his anxious eyes for the meet with the girl tomorrow fell prey to the light of the twilight to be the light of morning and got up for his work somewhat earlier than his daily routine. Hurriedly he got ready as the attraction of the girl made the house hot for him. Seeing her husband waking up early, Vaishali shouted, "What makes you wake up so early. It seems that you have not slept throughout the night. Sleep; there is time for you to work. I will get up you when you wish" Giving a cool response and avoided to converse with her on this issue. "It is not the problem. Today I have to go somewhat earlier as I have some other important work to do."

Shepherd hurriedly got ready took his articles and with his cattle moved towards the meadows on the side of the river. As usual the girl came there and started collecting cowdung. Shepherd took out his flute and played his melodies. The charm of the melodies of Shepherd's music made her forget the work of collecting the cow dung. She came and sat beside him and got engrossed in it. When the shepherd ended the melody, he found that a girl was sitting quite close to him closing her eyes as if she was still engrossed in it. After some moments Lajvanti came out of the spell of the melody of the Shepherd. Both looked at each other and began to converse. Shepherd, "I am the shepherd of the village. Caring cattle of the village has been a tradition of our family. My ancestors had been in this work for years. Now I do it. He takes a pause and questions what is your name? And where do you come from?" The girl begins, "I am Lajvanti the daughter of the milkman. I come from Vishrampur a small village on the other side of the river. Sometimes I collect the cowdung there in case if I don't get it there then I have to come here." Shepherd asked "How do you do it? What brought you here?" "By boat which runs between the two villages." replied Lajvanti. When their talk was going on, the boatman called Lajvanti. Hurriedly she collected the cowdung saying good bye she took leave of him and ran quickly towards the river where the boat waited for her. Seeing her going, Shepherd felt sad at heart but controlled him with a sweet hope that she would be here tomorrow morning to be with him. His mind got engrossed in Lajvanti. All the time he thought of her. He carried his physical presence everywhere but mentally he wandered in the world of Lajvanti. Vaishali noticed the change in her husband. She spoke to herself, "He was growing silent. What could be the reason? He was not like this previously. Something was going somewhere wrong. He should share but he did not do it. Perhaps it might be a secret he did not want to share with me. I will ask him one day."

Shepherd got completely involved in Lajvanti. His eagerness to Meet Lajvanti grew and passion of her burns him inwardly. His mind, his heart and every drop of blood sang the song of Lajvanti. When he was at home having talk with his wife Vaishali, he talked with her but it seemed that somewhere at thought level he seemed to be engaged in the memory of Lajvanti. His absent mindedness at home grew putting the head of Lajvanti in gyre of trouble. In evening time, the couple was taking dinner. Vaishali determined to ask him. "Is anything wrong? Ur silence is growing. You don't talk to me as you used to do it previously. What is the problem just share with me? If I can help you anyway I will do it. It would be my pleasure" "Nothing serious, don't worry. Everything will be alright at the right time.

He avoided to speak further and asked her to go to bed." Vaishali got nervous and went to bed muttering," something was going wrong somewhere. Let him hide it. One day, secrete would come out breaking the shield of silence. I will wait for that"

As usual, the Shepherd left for meadows. Cattle got scattered here and there in meadows. Keeping eyes on them, the Shepherd started his melody and waiting for Lajvanti at heart. He waited for long but Lajvanti did not come that day. He got sunk in despair. With great nervous and despair, he played his tragic melody expressing his grief for Lajvanti. It was for the first time that some tragic tunes came out of his flute. Hearing it, all the things around especially the cattle feel strange today as they had never heard such dismayed tune before. They too realized that their master was unhappy over their Lajvanti's absence. Seeing them together was great pleasure for all the animate and inanimate objects there. Really they are also bored with the absence of Lajvanti. When the darkness is about to fall, the shepherd asked his cattle to return back. Every day he returned home with a sweet wish in the heart that she would come tomorrow. But her today's absence hurt him a lot and he took it to his heart. On the way home, he got engaged in thought and said to him, "What could be the problem of her absence? Is anything wrong?" so many questions troubled his mind. He returned home tied his cattle in the corner and rested on the wooden cot at the middle of the front yard. Vaishali instantly came with a glass of water. He took water but paid no heed to Vaishali. It hurt her but she preferred to keep quiet. He rested there for long till the dinner was served. Vaishali looked at the silent husband and with an irritating tone says, "Where is your mind? Why do you observe silence as if someone is dead at home? I am still alive. Break your silence. Speak I am here in front of you. I am not a stone, a living human being." The Shepherd got annoyed at her, "Shut your mouth and your baffling. All the time you ask me the same question where your mind is. What do you mean by where is your mind? You want the answer, see it is here only and not anywhere else." The Shephered was really not angry but the absence of Lajvanti hurt him. Vaishali shout at him. "Why do you shout at me? What is my fault?" The Shepherd spoke with anger, "You speak too much that is your problem. You do your work and let me do mine. Remember don't poke your nose in my private matters." Hearing this Vaishali got shocked. Tears covered her eyes. She got up and went into the dark hut with dim oil lamp and sat in the corner and lamented over and eventually slept.

Already anxious and worried Shepherd over Lajvanti's absence took his cattle and with great haste walked towards the meadows with a hope that she would come. He let his cattle for grazing took his seat under shade of the tree. He began his notes of melody keeping his eyes on the footpath on which Lajvanti came walking. A smile flowered on his face and eyes started scintillating when the appearance of Lajvanti came on the canvas of his eyes. His heart began to dance and mind started releasing the happy notes of union. Seeing him happy everyone got happy. He played his favorite melody for her. When the melody ended, Lajvanti asked him, "Can you read and write?" "Not that much but I can manage." "Then why don't you put your melodies in writing. Let the generations read. It will be honor of your writing." The Shepherd looked at Lajvanti, "Not bad idea I never thought of it. But I will take words seriously."

Their meeting brought them close together. Their love started blooming. Their passion for meeting grew and they died for meeting. The next day he took with him a note book and a pen and began to put all the melodies in words. When Lajvanti came he read them to her. She appreciated him a lot. It ignited his poetic spirit and he created one by one outstanding piece of poems. The Shepherd was so much enchanted by her beauty of Lajvanti whatever he wrote reflected his love for Lajvanti. The fragrance of the poems of the Shepherd spread everywhere. Every day meeting with Lajvanti kept him ever fresh. At home also he was very friendly with his wife. Vaishali got surprised with this change. His love for Vaishali grew double. One day she questioned, "What makes you happy? Let me know the secret." The shepherd smiling at her says, "Why do you get engaged in unnecessary questions. You feel happy now that is important for you and me. Enjoy your life and let me do mine" It was a midnight hour. Suddenly the Shepherd started enchanting the name of Lajvanti and said something in her prayers. Vaishali got up and looked at her husband and understood that it was Lajvanti who was secret of his happiness. She made a midnight determination to unfold Lajvanti's secret.

Next day when the Shepherd went to the meadows Vaishali followed her hid herself behind the tree so that the Shepherd should not see her. When Lajvanti came and sat beside the Shepherd, Vaishali understands that this is the cause of happiness. A thought came in her mind to disturb them and scolded Lajvanti for alluring her husband but on the next moment realized that it was not fair to do so and it would hurt her husband. She returned home with a frustration at heart that her husband was being captivated in the charms of a girl and if it continued, her matrimonial life will be perished. She got entangled in a conflict either to save her marital life or to make them happy. It stole her sleep but she never showed the shepherd that she had unfolded the secret of his happiness. When the shepherd returned home he fondly called his wife, "Vaishali where are you?" "I am here. Wait I am coming." Vaishali came out in the front yard. What made you call me?" "I have written." "What? Poems! Wonderful!" "May I read them out?" It was not a shock to her as she knew that the magic of love changes the fool into a scholar and normal into an insane. She guessed that the poems might be in the admiration of Lajvanti. Like every other woman she too was unhappy at heart that her husband was going mad after another woman. Only to keep the mind of her husband, she said, "Please hurry up. I am excited to read whom you have addressed the poems." Shepherd started reading the poems one after the other. Vaishali observed the happiness on the face of the shepherd. Knowing all these poems are written to glorify the beauty of Lajvanti ironically asked him, "They are for me" The shepherd got bewildered with this unexpected question and to avoid the truth to come out he said to keep her mind, "Yes Darling these are for you only. Who can be other?" Vaishali got hurt with this sheer lie but did not let him know that she was hurt. Bringing an artificial smile, she exclaimed, "Really wonderful. It showed how much you love me." Shepherd felt sorry at hurt as he knew that he was deceiving his wife. As Vaishali had an important work, she left him and got engaged in her work in the kitchen. There were tears in her eyes as she could not bear the admiration of another woman on the lips of her husband. What hurt him the most was that her husband deceived her by telling a sheer lie? Shepherd was so mad in the love of Lajvanti that he forgot that he was hurting his wife by loving Lajvanti and keeping her in dark.

Every meeting with Lajvanti brought out a wonderful poet hidden within him. Lajvanti's inspiration made such influence on his mind that day and night he thought of her only. His excessive love for Lajvanti brought out wonderful love poems. There was a temple of some God. A banyan was tree with square like concrete structure where people gathered in the evening. One day Shepherd joined the gathering and presented some of his poems. Every presented poem brought him a great applause and appreciation. It became their routine to have such poetical gatherings. Graudally the genius of the shepherd reached to the court of the king. The king called him in the court and asked him, "Shepherd, I have heard a lot about your genius in poetry. I order you to present them. If I am pleased with them, I will confer upon you the honour of poet lauret of the court." Shepherd was astonished with the announcement. He took some pages from the torn cloth bag and began to read them out. It pleased the King and his ministers so much that everyone came up with a great appreciation for him. The king said, "You are really a genius. Your poems have moved us and compelled us to announce you to be poet lauret of our kingdom. The shepherded felt on the top of air. The news was spread all over and it also knocked at the door of Shephered. Vaishali got astonished at this unexpected achievement of the Shepherd. At heart, she thanked Lajvanti and held her responsible for this glory. The next day there was a grand procession. Shepherd was asked to ride on a kingly elephant. Procession went through each and every lane and finally reached at his home where Vaishali was eagerlywaiting for him. The shepherd got down from the elephant. They came face to face and exchanged a smile. It was the happiest day in the life of family.

The next day Shepherd got up early took the cattle reached to the meadows. Lajvanti came earlier. When he saw her there, he became happy. He shared the good news with her. "Lajvanti it was because of you that I have been honored with the poet laurite by the king." "Oh really! Congrats!" "Thank you." The talk continued for a long time. Before departing he expressed his will to marry her. She knew that the shepherd was married and marriage with him would put his matrimonial life in trouble and bring defame for her. But seeing excessive love for her, she assured her that she would consider it. It made him very happy. The next day the king called him in the court and asked him, "Poet Lauret where had you been yesterday." "Shepherd modestly answered, "My lord I had been after cattle on the meadow." The king got shocked and said, "Are you fool? Don't you know that you are the poet lauret, one of the most respectable persons in the court? You are not expected go after the cattle. It is the dishonor of the honor bestowed upon you. To save the dignity of the laurel, you are hereby ordered not to go after the cattle otherwise your honor of the poet lauret will be taken back." Shepherd got disturbed. The king kept the security at the house of the shepherd so that he should on meadows. The shepherd got disturbed. When the morning came, he got restless to go after the cattle. He was about to go but suddenly his eyes caught the security at house. Thus he got confined and could not meet Lajvanti for days. There Lajvanti came everyday waited and returned with dispair. She thought that shepherd had become a big person and in prosperity he had forgotten his Lajvanti. She sunk in despair and never returned on the meadows.

Shepherd got disturbed. He wished to see Lajvanti but he could not. His mind got engaged in her. Slowly he began to lose his poetic talent. At home he got annoyed at Vaishali. He stopped writing poems. Vaishali feared that if it continued, one day the king would take the honour back and again they would be thrown in poverty. Shepherd got diverted. He did not find his mind in anything. He stopped writing poems. Whole night he remained awake and thought of Lajvanti. Vaishali realized his state of mind. Shepherd couldnot bear the pangs of separation. To get relief from it, he began to drink. One day he overdrank and reached to the court. When the king asked him to present a poem, he took out a paper and was about read. Suddenly he fell down. The King got annoyed at him and declared that the Shepherd had hurt the dignity of the honour so he took back the honour of the Poet lauret and declared that whatever the asset given to him was being taken back. The king asked the security to through the poet lauret outside the kingdom. The news reached every corner of the kingdom and of course at the door of the Shepherd. Vaishail got shocked and did nothing but eagerly waited for him to be back. Till the hour of the midnight, she waited for him and finally she went to bed.

When the shepherd came back to sense, he realized where he was. He returned home. Vaishali was waiting for him. When he reached home, Vaishali was standing at the door. Shepherd did not have courage to face her eyes. He got in and engaged himself in some activities. She asked him, "What happened! Why are behaving like this? Let me know the reason." Shepherd knew that if he disclosed the secret, Vaishail would get hurt. So he kept mum. Vaishali knew the reason but she wanted to know from him." The next day the shepherd took his cattle and went to the meadow. Whole day he waited for Lajvanti but she did not come. It continued for many days. Shepherd could not tolerate. He became a frequent visitor of the wine shop. He became absolute drunkard. Once or twice he fell in the road and slept their whole night. When he didn't return home, Vaishali went in search of him. Picked him up wherever he was found. Whole kingdom mocked at Shepherd and Vaishali. The family got defamed. Who were jealous of them began to make fun of them. Vaishail felt very sad over their miserable plight. But she was helpless.

Everyday shepherd went to the grooves with the hope that Lajvanti would be there but nothing came but disappointment only. The more he remembered her, the more he drank. Wines made him weaker, ill, and pale. One day he was extremely drunk and with trembling steps, he returned home. He was almost unconscious and began to shout "Lajo where are you. I have not seen you since months. Why don't you come? I want to see you before dying." Vaishali heard it. She understood that Lajo was the secret of his success. If he did not meet her, he would die. She did not want to let him die. Shepherd fell ill and held the bed.

She invited her mother to stay with them. Her mother came. Vaishali narrated the whole story to her and told her that from tomorrow, she would be out of home on a mission to look for her husband's beloved and asked her to take care of her husband. She came to the meadows. The boat was already there. She asked the boatman to drop her across the river. During the journey Vaishali tried to collect the information about Lajvanti from the boatman. The boat man told her address. Vaishail reached on the given address. She got the house of Lajvanti but found it to be locked. She enquired the neighbor about the family. The family informed her that Lajo and her parents were out of station to attend the marriage ceremony of their relative and had not informed any about their coming back. Vaishali got the name of the place from the neighbor and hired a bullock cart and reached to the place. She visited the house where the marriage was taking place. There was crowd. Vaishali had seen Lajvanti. If she came within her view, she could easily identify her. When she fell to get her in the crowd she began to ask the people. Someone told her that Lajvanti was with the bridegroom and beautifying her in a room. Vaishali reached to the room and within a twinkling of eyes she identified Lajvanti. She called her out and said, "I am Viashali, the wife of the shepherd." The moment she came to know about her identity, she got scared as what to speak. Vaishali supported her saying, "Don't get scared. I won't get annoyed at you. You are the cause of glory and poverty. I want you to come to my home and save my dying husband who is mad for. If you do it I will be in your debt forever. Lajvanti assured her, "If it is so, I will be there but not now. Let me go back to my native. Vaishali who was eager to take her home anxiously questioned, "How long you are going to be here." Lajo answered, "Not more a few days." Vaishali took the word and returned to her native.

Shepherd was lying on the bed as if he was dead. Vaishali sat beside him and asked him, "How are you?" He looked at her and kept mum. Vaishali realized that he grew very weak due to frustration and being too much alcoholic. She looked at him and smiled and said, "I have such thing if I share with you, I am sure that you will be cured instantly." Fully frustrated Shepherd felt little rejuvenated and mustering all his left might questioned, "What is that?" Vaishali was very much happy with the way the Shepherd reacted. She could control herself and said, "I met your Lajvanti. She was coming to see you within a few days." Shepherd felt little confused over how she came to know about her. He knew that he had not told her anything about Lajvanti then how she came to know about. As if he was ignorant, he tried to pretend, "Who is Lajvanti I don't know any Lajvanti" Vaishali smiled at him and said, "To whom you are deceiving? Once I chased you to meadows there I saw her with you?" Shepherd got shocked felt guilty. Vaishali understood his state of mind supported him, "There is nothing to feel guilty. It happens. Get ready to welcome your beloved." Shepherd was doubtful and preferred to linger on the bed. He said, "Let her come." Vaishali said, "I had been to her native. If you don't trust me then you would see yourself." Though he did not trust it, he felt little bit relaxed."

One day morning Lajvanti came there and knocked at the door, "Vaishali was cleaning the house. She instantly came out to see the stranger at the door. She got pleased to see Lajvanti was standing there. She welcomed her in. Shepherd was still asleep. Vaishali asked her to sit down. She went near her husband and moved him with her hand and said, "Get up and see who has come?" Shepherd got up and questioned as he was not aware of Lajvanti's presence. "Who has come?" Vaishali excitedly said, "see yourself." Shepherd hurriedly got up and shocked to see Lajvanti was standing in front of him. He wanted to shout 'My dear Lajvanti' seeing Vaishali beside her suppressed his feeling. He stared at her and a beautiful smile appeared on her. Vaishali observed the gestures and felt a hurt that shepherd had never such pleasure when he was with her. It was the defeat of her womanhood but she accepted for the sake of his happiness. She understood that Shepherd wanted to talk to her but he hesitated due to her presence. She posed an excuse and went out so that they could have private moments. Vaishali went out.

Shepherd felt relaxed. Lajvanti looked at weak, thin and hopeless Shepherd and said, "What have you done to yourself? Nothing was left in your body only bones. How much you have drunk and suffered for me. I troubled you a lot." "It is nothing before you coming. You have come now everything will be right. Everything will be as it was. Let's forget about me and tell me something about you. Where had you been so long?" "I was at home only. I used to come on the meadows but I found you not there, I stopped coming and started going in another place to collect cowdung. I waited for you and felt pained as you did not come. I got the news that you were honored as the poet lauret at the court of the king. I thought that the honor might have confined you within the court and might not have time for me. I waited for you for some days and being hopeless, I left the place. But it was very painful to be away from you and missed you a lot." "I had to come but the king confined me within the court saying that going after the cattle on meadow was against the dignity of the honour given. He kept me under watch of his security so he could not come to see you. Once or twice came there but returned hopelessly as you were not there. But I tell you honestly that I missed you a lot and suffered you a lot. When I was not allowed to see you I got disturbed and became alcoholic. Once I attended the court in drunken state and got punished. All I had been given was taken back and as a punishment and finally I was thrown out. Then I realized the life at the meadow was much happier than the kingly prosperity. I decided to regain it. I came there but your absence hurt me a lot and in your thinking l lost myself. I realized how happy to be with you and how difficult to be without you."

They could not control and embrace each other. After sometime, Vaishali returned. They had dinner together. Looking at Shepherd, she said, "I am going. Don't wait for me. Take care of yourself.' Shepherd got shocked. Vaishali was observing all these things and read the facial expression on his face. She knew that if she was not there, Shepherd would not remain alive. She requested Lajvanti to accept her Shepherd as he could not live without her. Lajvanti was deeply in love with him and she also did not want to leave him. Vaishali asked her "Would you like to marry Shepherd?" Lajvanti looked at the dying shepherd and said, "For Shepherd's life I can do anything everything possible. If he would come back to normal life then I would do any possible sacrifice. I would marry. Shepherd became happy with that decision. Vaishali took the lead and performed their marriage in presence of the entire town. Everyone appreciated Vaishali saying, "A true wife lived for the sake of husband and love." Marriage took place. Shepherd got his Lajvanti back with that his lost genius as a poet. Looking at Lajvanti, he wrote wonderful poems which were taken note by the king. King got impressed and called him in the kingdom and gave him back the honor. Thus they lived together making compromises of life.

Nargis

Aravali was a wonderful place enriched with all aspects of Nature. Streams, rivers, rivulets, hills and above all deep forest have garnished Aravali. It was a place with thin population. There are houses but not of concrete but of wood just like wooden cottages scattered at some distance. There was a cottage at the foot of the hill. The cottage was so nicely built that its appearance was alluring one. Anyone who watched it wished to live in it. It was perfectly set to the surrounding. Distant view of it created the impression that it was not real but a painted picture of a landscape. It was a cottage of Shantilal a poor fellow who earned his livelihood by selling flowers to a nearby town. In the cottage he was staying with his wife Shakuntala and his daughter Nargis studying in eighth standard. Every day he had to go to forest to collect flowers. Shakuntala and Nargis were the helping hands in his business. He brought flowers and washed them and handed over it to them to make wreaths, garlands other flowers items. He had a handcart on which he carried the baskets of the flowers to Manali. There was a chowk where he parked his handcart and sold his flowers. He had good competitors so naturally income was not that much but fortunate thing was that there was not a single day when his flowers were not sold. Thus the flower business supported the family.

One day Shantilal had been to forest to collect flowers. While going through thick grass, his foot fell on a hidden snake which bites him in return and Shantilal died on the spot. The other flower sellers brought his body home. Nargis had been to school and mother was making breakfast. When Shakuntala saw a group of people were bringing the body of her husband, she hurriedly came out. She was absolutely shocked. She was not able to react to such a sudden and an unexpected situation. When the people declared him to be dead, she cried so loudly that people living nearby came running. One of the natives was sent to the school to bring Nargis. The native informed the school Head Mistress about the sudden death of Nargis's father. When Nargis heard the news, she started crying. Everyone consoled her and asked her to go home. The native and Nargis reached home till then people were crowded there. When Nargis saw her father's dead body was placed at the wall and mother crying sitting beside him Nargis shouted "Pappa, It is not possible. You cann't leave us in such situation. What happened, Pappa? Are you angry with us? Please ask us to do anything, we would do it but get up. Don't leave us in the middle of the journey of the life. If you are not there, who will take care of ourselves? Who will give us bread and butter? To whom should I call Pappa? Mummy, tell him na to get up. Does not he know we will be finished without him? Ask him to open his eyes. Mummy does something but give me my father back." She started moving her father when she found that he was not responding she turned towards her mother and held her tightly and both cried so loudly that everyone present moved by seeing their miserable plight. Finally the cremation was done. Ten to fifteen days passed in lamenting over the death, performing rituals and entertaining consolers. All left, the cottage was almost marooned. Only mother and daughter were looking at each other with faceless faces with a question mark indicating what to do and how to continue life." Father had left some saving behind but not enough to continue life without doing anything. Shakuntala said, "Nargis your father left and left a lot of trouble for us. Without his presence we have to continue our lives facing challenges of life. His departure does not mean that everything is finished. We have to make new beginning. I have to think of you also. You are great commitment of mine. As long as I am alive I will do but after me you have to stand on your own feet. The moment Nargis heard last words; she locked her mother's mouth with her palm and said, "Just a death is out of the house why do you speak of one more. If you are fed up with me then live me alone. I will survive because death does love me and destiny wants me shade tears on others death." Both held each other and started crying. After sometime mother said to Nargis, "I will continue your father's business. It is kasart but I will do it as there is no other option. You continue your schooling. Remember your childhood is over now. You have to be mature though you are not. Perform your own responsibilities and don't depend upon me. Now I have to perform additional job which may let you pay attention on you. Learn to take care of yourselves.

Mother continued her father's business. Nargis continued her schooling. After returning from the school, Nargis engaged herself in household activities and when she was free from all she sat for her studies. Years passed the family stood firmly in all stormy and calm days. Nargis finished her matriculation and was dreaming to get admitted in the college. But the destiny did not want to lead her life smoothly.

Collecting flowers and selling them by travelling some distance was really an ardous job. Shakuntala could not bear it. Shakuntala fell hill. Nargis' dreams got shattered. She had to give up her education and be with her ailing mother who was stuck to cot with no hope to regain her health. It threw Nargis from fire into dust. Life became a great confusion for her what to do? Whether to be with ailing mother or to continue educational aspiration or continue father's business. How to manage all responsibilities became a great question for her. She learnt one thing that her mother won't support her now. She had to support herself. She took her to doctor. Doctor examined her mother and said, "It is case of physical depletion. Due to arduous work she has lost the power of body and now she can't do such work better she should not do as it can put her life in great risk. I advise you to let her rest. She won't recover from this illness." Nargis realized that she had to take the hold of her life.

Nargis was a traditional girl not with any special feature that someone should fall in love with her and not very beautiful but not too ugly. She was a girl with medium beauty. The continuous attack of adversity had stolen the charm on her face. One day she told her mother, "I am going to stop my education and continue our traditional business. You be at home to do something possible. But don't trouble yourself otherwise it will add to your trouble and mine too. I am going to sale the flowers from tomorrow." Mother said, "Stopping education would spoil your life." "I think survival is much more important than education. If there is no bread in stomach, how can my mind find pleasure in books? Let me survive now, we will see what to do with the education. If it is in my lot, I will have it better I forget it now."

The next day she woke up rather early and went to the forest to collect the flowers. She herself did all the activities took the handcart and went to Manali to sell the flowers. It was the first day but she enjoyed as it taught her lesson of survival. For the first time she was exposed to the world outside. Initially she felt it strange to stand in chowk among men and women facing strange and unknown people. When evil people cast their evil eyes, she felt somewhat awkward but she had no other option but to survive. Days passed. Nargis was becoming mature and of marriageable age. Mother was in great tension about the marriage of Nargis. Through neighbor or her relatives, she was trying to get a boy for her but marriage was not being fixed. The income which she had through the business of flower selling was not much enough to pay dowry and get a good boy. Second thing was Nargis was not that much pretty to have a husband easily. Mother being sick could not go to the families find a boy for Nargis. Problems were many but answer was not there. Mother was frustrated as only years were passing but marriage was not being fixed. One day she called a horoscope maker at her cottage to know about the stars of her daughter and her future specially her marriage.

Horoscope maker made the horoscope said, "Marriage is there but it will be delayed." Giving smile to her further added, "Girl is quite lucky as she is going to have a very rich husband." "Really. She will have rich husband." "Yes." "But when?" "She will get married when there will be a complete rainbow in the sky." "Rainbow in the sky. What does it mean" "Yes. When she will see the complete rainbow in the sky, she will get her husband and it is bound to happen. Her fortune is bound to smile upon her. Wait and have patience. Everything will be alright."

Shakuntala was happy with the prediction but the problem was the waiting of the day. None can surely tell when that rarest day will come. Her concern was growing day by day with that her sickness too. Much of Nargis earning spent on her illness. So survival was growing harder and harder. One day both were taking dinner together. Mother asked her, "How is your business?" "It is not that much well. As number of flower sellers are increasing. Everyday a new seller is coming and opening his shop adding to my trouble. I don't find any future in this business. Very soon I will have to find out a new option otherwise difficulty will be enhanced" Mother observed her and concerned face. In order to relive her from that she said, "I wish to share somethingworth delightful to you." What!" "A horoscope maker had been to our house. He made your horoscope and predicted that you will have a very rich husband." "What! A rich husband! I don't believe all these predictions. They are for short time happiness and long time grief." "No its true and he also added that rich boy will come in your life when there will be a complete rainbow in the sky." "Complete rainbow. When it will appear?" "I don't know but it is bound to happen." It gave a little relief to her that at least marriage was there in life and it will be with a rich boy. Every day while going to the market and returning back home, she looked at the sky with the hope that rainbow will be there but every time her hope got shattered. For years she waited. Finally she gave up hope thinking that it was just prediction and nothing else and not necessary all predictions should come true.

With the advent of every rain, the hopes of mother and daughter got rejuvenated and ended with its end. Hopeless daughter and mother became hopeful for coming rain that the rain coming rain will bring the rainbow and the fortune of Nargis would smile upon her.

Their life was going on a hope. Though not Nargis but her mother was cocksure that the day will come Nargis will get her husband. It was the hope which made them continue their life in all ups and downs. One day it was about to rain. Clouds were engaged in athletics. The sun rays were trying to shine the world by piercing through dark hearts of clouds. At that time Nargis was selling flower. When the thundering sound struck her ears she looked up in the sky and found a rainbow but it was not very clear somewhat faint. Before she took its complete view, it was getting disappeared as the dark carpet of the clouds covered it. Rain began to fall. Nargis picked up plastic cover to protect herself from the rain. She was very much disappointed as she saw the rainbow but not complete and clear. It killed her hopes. She sunk in despair and thinking that will that day come? Or she will have to continue life on hopeless hope. Suddenly a car came there and stood in front of her handcart. A handsome young man got down with an attendant holding an umbrella over the boy. He started walking towards her. Nargis eyes fell on her. All of a sudden an idea struck her mind, "Is he coming?" on the next moment she thought it was not possible as rainbow was not seen completely. She was in deep thinking. Suddenly the boy came and stood in front of her. His eyes were caught by the appearance of Nargis. She had covered her hair with a pink color cloth. Over her head there was a plastic cover. The streams of rains were gliding down from her face. The plastic cover was not enough to cover her body. She was getting wet. Her clothes were almost wet. They were torn at many places. Her face was serene with simple but appealing beauty. Her torn and tattered clothes indicated her hidden poverty. His inner voice said, "It is the girl that you have been looking for. Your search has come to an end." He said "Hello!" Nargis was still in her world of hope. He repeated, "Hello!" Nargis heard and came out and looked at the boy. Both stared at each other for some moment. Nargis looked down with a smile. Boy also became happy. Both felt that they had been waiting for each other. Boy also felt that it was the girl that he was looking for and Nargis too felt that it was he that she had been looking for. He took some flowers and paid the money. Both exchanged smile. The boy walked a few steps towards his car. Suddenly he felt at heart that he should know her name.

He turned back and found that Nargis's eyes were still on him as if she was also waiting for him to be back. Both seemed to be very happy as if they wanted that they should part but be together. "Hi! I forgot to ask your name." "She blushed and said, "I am Nargis. I don't have father but mother sick at home" "I am Divakar son of a popular businessman Mohankumar in the city. I think it is enough for this meeting. When I will be back next time we will talk a lot." "Nargis became happy. She felt at heart it was the boy she had been waiting for. Hope revived but no one knew anything about its fulfillment. It was a very happy day for her. She went home in a jolly mood and narrated everything to mother. It gave life to her ailing mother. "Remember every dark cloud has silver lining. I was sure that one day or other your fortune will smile upon you. I think that day is coming. Have patience to enjoy the fulfillment of your dream" Nargis' hopes became alive. She thought that one day or other Divakar will come and end all her miseries.

There was a huge bungalow at the center of Manali. It was the bungalow of Divakar's father, Mohankumar, a giant in the business world. He had his business not only in India but abroad also. Its front yard was magnified with a wonderful lawn and presence of imported cars. People might be waiters were busy in going and coming in. Suddenly voices in the dining table disturbed the ears. A woman shouted, "Divakar, where are you? Your breakfast has been served. It is getting cool come quickly otherwise it would lose its taste." "Just a minute. I am coming. Wait." Replied Divakar. Divakar hurriedly reached there after a short interval. They had breakfast. Mother said to him, "See your father is coming tomorrow. He is in hurry in fixing your marriage. We have received ample proposals from girls from the rich and richest families. I want you to select one of them and get ready for marriage." "Mother, I don't want to marry a girl from a rich family." "What!" "Yes. They don't value the property earned through hard work. I want to marry such a girl not needed to be beautiful but never seen prosperity in life. I want to marry such a girl who sweats for single rupee and cares for property. I think my property will be safe in the hand of such a girl. I think I will enjoy life in real sense. I will marry such a girl." Mother got confused with such a strange choice of her son. She said to him, "How to get such a girl who is not beautiful and rich too." "Have you seen any such girl?" "Yes mother."

"Where?" "In the market." "What does she do?" "She sells flowers. Her name is Nargis" "What? Are you mad? Marriage with a flower seller; what the society will think. The son of the richest person married with a flower seller" "No. I can't bear it. What will your father think of it? I don't think he would accept it. Better you change your mind." "No mother none can change me. I am firm. You have to accept it if you want to see my marriage. Otherwise I won't marry." "Divakar, you are growing obstinate." "You have to accept it. I am quite firm on my demand." "Your father won't accept it." "Don't worry about his acceptance. I will make him accept my choice. I am sure that he won't say no to me." "If you are so firm on your idea then I won't come in your way." The phone rang and their conversation got disturbed. Divakar picked up the phone and heard the voice of his uncle. "Hello!" His uncle started crying. Divakar got confused. "What happened? Why are you crying suddenly? Is anything wrong there?" "Your father is no more. He died of a severe heart attack. We are coming." He cut the phone. Divakar started crying. Mother got up from the dining table. She came there hurriedly, "Divakar, what happened? Why are you crying? Let me know?" "Mother, father is no more. He died out of heart attack. Uncle is bringing his dead body." Mother cried, "No it is not possible. How can it be possible? He was quite fit when he left." "Yes it's true. It is true." Both started crying. Within a minute the news of the demise of Mohankumar spread in the city. Relatives and people started gathering at the Bungalow. The next day the dead body of Mohankumar was brought in Manali and was kept for antyadarshan. A grave silence was there. Crowdy and noisy Bugalow turned into a grave yard. At the end of the day cremation was done. Everyone rested in dark silence.

The issue of Divakar's marriage postponed. Responsibility of his father's business fell on his shoulder. He had to go abroad with his uncle to handle the business of his father. The business concern became so supreme that he too forgot his marriage and of course the thought of Nargis almost wiped out from his memory. He took two years or more to get the grip in his business. He handled the business in such way that the people were saying about him 'Like father Like son.'

In absence of Divakar, Nargis's financial and physical condition deteriorated. The continuous standing in rain made her sick. She was so sick that she had to stop going for her business. It created tension in the family. Healthy cottage with sick lives became the scene at her house. Nargis rested on the cot. Mother was able to walk. One day when there was nothing to cook and not a single rupee in saving, Shakuntala went to the neighbor and borrowed some money on the word that she would return it when Nargis would restart her business. On the borrowed money they continued their life.

One day he returned home. Mother and son were taking breakfast. Mother said to him, "Almost two years have gone. You have handled the business in a nice way. I think you should think of marriage now. The issue of your marriage has been not discussed in the home since the death of your father. I think you have become of marriageable age. I think you should marry now. Parents are knocking at our doors. I have to answer them. Tell me your stand please." "I am also serious about the marriage. Suddenly the old memory of Nargis revived." Mother disturbed him and said, "If you want I will start calling the parents." "No I am firm on my stand. I have seen the girl. I am going to bring her home." Mother knew that nothing will change her son. Finally she gave her consent.

Divakar took a car and reached to the market of Manali to meet Nargis. He got shocked to see that she was not there. Her spot was captured by another flower seller. He enquired him about Nargis. He told him that she had not been seen in the market for many months. Somebody told him that she had been ill so she closed the business. He collected the information of native of Nargis and reached to Aravali.

Heavy rain was going on. After sometimes rain got stopped when he reached there. A complete and beautiful rainbow appeared in the sky. Shakuntala came out of her cottage to bring firewood. Her eyes fell on the rainbow in the sky. She got excited and she went in running shouting, "Nargis get up. Nargis get up. Your day has come. Your day of marriage has come. A beautiful and complete rainbow has appeared in the sky. Shakuntala took sick Nargis out to show her the rainbow. Nargis became happy but in disappointing tone said, "Forget the prediction. He won't come. I have accepted the truth. You too do it." "I won't. I am sure. He would come. Keep patience." "Patience! Patience! Patience! How much patience to be kept? Death seems to be approaching and you say patience. Better not to wait and accept the truth. At least it will let me die peacefully." "Why are you so hopeless? Nargis don't get upset Everything will be alright." "No more talk on this issue." A cold wind started blowing. Weak and deceased body of Nargis could not bear it. Mother took home and shut the door to avoid the detrimental entry of the blowing wind.

Divakar finally reached to the cottage of Nargis. He knocked the door. Shakuntala opened the door and got shocked to see a handsome young man with a motor car parked outside was waiting outside. Shankuntala doubted that he might be the boy. But she kept quiet and let him started. "Hello! I am Divakar. Nargis stays here." "Yes! Please come in ask him to sit in one of the rooms." Mother hurriedly with dancing heart ran into the room where Nargis was sleeping. With a great excitement she said to Nargis, "Nargis get up. Your boy has come. Divakar has come to meet you. Nargis got shocked hearing it. Mother took her out as she was not able to walk due to illness. When they came face to face, the old memory of their meeting got revived. Divakar asked her, "Do you remember me when I came to buy flowers on a rainy day." "Nargis nods her head positively." "I have come here to take you with me. I want to marry you." Both get shocked. Shakuntala looked at her and said, "See the prediction has come true. Your boy has come. Get ready for marriage. Nargis felt on the top of the air. She looked at her mother and gave her a blushing smile.

End